ARMOR

OF

GLASS

A Novel

R. M. A. SPEARS

authorHOUSE®

AuthorHouse™
1663 Liberty Drive
Bloomington, IN 47403
www.authorhouse.com
Phone: 1-800-839-8640

This is a work of fiction. All of the characters, names, incidents, organizations, and dialogue
in this novel are either the products of the author's imagination or are used fictitiously.

Published by AuthorHouse 11/03/2015

ISBN: 978-1-4918-9966-3 (sc)
ISBN: 978-1-4918-9967-0 (hc)
ISBN: 978-1-4918-9968-7 (e)

Library of Congress Control Number: 2014905538

Print information available on the last page.

Any people depicted in stock imagery provided by Thinkstock are models,
and such images are being used for illustrative purposes only.
Certain stock imagery © Thinkstock.

This book is printed on acid-free paper.

CHAPTER 1

A somber ashen tomb of leftover snow and ice, the Missouri January matched the way I felt. The urgent snow turned to icy chards, reprimanding. The gods were pissed. The small ranch house I had raised a family for fifteen years was dark and empty, past. Whatever belongings were not packed in the hitched trailer or car had been sold in the classifieds to scrape together cash. I wouldn't need a trampoline or a trumpet where I was going.

The least of expectations was for average—college, a job, a two-by-two family. The bar set barely off the floor and should have taken little effort to step over. I didn't want a lot, not millions, a Mercedes, or oceanfront property in Malibu. Love and war, I learned, were synonymous.

Men. We don't do emotions well. We love indifferently, waiting. Passionately placid. We carve shallow pits, toss the feelings in, then skim it with dirt. At least I should have. Gaping holes in my shield exposed raw tips of sheared nerves that needed to be cauterized to stem feeling. I should have used a backhoe instead of a shovel.

Returning to familiar structure, to regimentation, I was returning to active duty. Civilian life had been experimented, tormenting. I couldn't hack it. I couldn't be normal.

Approaching my brimming car, my shoes filled with cindery ice water, hastening my departure. My dear brother was in the driveway, sobbing. Daughter Izzy said it was the worst day of her life. I wanted to agree, but I had known worse.

I couldn't look back.

CHAPTER 2

Years Later
Bush Turnpike Station

The next ex-Mrs. Me will be a gorgeous deaf mute. The yakking over my shoulder focused my steps to the pickup. Under the halogen umbrella, where the truck was parked, I unlocked the doors, swung the bags into the backseat. One, a physical training, or PT, bag, hiding lunch, I've been running close to forty years, since they invented it. The other, a green flight or helmet bag was a combat briefcase of sorts, I'd bought it ten years earlier in Seoul. Most soldiers and Marines had their names and rank stitched on the bag, chances were slim to none I would be promoted.

I opted against having the less-than-endearing call-sign "Grumpy" embossed on it. You don't get to pick your call-sign; they smack them on you. I didn't know that character, thought I was getting better. I couldn't shake it, the exposure of its meaning. A lieutenant colonel once warned me I was brutally honest. I considered myself a realist, not a skeptic or cynic. What I thought to be brash and bold, many took as ass and a hole. I think not, therefore I am not.

I settled on my first nickname, Brick, telltale enough, as it turns out. Things were not always miserable, and they won't be again—someday. I repeated aloud to myself, "I am happy, I am rich, and I am successful."

Climbed in and it was on. Engine- check, mirror view- check, and seatbelt ignored- check. The clock on the dash read 0607. On time. The

2

window was 0603 and 0608. Had it been later, I would have had to step on it to maintain my lead. Yawning, I slapped myself to reinforce I was awake.

Our brick foursquare hunkered between nooks of golf course greens at the end of a cul-de-sac, tucked in the middle of a drive-by subdivision. Yanking the steering wheel left, a wide sweep to get out, I waved to the current wife. A couple of rights and lefts later, I exited the middle-class hood via a side street, bypassing the traffic signal and accessing the main road, saving half a minute. No light here. The route did not mess up the practiced timeline. This pace shaved seconds off the daily haste.

Pulling up to Renner Street, one of the feeder roads to the interstate, I looked left and right, as one is supposed to, then left and right again for double assurance, and pulled out. It was a mile-drive to the Bush Turnpike parking lot canopied by the toll way and the intersection with I-75. Sweeping under the bridge, I whipped past the umbrella plants I liked so much I'd planted some myself but in the wrong place and then had to change their origin to spare them the brutal Texas summer heat.

Once I reached the lot, I scanned the random cars parked there to see if my normal space was vacant. I skirted the mostly empty lot and turned the truck in a big loop another hundred feet to the exact slot—mine. Everyone has their fave, the most convenient, the habit-formed comfortable one, the *one*, like the many inconsequential things that people assume as theirs, one of their assumed rights, almost. It had not been available since gas prices went through the roof. I wasn't used to the truck's lack of turning radius. I backed up and lined it up to take only the precise space allocated by the lines. My spot from a year ago was actually open.

Of course, it was Thursday. Not as many people worked on Thursdays. I always did. The world was off and the parking lot emptier. Mondays were the busiest, with volume dropping each successive day. Fridays were ghostly light compared to Mondays, as parking lots indicated. I'd half expected sluggish zombies plodding to work in their dull-eyed trances. *Perhaps I'm one*, stifling another yawn, writhing to enliven my body.

I was too early by DART time, the Dallas Area Rapid Transit. The train before mine had not come through. I poked the radio button for a dash of conservative talk radio. More of my kind of radio was available here than in Washington, DC, Los Angeles, Miami, or even back home in the Midwest. They had a firearms program on Saturday mornings. Good. NPR sucked. Reminded me of Goody Two-shoes and pansies.

The reflection of a train's lights on its hovering power lines flashed in the rearview mirror. The southbound Red Line rose over the pass, north of the parking lot, and under the Bush Turnpike toward the station. I collected the requisite transit trash of coffee cup from its holder and the helmet bag and PT gym bag from the backseat. Off to the right, I detected an obvious competitor. The man acted like I didn't know he was there. Walking at a fast pace, the man was trying to get ahead of me and hijack my standing spot, the best spot to wait for the next leg of this course to stage himself for claiming my seat. He knew where I stood, and I knew where he normally ended up.

He had too much of a head start. At the station's waiting ports, a probable illegal was handing out the daily paper. The *Slick* was the local left-leaning, pop rag trying to pass as hip, a waggish, crap-alogical chronicler of propaganda passing for news. Everyone grabbed a copy before they boarded, whether they read them or left them on the floor as litter. I read it to know what the fanciful clueless thought and talked about and what I'd fight or bitch about later to someone who shared my colors. The other pretending-not-to-be-racing non-racer accepted a paper as I crossed over to his side of the track, having caught up. Snatching my copy of a *Slick,* I noticed the guy had assumed the silver-medal position for his wait, but he had not figured it out. Smirking, he was content with whatever position he received. His target had been one car length ahead of mine, the chap obviously into frivolous spontaneity with regards to his travel plans. *Amateur.*

My real and only competition was the older bald guy, not with a bald spot but the ring thing. Think Homer Simpson's boss, Mr. Burns. He and I were the only two who knew what the best time was and where to plant our toes to wait the train and execute the exacting moves to attain the sweet spot. The seat that each of us thought of as ours was the seat on the train affording the least number of interlopers as possible for the trudge of a journey downtown. The crème de la crème of seats was not too close to the front, not too close to the rear, and shy of the middle. Out of hundreds of travelers, only Burns and I had it successfully calibrated, except Blue Hair, but thankfully, she was not here anymore. She knew what she was doing. The grande dame would stroll up to me at the last minute and strike up a friendly conversation, ensuring her place in line in front of me. Most certainly, I had to let her go in front, even if I'd stood there fifteen minutes prior.

They're like that; they know what they are doing the whole time pretending the contrary. Now, don't get me wrong. I love women—make mine blonde. They want it all but don't know they already have it. Men are brutish, vulgar, judgmental, and competitive, but what you see is what you get. Men know they can't have it all and that sacrifices have to be made.

Off to my left rear, a quickened pace signaled Burns' approach. Burns used to stand in the spot that I now commanded. By tweaking the schedule, I arrived as the last train departed. He passed behind me to take his mellow game to the on-deck circle, where he would enter the same car I did but enter from the front, aiming for my seat. From that position, we both knew it added a second to his approach.

The 0624 train was the golden window in the morning commuter surge. Don't get me started on the afternoon goat rope. DART newbies' inexperience was a hindrance, but the timeline remained the same, despite working around them. When gas was two dollars a gallon, few rode the DART. At three dollars, there was no change, but when it finally reached four bucks a gallon, everybody grew infinitely wiser and flooded the DART system. I rode grudgingly for years to save hundreds of dollars per year. I didn't ride the DART for the environment or for convenience, I did it for the money. Unspent money is the easiest to come by.

The hint of a breeze raked the hair on my forearms, tripping my mind into thinking about fall. *Silly*. For the past two months, days had been near or over a hundred degrees. Someone on TV said there had been sixteen days in a row over a hundred. A little hint of cool and mentally, I shifted a season. Perspective is a kaleidoscope. No two ever see the same.

Train crossing bells clanged; the flashing striped arms dropped.

I grabbed my bags and armored coffee before the train pulled into the station. Ready. Weird to lean forward at the same moment the train arrived. It would be effortless to kill someone, an accidental nudge to eternal sleep. A lady was killed a couple of months ago at another station. I wonder if it *was* the accident they claimed it was. Hard to tell.

The draft from the train splashed the waiting herd as the seated engineer whooshed by. The snooty-looking chick on my left started moving away, indicating Snot wouldn't oblige me to be the gentlemen and would just butt in front of me. Of course, I would feign gracious allowance, even though I would not want to. Snot might have been the spoiler in my quotidian scramble.

Lean forward but don't appear to.

The doors paused, beckoning their entries in unison. The alarm would announce the gates unlatching, much like a starter's pistol sharp pop.

Wait.

Opening... *Wait for them to fully open.*

Clang-bump. All doors opened, front to back, welcoming the programmed throng. The Pavlovian herd spilled into various cars, scurried about, checking fore- and aft-facing seats and unwanted port- and starboard-staring benches. The assembled creatures flurried about the spoils of seats and picked their poison for the downtown launch. With collected belongings in hand, I bounded into the car, hurdling over the bottom step to the middle. Elongating steps as I turned, I leaned forward and right to speed the reach. With three stretched steps and swinging my PT bag in front to chocker-block Burns, I turned into *the* seat, the second one from the rear on the left, not counting the seats facing each other.

Aha, I win. Burns is the putz, I silently regaled though trifling, and cared more than I would admit. Burns pretended it was no bother but couldn't help scowling. He and I knew better it mattered. He took the seat in front of me, summarily guaranteeing a guest would sit with him to sour him more. *Hope it isn't a talker.* They have been known to inhabit the trains, and both the talker and Burns would be too close.

Time, days, months, weather, seasons, holidays, people, traffic, sports, astrology, and schedules factored, *the* seat, my seat, was the premier point, tabulated to be the precise spot to ride, minimizing annoyance in the daily travel drudgery.

Once upon the throne, the PT gear was nested under the seat in front of me and the helmet bag propped between my feet. After a last drink of my coffee from my non-spill, non-crushable cup, I tucked it into the helmet bag. Rebel that I am, this was the extent of my hippie coming through—food or drink wasn't allowed on the DART, but I had to have my coffee, a gallon a day before lunch. On hot days, I can't drink hot liquids after lunch but need all the caffeine I can get to tolerate the boredom. It is Groundhog Day number four hundred or five hundred something. In the Marines, we said, "Same shit, different day." *I am happy, I am rich, and I am successful. Okay, maybe not today.*

No urban wayfarer consciously ogled. Avoid eye contact, but assess the assemblage, forward to behind, watch without appearing to do so. Peripheral circumspection was sufficient to survey the assembled lot. Opaque reflections from the windows of the shuttling bubble enabled deduction and judgment without committal. Have to be conscious of my surroundings, everything within sight and sound, as trained, and to elicit her eyes hunting mine, if there.

I didn't think of her all the time, but burrowed parts of me never stopped. She had to be okay, had to get back to me. Her smile would be my confirmation. I wanted things *not* to be as they were. The crowded train offered no such composure.

The black gal two seats up had nice hair. I mused, *Can't think or say "black," like no one can see her.* Everyone was prejudiced in silence. The minorities tended to be the most so, or so said a headline of a recent ABC News-Rasmussen poll that was crumpled in the aisle under imprints of shoes. In a race-relations class at The Basic School, we had a black lieutenant who said that "prejudice" meant whitey putting down blacks. The class tone changed to educate him on precise definitions, and in doing so, a prejudice could be favorable. We are all prejudiced; it just depends on how we deal with it.

I had a black friend once. We did everything together for months. Thought we were close until one day in conversation, I mentioned I'd had a black friend in high school, as part of establishing greater depth in dialogue with him. He thought *that* comment was racist and replied, "Here we go." We never talked again.

Upon my further undetectable inspection of my fellow passengers, I noted that attractive hair didn't delude her idiocy—the ditz. Manners ordained that the first one to sit should scrunch against the window, allowing room for another on our downtown cruise to whack-a-mole land. But Ditz was sitting alone on the aisle side. Her shit was piled on her seat, like she owned it, and projected her unwillingness to share— the selfish, arrogant, ditz-bitch!

In her defense, Ditz was not the only unrepentant. Several others surmised their own importance was grander than sharing. Provoked by one of these grander ones, leftovers would be coerced into squatting next to me, with my indication of selfless seat assignment, despite curdling misgivings to do the contrary. Everyone preferred sitting alone. Thursday's and Friday's travels were best, as all traveling workers were in seats solitary, and unknown to each other, the greatest extent of their sharing was their equal sentiments for unencumbered seating selections.

I didn't want to be discovered or tethered, to flinch at the violation of my sphere, my space, my person, my personal-ness but couldn't appear to fetter about either. Didn't want to be noticed, or readable, or appear unhinged or bothered, either and both. Didn't want them to know me.

Ditz was plugged into another world, commanding her cockpit in time with the latest musical convention—one she probably could ill afford. All her other superficial stuff, a big purse and ten-gallon, open-top luggable, full of her essential girl-crap, magnified her elevated stature, one that deserved a whole seat for her whole bitch self. As they say, "All hat, no cattle."

My brain ping-ponged relevant thoughts with those that were not. I listened to the sound of my thoughts instead of to iPods, MP-3 players, or music in general—or those iPhones, or whatever "Facepage" and "Tooter" were. I guess I never got up caught up in trends or liberal, social attachments and contraptions. It could be why I had few friends. I had a career to make, a life not to live but to lead. I had no stereo equipment or CDs, or in times past, the odd cassette tape, eight-track, or LP. It was a waste of money; plus, I didn't even know the names of the songs I did like or who sang them—except for Pink Floyd and the *Dark Side of the Moon* album and some Electric Light Orchestra eight-tracks back when.

Still, initial interest could become obsessive, and then I would fall prey, like the rest of the lemmings. I didn't do music or logos, if I could help it. High-priced fancy clothing with the embroidered horse or croc or kangaroo on it or some bozo's name like DeLauren or Hans Polo was meaningless hype. It seemed silly to waste money hiding in someone else's clothes with their name on them.

I wanted to emblazon my shirt with "JUST" on the breast, so when asked "Who is that?" I could say—just—me. I alone am responsible for the guy in this shirt, to accept or deny the faults and guilts, to decide whether he laughs or cries; the one that has to live with him.

Was I unconventional and out of norm? I'd always had this tit-for-tat Q&A in my head. Too busy working, I had no time for the extracurricular immersion and familiar distractions. I studied and trained how to survive the battlefield, to live and breathe and bleed, and to kill or be killed. Yet the wrong one was dead.

I covered my gaping mouth and yawned again—a big one. *Damn. I have to quit waking in the middle of the night.*

To disappear, I read a lot more than I used to. I needed to retract into my own oblivion for this diurnal excursion, invisible, to tarry away the time from the bustle. From my helmet bag, I took out this week's travel log. Having read several hundred books over the last couple of years, I knew I'd have to order more after checking the wish list on Amazon. I switched my book list around—a topical book, a novel, limited sci-fi, self-help, financial independence, history, biographies, or an anointed twentieth-century classic that I was supposed to have read in high school but didn't care then; I didn't like better now. I started appreciating fiction and futuristic science fiction. Romance—gag!

Bought used, if I could; new anything was rarely worth the increased cost, including women. The current model wife had been married four times previously. She was more practical than one new to the marriage gambit, with no required break-in period.

Transcending time and predicament, I opened my portal at the bookmark to step into another world, rereading a high school English lit requirement.

I rocked my head back and stretched, arching my head from side to side. I rolled my head on its socket. *Easy*, the skeletal pops and snaps warned. *Don't want to entice the old injury from the fight.* Aging is not kind. Most injuries heal in time, but guilt is a cancer that knows where to hide.

A face appeared. Dark red pores bored into me, projected from beyond the blackened windshield fore me.

I froze.

Memories flooded.

No.

I was not responsible.

The sardonic sneer brightened in disagreement. Shuddering, I turned to face the one in the train who was accusing me. All heads were down, compliant and passive. No one around matched the emblazoned image that was presented.

I hesitantly turned forward to face him.

One orb started blinking.

Then white ones appeared. I glanced out the windows for answers.

Stealing forward again, I saw nothing familiar in the image. Multiple red and white reflections darted. Yellow and green ones emerged. It must have been traffic lights.

I couldn't run away from myself.

Images rose from the dead and danced in my head. *Too tired*, I thought, daring to settle my eyelids. *I'll shut down for a second.* The reels continued to spin in specter-vision. I was forced to watch these episodes, repeats of a canceled drama—no escaping my role.

CHAPTER 3

LBJ/Central Station

The DART jerked. I blinked. What day was it? What date, or the season for that matter? Every day was like the others in this hamster wheel to a feckless job and then back for a do-over.

The seat next to me was still empty. I hadn't warmed up since I boarded. The heater in this car was broken. It was dark outside. I could make out wispy images in the street lamps, white streamers crashing to earth, snow. That's all it would do and then melt in minutes. Drivers had to worry, but no fuss for DART riders.

The turbulent, dry winds of the American southwest twirled and mingled with moisture up from the Gulf of Mexico. In spring, it meant tornadoes here and for the Midwest. In winter, it was anybody's guess. It rarely snowed in Dallas; mostly, it hailed.

An article open on my lap stated that the period for damage claims from the massive hailstorm a couple of years back was closing this week. Thousands of homes needed new roofs. The area turned into a Seuss-inspired golf-course extravaganza, with blue-tarped homes, and everyone driving four-wheeled "golf balls"—vehicles coated in dimples.

The train braked at LBJ/Central to load riders. More people disembarked than loaded. This lot was the closest for the Texas Instruments employees.

A five-and-a-half-foot oversized ball of a man stepped on the train, looking more like a human orange with a five o'clock shadow, as he penguin-walked down the center of the car in search of a seat. He wore a Rangers jacket and complementary cap. He reminded me of someone, and that brought the sound of fingernails scraping a chalkboard, but it was on the inside of the back of my skull, prying loose disgust.

I slowly ducked to grab my PT bag and placed it on the open seat. The baseball fan and his bulk were inclined to a more considerable seat near the front.

I quivered but not from the chilled atmosphere; it was my past, pulling me in.

* * * *

Buried in mush were greater details—though perhaps not. The incident scorched, imprinted, and then scabbed over. It required great effort to strip away the denial and the disgust to access the latent marks in my limited recall. Interred for years at a time, prying and grating for specifics of the haunt would jar lose chunks of hatred, disgust, and self-loathing. Did branding the soul alter the make-up of the person? Callous and pathetic—the specifics that the authority figure used to lure and beguile me were then and now unthinkable. Distance and time, however, had not helped to resolve or heal.

Young, impressionable boys dream large but think small. As coaches should, he befriended me, as he had befriended other teammates. Many were okay ballplayers, but I was not athletic yet and was reduced to playing outfield, where I could do the least harm.

Fat, ugly, and scraggly—that's how I now made him out to be, whether he was or not—Coach practiced his cunning. Judged less by appearance than the authority of the figure, he was the purported instructor, the elder, the one we were taught to respect. Unsuspecting and trusting, the younger me was at the dangerous abyss, facing myself, a youth growing older. All things anew crossing over from boy to youth, to grow and do new things, to learn, take responsibility, and be oneself.

Some boys mature faster or better than others. Weak and gullible, boys are too vulnerable. Advantage goes to the greater power, and when that greater power is an accepted authority, which adults are still believed to be, they win by default. Coming of age exposed my raw naiveté—a nicer word than stupidity. I was an imp out of time, forced to grow, to move to the next level, but the puzzlement and dilemma was beyond my comprehension. I was ill-prepared, mentally and emotionally, to handle the harsh, cruel realities that others could bring to bear. I struggled to cope, to understand, to tackle new challenges at the crossroads. I suffered in silence, in the preparatory stage to becoming a man.

My baseball coach lived six houses down on the other side of the street. I can no longer remember our team's name, colors, or whether the team won or lost. I only remember the coach's name and his wretched face, which was seared into the lining of my skull, as well as that he kept girly magazines in his car—the first such magazines I had ever seen.

He had invited me to his home one summer evening to babysit. Watching his one-year-old daughter, Stephanie, while he and his wife went out was my first paying job, a chance to prove my maturity. While watching TV, I looked at the family portraits, the image of the pope, a picture of John F. Kennedy, and I admired several certificates on the living room wall. One read "Specialist, Honorable Discharge, United States Army."

Everything went fine for the short two hours with Stephanie. And then Coach returned home alone. He asked me how much he owed me. We agreed on five dollars. He asked if I could babysit again, and I agreed to come back the following Saturday afternoon at one.

He started to hand the five-dollar bill to me but then put it down his pants. If I wanted it, he told me, I had to get it myself. I stood there, dumbfounded, for what seemed like hours, saying nothing, as he kept explaining how I was to get paid. Raised to be kind, not fight, and to never say anything if I could not say something nice. I was in a mental vapor lock. Fight or flight were better options. But then I would be without my five dollars. Was this one of the bullshit rites of passage— surviving the unspeakables of growing up?

I decided on flight, but Coach grabbed me firmly on the shoulder as I stepped away. He pulled out the belt that corralled his baggy trousers to his protruding belly and forced my hand to find the five dollars, then let go and played it all off as it never happened or never would happen again. As I quickly pulled back, I slammed into the wall, knocking off the framed honorable discharge. Dishonorable fissures spoked through the glass covering the army emblem as it crashed to the floor. I turned and stepped on JFK and the pope as I ran out the door.

Locked in to never say anything, like so many other things of tween-hood. I could never share everything with my mother, not ever again. I raced home and quickly forgot the incident, until the following week. Mother answered the phone and said it was Coach. I told her that I did not want to talk to him, but when she asked why, I took the phone receiver without replying. Coach chitchatted for a minute and then reminded me, "Don't forget you are coming over here today at one."

Stalling, I tried to find the words to tell him no, I couldn't make it. He said to ask my mother if it was all right. I tripped over words and excuses, elusions to void him without seeming obvious to the matron in the room.

"My wife will be here," Coach assured me. "You don't have to worry about anything, and I am going to pay you double what you got last week."

The mind must work at multiple speeds and levels, crisscrossing and confounding, blinking and blasting, wracking to find clues, hints, or snippets of patterns to get what you want now and avoid danger. A boy's reasoning capabilities diffuse into strange feelings, internal microscopic buzz bombs, hormones colliding and grinding, exploding like landmines in a DMZ, a vacancy where critical thinking should be. Crossing over to boy-man, alarm bells and red lights should have been blaring, but mine must not have developed, or were busted, frozen, or died off. I told him I would be there, just to get him off the phone and shut up.

After knocking on his door, I heard rustling, and he stepped into view. Once the door closed behind me, I stood and waited. Mrs. Coach-Scum was nowhere in sight. I wondered if she was in the kitchen or in the back of the house.

Coach called me, saying, "Come back here. I am just putting Stephanie down. I want to give you some specific instructions for her."

I did not see Stephanie or Mrs. Coach-Scum. He walked past me and said, "Hold on. I'll be back in a minute."

No sooner had I turned around than he shut the door and locked it. He pulled out a ten-dollar bill, laid it on the bed, and said, "There—take it."

I reached for it too slowly to make my planned escape. He trapped me to keep me from stopping or thinking. He grabbed me and ██████████████████████ me. A flood of panic cooked my head and froze my legs. Then he ████████████ and lay down on the bed, where he ████████████████████████████ ██ onto his ███. Once he had ███████████ enough, he told me to go to the bathroom where he ██████████, put some kind of ████████ and forced ████████████, while ████████████ ██████ to keep me from stopping or thinking, now his perverted accomplice, a dolt, an idiot.

Too shocked to scream, too weak to flail at the shaggy beast, whatever he was, I wanted no part of his disgusting act. I was embarrassed, confused, lost, used, afraid—all that and more, he cornered me once more before I could make it stop.

I never played Little League again and never liked baseball.

My innocence queered from me, erased at age eleven.

I would not be conscious of the events of that year very often, but when I was, I would hate the weak me more than wretched, filthy him. I spent the rest of my life running away from that boy in me.

* * * * *

Life was idyllic until my childhood was taken. We were the suburban version of the Waltons, which made me John-Boy, in a way. The transplantation started a few years earlier. My parents, Bryson and Ellie, were high school sweethearts. She fell in love with my father when she was fourteen and never dated another. Mom grew up in Buffalo;

Dad grew up in the nearby town of Reading, Missouri, astride the Mississippi River, an hour north of St. Louis. Mom's farm township, church, a rocky knob, a creek, fire station, and post office were all named Buffalo. What made up Buffalo was the dearth of pioneer descendants, all farmers, who inhabited the hills. Most knew their heritage and were humbly proud. Mine no different. Dad was the city kid, despite his town's population of less than three thousand.

Before traveling to town for high school, Mom's education came from her parents and attendance at the one-room school a half-mile walk through Lick Valley, where they taught first graders through eighth. As family historian in addition to mother, Mom made it a point to remind us of our stock. Good works and deeds not attributed to her father belonged to a brother, cousin, uncle, or ancestor. We were the sons and daughters of no less than eight Revolutionary War soldiers. Two family members served in the War of 1812. Another was the first white man born in Tennessee. Yet another family member fought in the 1850 Florida Wars and was given deed to land in Nebraska by President Lincoln. Two served in the Civil War, one on each side. Another, a slave owner, lost a farm of three thousand acres due to the debt on his property, the slaves set free by the Emancipation Proclamation, and a paddlewheel boat, the *Molly Glen*, that cracked up on the ice of the Mississippi River. Yet another family member served during World War I and went on to be a millionaire oil man in Houston.

Dad and Mom were married in Buffalo Church, a one-room church built by the great-grandfathers of all who attended. Mom's dress was her Sunday best and Dad's was his new uniform. Answering the call to duty during the Korean War, he joined the former Army Air Corps, the new Air Force. When the couple had married and were ready to depart, Mom's father, the patriarch of Buffalo, could not be found. He feigned being busy in the barn so she wouldn't see him sobbing. Their life together had been one of storybook charm, as Mom always told it.

The military couple moved to Texas, their first of many destinations. Mom learned to cope with the desolation of being transplanted in a stark, white clapboard rental house outside the air base of Goodfellow, in the middle of the dusty, arid plains of west nowhere. While her B-25 crew-chief husband fulfilled his consuming duties maintaining his aircraft and flying across the country, she met with and exchanged niceties and recipes with the other young service wives at the shared clothesline behind the rental complex. With no phone or TV, she spent much of her time babysitting the neighbors' children, learning to cook what they could afford, and endlessly transferring the dust and dirt back to the yard where it belonged.

Mom was not alone for long, as I was born the next year. I arrived, she later would tell me, not by stork but by night owl, having been born at midnight thirty, the early hours of the morning before dawn. It was a nocturnal beginning that set in motion a penchant for prowling late at night. Within no time, Dad and Mom would be exhausted by trying to get me to sleep and turn in, leaving me alone to explore my confines until I succumbed to sleep.

While visiting the farm a couple of years later, I fell off a tractor while playing and split my forehead on a brick at the base of an outbuilding, requiring stitches. Although I was given the name Elijah, or Eli, when I was born, I returned from the hospital with a new name. Mom's character of a brother, Bob, quickly untied the bandage on my head, stared at the sutures holding my head together, scratched at his head, noodling for a name and anointed me as Brick, then tied the medical wrap into a pirate's bandana. Mom had her hands full with a son prone to earning his name.

Any trouble stirred up as I grew older was tied to the story of the windmill I climbed when I was two. She had to rescue me while seven months pregnant with my brother. And then there was the iron-framed swing I ran into on the first-grade playground, which put a matching scar on the opposite side of my head. Because I didn't cry, the teachers thought I was in shock. "No," Mom would tell them, "his head is like jawbreaker candy."

Typical for military personnel to move every couple of years, Dad served at three different bases in Texas then we were off to various states for training, which made roots hard to plant. Don't remember Texas much other than visuals Mom would paint.

Or Illinois. Dad told of a rocket test conducted at Chanute Air Base. The rocket fuel to be tested was Red Fuming Nitric Acid, or RFNA. The general officers and contractors brought their wives and girlfriends to attend this momentous occasion of a new and exciting propellant. The crews laid out the platform-mounted rocket far afield in front of the reviewing stand and rigged large makeshift gauges to showcase the thrust generated by the ensuing performance. What the crews failed to calculate was a shift in the winds, which whipped around and engulfed the dignitaries, to the special horror of the ladies in attendance. The toxic crimson plume began to nibble and melt articles of clothing the assembled ladies were wearing. The show quickly came to an end as the ladies and their senior officer escorts raced back to the safe confines of their parked cars. Dad was low enough in rank that nothing befell him but he never said what happened to his bosses at the disastrous demonstration. He giggled when he spoke of it, often repeating the story of the ladies running out of sight, with their underpants and nylons clinging to their ankles as they ran out of sight.

Images flashed. On to New Jersey and Lemons, not the citrus but the neighbor's name. Virginia was the soft peal of the bells of a Mr. Softee truck traversing the early evening freshness of spring. Oklahoma was living in a trailer, while above, the gray-green clouds piled onto the flattened coral sky with pink and orange rays, light lancing from the west—Tornado Alley in the spring. Kansas meant tulips at Easter and an erect missile refueling with LOX that looked like a giant Popsicle cooling. I could recognize the distant skyward rumble of a C-36 versus a B-29 or B-25 as we drove the highways. Dr. Seuss and Piggly-Wiggly squiggled into my vocabulary in Florida.

As a family, we sprouted a brother for me, but transiting the country wasn't thought about much. We were together, exploring nooks and niches of the world outside of the folks' Smallville upbringing.

With the American shock of the Sputnik launch, Dad retrained in the lucrative field of missile mechanics and left the service. Dad worked at General Dynamics in Ft. Walton Beach, Florida, for a year, and then work ceased on the land-based Atlas missile, and he was laid off. Government cutbacks forced the Kennedy administration to cut defense projects. Dad blamed Kennedy for favoring his navy's competing Poseidon project. He took this opportunity to return to Missouri to be near his ailing father.

The move closer to home brought our young family to St. Charles, Missouri, west of St. Louis. From here, Lewis and Clark had left civilization behind. A 152 years later marked the launch of the interstate highway system.

Fearful of taking a job with another defense contractor, Dad turned down offers from McDonnell Aircraft Corporation (MAC) in Bridgeton or another relocation to Long Beach, California. Enlisting the assistance of a headhunter, he took a position with an insurance company as a safety inspector for half the money he'd made as a missile man but with greater stability and job security. It would be the job he kept until he retired.

Despite Dad's misgivings, St. Charles was exploding with construction to meet the demand of homes for machinists at MAC, the expansion of the arms race, and the race of arms and legs from St. Louis. Mass migration in the mid-sixties contributed. Laws and changes initiated white flight from Berkeley, Jennings, Maplewood, Riverview, Normandy, and Bridgeton, before property values dropped with the influx of forced equality.

Corn and wheat fields abutting old town St. Charles for a century were dozed over and marked off for new subdivisions. We gave up our mobile home life and staked a claim on a quarter-acre lot and a three-bedroom ranch house, a mile from Lindenwood College. Growth was not instantaneous. We were the third house built on the street and would live ten years before all the lots on the street were filled with homes.

Ongoing building choked the streets. Concrete and pickup trucks constantly bounded down the pavement, scattering mud, dirt, busted bricks, wood chunks, sand, and bent nails. Weeds and small trees sprouted in the undeveloped lots. Ditches etched, washing topsoil and clay into the street. The constant din of hammering and sawing filled the air as soon the sun came up. Dirt clods were common implements of play. Though we were not to throw them at each other, we did. During those first years, the only friends my brother, Beve, and I had were the carpenters and Mom.

Growing up, I would hear the sizzle of bacon or smell the coffee as the day came alive. I'd get up, regardless of the time, and walk down the dark hallway on the cold hardwood floors into the incandescent kitchen. Mom would turn down the level of Elvis, Jimmy Dean, Momma Cass, Patsy Cline, Johnny Cash, or the song about the Green Berets she had been listening to on the simple AM-FM radio. She kept an ear out for the weather updates, traffic reports, and hints of school closures in the case of possible snow days.

I would kiss her good morning and take my position on the linoleum floor, with the heat register at my back, as she prepared breakfast and lunches for Dad and us kids. We would talk about nothing and talk about everything. I didn't know what I would do when I grew up, but maybe I'd be a coach or a teacher, since they had summers off. We talked about school mostly, and I would tell her about this teacher or that. I would ask about purchasing a new pair of jeans, or what project I should work on for 4-H, or how to approach the childhood dilemma of the day. As I grew older, increasingly the conversations centered on two things: what I was going to make of myself and what girls were about? The latter, I would learn, was one of the most illusory mysteries of mankind.

This dope at school was telling the others that to "have sex" meant the guy put his peter up into a girl's butt and peed. We all thought he was crazy, but nevertheless, this was also before our sexual indoctrination in fifth grade so I had to double-check it with Mom. They split the guys from the girls so they could tell the girls something special in private. I didn't know what they had told the girls, but Mom explained it later. She told me other things too foreign for my tender ears, and I got more than I'd bargained for. As I got older, she expressed openly she liked sex—it was natural.

Eventually, other houses were built on our street, and families with kids moved in. None of the remaining home lots was ever big enough or had the right slope or smoothness for baseball, so we played kickball in the middle of the street, using a crack in the asphalt for home, manhole covers for first and third, and a piece of waste lumber or cardboard for second. Dug-out holes waiting to be basements and partially framed houses pot marked the areas of right and left fields and made for the best home runs, as the balls would ping-pong their way around studded open walls and construction debris. No place was ever considered an automatic home run, as we jumped off minor cliffs and traversed an obstacle course of plywood, spoils, and foundations to scoop up the ricocheting balls and attempt to knock out our buddies before they made it around the bases and back to the home-plate manhole cover.

In time, the growing gang of children on the street would work like army ants, ferrying supplies of construction debris up the hill, where the empty lots remained, to build versions of cities to prosper and defend. Scrap-pine planks, plywood sheeting, 2x4 chunks, and other cast-off building materials formed shaky forts in the eroding landscape. Loosely built, they quickly fell apart with a gust of wind or a rain burst. They were hastily cobbled together, as needed, on each side of the road. Territories aligned, and our kid armies defended them from plunder. There was always a war to be fought, a contest against another, outmaneuvering and outsmarting all comers, whoever they were. Boy against boy emulated man against man, with lumber as walls, stick swords, and spears, and dirt clod grenades took loft.

The war went nuclear when someone (okay, me) hoisted a brick at a wall of an enemy fort. The brick was lobbed, but the elevation was incorrectly tabulated. Over the wall the bomb sailed and abruptly impacted the brow of my new buddy Boogie, knocking him into a puddle of clay. Wailing ensued, bringing a quick halt to hostilities as we ran to investigate the cry. When Boogie stood, he resembled a chocolate fountain. His eyes were closed, but we could readily see the impression across his forehead. We found the welting implement and matched it to the ridges forming on his noggin, while busting our guts laughing as he bared his teeth.

We escorted him home, where his mother made him stand on the back stoop as she hosed him off. When she saw the swelling on his forehead spelled out the last two letters of "LACLEDE" backward, the "ED" making a square-looking "3" and a funky "D," she called him "poor 3-D" as she rubbed butter on the imprint. Boogie didn't much care for being called Boogie, since his cousins had named him that, nor did he care for his sixth-grade nickname, "Pudgy," either. That term of endearment was given him by our teacher, Mrs. Ellis. He readily accepted the battle-scar and the hipper name of 3-D.

Breakfast meals were cold cereal, whatever brand was cheapest and on sale the previous week. No sugared cereals. Lunches sometimes consisted of bologna or salami, but mostly it was PB-and-J sandwiches—so much so, I hate peanut butter still. We carried lunch bags to school through high school. I prided on how long I could keep the same plastic baggie and folded-up lunch bag in my back pocket throughout the school year before having to cycle in new ones.

Evening meals were fried chicken, fried pork chops, fried hamburgers and homemade French fries, fried Swiss steak, friend round steak, fried pork-n-beans, fried hot dogs. Mom made the occasional lasagna or spaghetti but the fried variants were more regular. Salads consisted of iceberg lettuce with only Miracle Whip for salad dressing. I ate everything in sight and if insufficient, I filled up on catsup or mustard sandwiches.

Baking from scratch was Mom's loyalty to the old tastier ways before box mixes and frozen dinners. Special events brought on homemade cookies, mile-high meringue pies with homemade crusts made from the family recipe, bran and Anadama bread (made with wheat flour, cornmeal, and molasses), Twist bread (a secret recipe but declassified by 3-D's mom), cinnamon bread and rolls, yeast rolls, and cakes. The most common cake pitched together was named Wacky, due to simple ingredients, but it should have been named "Weekly."

At Christmas, the kitchen oozed dozens of pastries and candies. Mom was Martha Stewart, without the billion dollars and before Martha was cool. This was during the rant of the women's movement, which made Mom feel small for being the archetypical stay-at-home mother.

Every other weekend, we drove up to the farm to be with Mom's parents. At an early age, I named them Daddy Walter and Momma Honey. In the spring and summer, we fished and shot bullfrogs with our BB guns, lassoed locust, and ran around several hundred acres, catching lightning bugs. In the fall and winter, Dad went quail hunting, and we were fortunate when allowed to tag along.

Summer vacations had us take up tent camping as the cheapest way to see the world. Each year brought a different destination: the old version of Branson, before it was discovered, taken over, and ruined by country music. Smoky Mountains one year; the Badlands and Mt. Rushmore another; Yellowstone and Elk Park the next; Black Canyon of the Gunnison and Four Corners later.

We squeezed in the Black Hills one last year before Beve and I were old enough to start summer Little League. Like the birthdays we brothers shared equally, I had to wait for Beve to reach beginner's age.

Mom hadn't wanted us to play baseball, but I did. So I went straight to the non-talking head of the house, I took it to Dad. This was an unusual occurrence. Although he was there for us nearly all the time, Mom was father by proxy. Anything he thought or said was translated by—and enforced by Mom, while Dad spent his time at work, or enjoying his newspapers and everything sports. He normally did not have conversations with us children, but I took the chance with this special request, thinking we guys could see eye-to-eye. I levied the possibility of playing baseball directly to sports-aficionado Dad, instead of using the circuitous route through Mom. As it turned out, he felt obliged to agree that Beve and I should play.

But Little League was a mistake.

* * * * *

For the next two years' survival, I buried myself under the house when I wasn't at school. Our basement was dark and dank, perfect for stewing, evading rays of intimidation, and penetrating introspection. The water table altered by the subdivision development left a small stream in the back room against the concrete wall. A French drain was hammered out, but it never quite worked as planned. Mold trimmed the outline of me as I wasted away on the damp indoor-outdoor carpet. Tattered, I might move to the matching couch, where I'd watch TV on an old Zenith with the channel selector missing. A pair of needle-nose pliers was enlisted to change from channel 11 to channel 30.

The crystalline shuttle to alternate realms channeled faraway lands, adventures, and happier endings that filled in the hours and days. The gamut ran from Bowery Boys, James Cagney, and Charlie Chan and his number-one son, to the *Mighty Sons of Hercules*, the Stooges, westerns, *Combat*, and *The Longest Day*.

One of Dad's old Air Force buddies got a part in *Twelve O'Clock High*. Mom told me how he lost the most beautiful baby boy she had ever seen when we were stationed in Texas. The child scalded himself while bathing in the kitchen sink when his mother left for a brief moment to fetch a towel from the bedroom. The baby died a couple of days later.

Black-and-white images trickled over the crevices of my percolating mind, unthinking and unnoticed. Strength, courage, and conviction—attributes unknown to the interred me—possessed the icons of the silver screen. Chivalry incarnate was a man nicknamed Duke, who was the same imposing figure whether rancher, roughneck, marshal, pilot, or Marine.

I wanted to be a strong, dependable person like the Duke, but which flavor of Duke could I be? I couldn't do all of them, and I couldn't help but notice he was seldom good at being married.

"Brick?" Mom hollered down one day, "3-D is here. He wants you to come outside."

"I don't want to right now. Tell him I'll see him later."

Several days (or weeks) passed, and then 3-D stomped down the stairs. "What are you doing?"

"Nothing," I answered. "Watching *Beverly Hillbillies*."

"Let's ride our bikes over to McNair Park."

"Naw, I don't feel like it. *McHale's Navy* is on next."

"What do you mean? You can hardly make out the picture. I got a new glove for my birthday. Let's go play some ball."

"Maybe later. I don't think I can find my glove. Ronnie Howerton borrowed it, and I have to get it back from him."

"Well, let's go over and get it," 3-D said.

"I think he is on vacation and out of town." Silence ensued as we watched Jethro throw Elly May into the "ce-ment pond" while Granny held on for dear life, trying to stop him.

"All right," 3-D said. "I'm going home."

"See ya."

"I don't know what is wrong with you, but I'm not wasting any more of the summer waiting around for you. I'll call Mikey and go to the park. This basement stinks."

"You stink."

"No, you stink, asshole."

"Well, your mother stinks," I retorted.

"Shut up."

"Bye."

"Shut up."

Afraid I was rotting in the basement, Mom forced me outside into the open, sweltering, corn-fed air. As the summers went on, and 3-D wasn't around, I grilled myself on the driveway, staring into thin air. Jets interrupted every two minutes, plying their eastbound approach to the Lambert Field airport. Belching black from their tails and with the whine of their engines screaming, green F-100 Super Sabers and orange-painted experimental F-4 Phantoms dashed in turn between the airliners as they announced their intentions of landing.

As time went on, I wondrously gazed into the stratosphere for a divine vision of a world away from the crowd… and an image took hold of whom to become.

An image of anyone but me.

With the next grade, school activities increased, I kept my grades up and joined every extracurricular club and sports team I could, trying to make myself less vulnerable. I wasn't very good at any of them in the beginning, but I kept going out. I started running every day in the summers, ran once a month the distance equal to my age, and ended up running for the next forty years. I played a sport every quarter for the rest of school. Free time was push-ups, sit-ups, and working out on the school's new universal weight machine.

Slowly, I gained twenty pounds of shoulders and legs each year.

CHAPTER 4

Arapaho Station

J ostled awake, I stole a glance at the other DART-ers to see if anyone noticed my head unhinging from my neck. I flogged my inner self for sloth before nodding off again, seconds later. I needed to read, learn, energize, and unearth the hidden clues to the elusive comfort life offered. Constant uneasiness was not living. Indicators for repair had to be somewhere. Normal people didn't go to therapists, couldn't afford them. We fixed ourselves, even if the solution was at the bottom of a bottle. More people these days chased drugs, made too easy, and convenient. I was too cheap and conservative for that trendy salvation, or for the prescriptive alternative.

Parables in the Bible were valuable and precious, but only if *everyone* else went along with them. Folks kicked the church around as being too stodgy, antiquated, and old-school, something your parents or grandparents did. Many Bible verses I'd read in my younger life made perfect sense in a perfect world. I'd enjoyed listening to various preachers explain passages and relate their currency. The lessons and examples were classic; none better could be written.

The hymnal singing and ceremony of churching, cloistered tightly with Sunday-best garnished sinners, was the unsettling. I didn't like being around people extolling a blissful life when I felt mine was crumbling. An admitted sinner in a house full of them. Hypocrites, all of us, a lay leader had stated, were in church where we were supposed to be. I preferred not to be one and set out on my own to find myself. I'd have to take up reading more and everything, which is what I did.

The seat jumped. I stirred and readjusted, and the book I was holding slipped to the floor. As I reached down, the large man seated next to me was conscious of the inconvenience his bulk created, but it didn't stop his fat thigh from hugging mine. He sat with one cheek on the seat, suspending the gross weight of his carriage, half on and half off.

Reminds me of Boscoe, I thought, as I shrunk into my dozing.

* * * * *

I had to get to Boscoe's office. We called him that when he was out of earshot. Didn't sound right, calling him Mr. Blemings. He looked like a Boscoe. To his face, we called him Coach. He was assistant football coach and one of the counselors. My classes were in the back of the school, generally and I had to make my way through the quad to the front original high school building, where the administrators' offices were. I plied my way through a sea of hair.

Two years prior, students had been neat and trimmed. Then an ACLU lawsuit somewhere in the country overturned dress codes, and a sea change engulfed the schools across the nation. Now, the waters parted as a crew-cut jock waded through the flotsam of bobbling blond Afro puffs in tie-dyed T-shirts, olive-drab fatigue shirts with sleeves cut off, and shredded bell-bottoms shading flip-floppy footed sandals.

"Hi," a cute girl spouted off as she slowly passed.

My eyes lifted from the invisible trail I was following, and I glanced back. The books I was carrying slipped and then crashed to the tarmac. *She wasn't talking to me, was she? She must have been talking to someone else.*

"Stuck-up," I heard her say as the words knifed my back.

Guess she was talking to me. Why did she call me that? What does stuck-up even mean? Boring, maybe, but I didn't know she was talking to me. As I collected the books, I leafed through the US Air Force Academy picture book I had permanently checked out. I couldn't keep it longer than fourteen days at a time, so I rotated it with the Naval Academy or West Point book. They had been temporarily permanently mine, one or the other of them under my arm at all times.

Reaching Boscoe's office, I knocked and waited.

"Come in," I hear from behind his door. "Sit," he said, spitting words without breathing. "Your grades are great, but grades aren't everything, you know. Don't get me wrong. You have to have good grades, but the academies, you know, want more. What else do we have here?"

Silently, waiting to hear, I squirmed in the tight office. I didn't like sitting too close to anyone, and Boscoe filled the room without me. It wasn't that I had an overarching fear of coaches, it was a general mistrust of everyone. Coaches ran the programs that enabled me to be someone else. I wasn't the best athlete, but I was better and stronger each year.

Coach Boscoe Blemings reviewed my student record of the past three years. "With the classes you have now and the ones you're scheduled to take for your senior year, you have met all of the requirements needed to graduate. We have your sports participation with football, track, and wrestling. Would be nice if you'd won more of your matches, though. Need a winning season to your credit… ahem… but you can't count on football in this league." Our school tied Pattonville as the smallest school in the baby-boom swollen Suburban North League, which included the largest schools in the St. Louis metro area, and which unfortunately meant Pattonville and our school tied for worst. The other schools had four and five thousand students to our two.

"Your membership in the National Honor Society, Fellowship of Christian Athletes, Key Club, and Letterman's Club is good, too. They like to see club participation. Shows development of social skills."

"Yes," I said, but I thought, *What social skills?* Club membership required the minimal joining. *Skill? Where do I buy some? I guess he hasn't heard about my inability to find dates.*

3-D and two wrestling buddies, Finnegan and Kiernan, joked about how many phone calls I made to get a date. I used the phone because I couldn't talk to girls face-to-face. I hadn't attended the junior-senior prom because no girl would go with me. My last reject count was thirty-five. Straight-A student in trigonometry but couldn't put two and two together when it came to girls. Years later, I figured out why.

Earlier in the year, I'd heard from a buddy of mine on the wrestling team that a cute girl I met once was pretty loose. He had gotten laid at the Boys Club after swimming practice the week before.

"Everyone who tries gets lucky. I heard about her from Mike Woolworth," he said.

"I could use some of that," I said. I meant luck, but the sneer on his face was "right on," and he gave me two thumbs up. He meant the other stuff.

I bumped into the loose-goose Tracy intentionally the next day, but instead of asking her out directly to meet up somewhere, I asked for her phone number, which I thought was still pretty bold.

We went out the next Saturday night to the Plaza Drive-In—the best chance to score. We started watching the movie and talked for about fifteen minutes, and then I leaned in.

I wasn't smooth as I put my arms around her. It seemed like I had boxing gloves on as I traced my fingers along the top of her breasts in her V-neck sweater.

"Don't," she said.

Huh? I sat upright. *I'm as nice looking as that other schmuck, aren't I?*

"You're nice."

"Hmm?"

" You actually asked me out. I haven't been to the movies for a long time. It's nice to just sit here and enjoy the evening air. You're not like the other guys."

"Uh, thanks," I said, but I wanted to be like the other guys, dammit!

"I had a hard day at work, and I am beat. You know I'm a waitress at Moe's Grill, right? Please, I hope you don't mind my pooping out on you, but can't I just lie here on your shoulder and sleep?"

Crap. "Sure, why wouldn't I let you do that?" *Dammit!* "Sure, you go ahead and lie right here. I don't mind watching the movie by myself."

"Thanks."

Story of my life.

Nice? I hated being me. Too nice, polite, and proper, and where did it get me? Her bad reputation was mine now, though I didn't know it, and without any of the perks or benefits. Add my short hair and desire to join the military in the sandal-wearing, hippie pot-smoking, anti-war days, and I was a three-striker before I stepped out of the dugout and picked up the phone receiver to ask a girl out.

"I talked to the colonel with the Air Force Junior ROTC class," Boscoe said.

"Huh?"

"The colonel."

"Ah, yes, the colonel. And he said?"

"He agrees you have a great shot to land an academy appointment. Do you know him?"

"No, sir."

"He said you could do better. If you were in his class your senior year, it would ramp up your appeal and qualifications before the Air Force acceptance board."

Joining ROTC was not what I wanted, it was totally uncool and getting colder. I wasn't much of a dresser, never had been, but I was improving. I hadn't worn a dickey since seventh grade, mind you. I started to fit in more, despite date shoot-downs. I would hang out with the school superintendent's son and his buddies and play nickel-dime poker. They drank foraged beer while I drank soda.

I suspect they liked me at the poker table because I wasn't any good. I didn't care about winning when I had a handful of friends and somewhere to be on a non-school night. If it took losing a few rolls of nickels or dimes, it was worth it to me. They were part of the clique, and I went along for the ride. When a party came up or someone needed a sober ride, I fit right in.

Why would I want to join a group of chrome-domed nerds wearing blue suits every couple of weeks?

"I hadn't thought about it, Coach. Are you sure I don't need advanced physics or chemistry?" I said, disbelieving the words as they spilled forth.

"Take a week or two to think about it. Get over to the Industrial Arts building and talk to the colonel. He'll help you decide."

* * * * *

Dad and Mom could not afford to send me to college. The US Air Force Academy was my focal point, as Dad had been Air Force. But to hedge my bets, I explored other low-cost venues, such as ROTC scholarships. West Point was the oldest, most prestigious military school, steeped in a long history, with numerous illustrious alumni. MacArthur, Eisenhower, Patton, Bradley, Grant, Sherman, McClelland, and Lee—all the great generals were West Pointers. I wanted the school for that reason but not the army. The Naval Academy had a storied history as well, but their officers and sailors spent too much time at sea. What if I got seasick? I didn't even like to drink water and joked I was allergic to it—and to the white uniforms and the boating stuff and I didn't like to eat fish, either. But I would apply, as a last resort, in case none of the other options panned out.

The ROTC class was less structured than other classes; scholastic credit was given for mere attendance. I noticed Cameo immediately. She was the more attractive of the two girls in ROTC. She did not have long, flowing hair and did not wear the nicest or most fashionable clothes. What Cameo did have was a constant smile and a twinkle in her eye. She appeared to beam when I walked into the room. The sun in my world emerged.

It took several days for me to respond. Guys and girls preen and posture to solicit interest or discover indifference. To demonstrate I noticed her was to place tacks on her desk seat.

Cameo was out of her desk, talking to the senior enlisted advisor in his office at the back of the room. She returned, aware of the class of muffling guys. At her desk, she neatly leaned over and deftly plucked all the little pointy weapons. She grinned, gazed around the room, and then abruptly planted herself in her seat. Her shriek indicated her failure at total tack retrieval. Laughing in unison, my role as prime instigator was hidden in the chorus of guffaws and hilarity. Cameo vowed to get the perpetrator of her blush.

ROTC was the school day's last class. We tended not to rush out as fast as after the other classes. I was off to football practice. Cameo beckoned me over, pulled something from her purse, aimed it at my face, and fired. Her version of mace was perfume.

I ducked away, dashed to grab my books, and bounded over desks and chairs, aiming for the door. She beat me there. I flung my book bag toward the exterior wall and sprinted for the open, unscreened window. I was straddling the sill when she shot me squarely in my puffing mouth. *Blah, yuck, spit.* I dragged my kit to the locker room, not letting on how good she nailed me.

It took ten minutes to rinse the flowery blast from my mouth and off my face. The guys ribbed me unceasingly about the overpoweringly sweet stench clinging to me like wet gym clothes. I kept spitting at practice to lessen the lingering taste and had a headache until bedtime that evening. It was hard not to keep thinking of Cameo.

Several weeks later, the colonel arranged a field trip for the class to visit the 131st Missouri Air National Guard at Lambert Field in Bridgeton. I sat next to Cameo and her friend, Peggy Sue Something-or-another, on the bus ride. After our ride on a T-39 transport plane, we sat and talked at a table in the canteen area. Cameo got the wise idea of putting water down my back. I had to top it. I teased her with the pepper shaker in the middle of the table. Cameo tried to pry it from my hands before I twisted the lid off. We struggled, and I reclaimed control, popped the lid, and blew. A pepper blast, bigger than intended, flew in her eyes and into startled tonsils.

She coughed, struggling to breathe. I thought for a second she was going to die. On the way back to school, we laughed about it, which caused her to gag up residual pepper, and then she laughed as she choked again and tears ran down her cheeks. Taking it in stride, she warned me to watch out—her turn was next.

Our first date wasn't really. A bunch of us ROTC-types decided to put on our uniforms and go to Collinsville, Illinois, to another ROTC unit's military ball. Five of us piled in to my folks' car. Once we crossed the river, we spent an hour finding the place. We were there as a group, not couples, but I spent most of my time dancing with Cameo. Dancing seemed inappropriate and too sterile in uniform. Afterwards, I dropped the others off at their homes, so I could try to kiss her. She was more receptive than I understood. She must not have known who I was. Nerds of a feather, she was as uncool as I was and thus, not privy to the "word on the street" about me. The year prior, I was the leper that other females scoffed at as they ran away as if their hair was on fire.

Her parents had gone to bed, and we were on the couch in her living room. We "made out," as they called it, but I never understood why they called it that. It seemed dumb to me and inappropriate English.

Taking a breather, she asked, "Why do I hear some kids call you Captain America?"

"It's a nickname I picked up in junior high. Wrote an article for the school newspaper my freshman year against the draft dodgers and draft-card burners. I said we should do our duty, as the government determined."

"What did you say?"

"I reminded them that we, as a country, were weak if freedom for all wasn't worth fighting for. If China and the Soviet Union forced their Communist views on the weak and powerless Third World countries around the globe, then we would eventually have to fight the whole world to remain free. You know, the domino effect."

"Did the kids laugh at you?"

"Not really. They called me names until Captain America stuck. Everyone else went along with it."

"What did you do?"

"Didn't bother me so much. Thought maybe it was who I was. One kid picked a fight with me after the school dance, though. He tried to get me to take a swing at him. I wouldn't. I told him I didn't want to fight. I had no beef with him, no reason to fight. He kept egging me on, but I stood there, trying to reason with him."

"So nothing happened?"

"Fortunately. When he got tired of pestering me, and I started to walk away, he revealed he had a knife hidden in his right hand."

"Weren't you scared?"

"Not at that point. I had beaten him without lifting a finger."

* * * * *

The University of Missouri at Columbia regularly hosted ROTC drill competition. It was two hours' drive away. As if the ill-fitting blue uniforms were not bad enough, add a chrome-dome helmet to the ensemble for a drill competition, that's a real geek-treat. Rather than buses or school vans, our instructors asked the local recruiters to chauffeur the drill team to Mizzou with their government vehicles. In the car in which Cameo and I rode, she sat in the middle of the front seat.

Cameo's endowment was not lost on the driver. He could not keep his eyes or his attention on anything but Cameo. I bristled as she enjoyed the flirtations, while the rest of us were uncomfortable witnesses. On the return trip, I ensured that Cameo and I rode in the back.

Cameo and I hadn't been on a real date yet, but I felt confident she would go out with me. The first opportunity was the upcoming military ball. When I asked her to go, she said she would have if she had not already made arrangements. Before we had met, she agreed to attend the ball with a former alum who was away at college. His name was Francois. When I met him later, he reminded me of the cartoon skunk with a pencil-thin moustache, Pepe Le Pew.

By virtue of trying to qualify for the academy and having the rumored good shot, the colonel-instructor promoted me above the third-year cadets and appointed me the flight commander. I was assigned as the top-ranked cadet officer in the school with three months experience. The veterans understandably groused. I knew it was wrong, but no one else was vying for the academy. I obliged the patronage, despite the fact that it came with the additional duty of being in charge of the ball for which I had no date.

I shook off the dusty mental datebook for girls I could solicit and found the list of my past defaulted queries and those who had built résumés of ruses and excuses as to why I was not to be dated. The list consisted of all the females left in the school, as I worked the phone like a congressional aide. The girls I contacted saw a military ball as too stiff and staid. I could have gone alone, but didn't want to look destitute in front of rosy-stink-sweet Pepe, Cameo, and the rest of the blue-clad crew.

I shouldn't have broken it off with that busty gal with the short black hair. I had almost run her over in the hallway outside the school auditorium, after a school meeting on bomb threats.

"Hi," I uttered. *Hey, I can talk to a girl.* "I'm sorry."

"Hi," she said.

"My name is Brick and—"

"I know who you are," she said.

"Oh, and you are?"

"My name is Sheila. Sheila Treason."

"I haven't seen you around before. Why do you know who I am?"

"You play football. I go to the games. You almost scored a touchdown last week."

"Yeah, couldn't make that last yard. Maybe next week, when we play Pattonville. Our chances are better, you know."

"Do you want to go out?" she asked.

"Huh?"

"You probably know my older sister, Paula."

"I know of her. Wasn't she dating Allen Rogers? He graduated last year."

"She still does. They've been a couple since she was a sophomore. So, would you like to take me to the movies?"

"Sure." *I mean, hot damn—and she wasn't ugly.* "That would be great." *Slow down, old boy. Don't sound horribly desperate like you are.*

"Here is my number. I am not doing anything Saturday," she said.

"That sounds good. I will call you. Good to meet you, Sheila."

Drive-ins in the county outnumbered indoor theaters five to two, and the Strand Theater in old downtown St. Charles showed movies that catered to teens, not adults. But the Strand was only where we went on Saturday afternoons for dollar shows and old Vincent Price horror movies. Cold didn't stop us from going to the drive-in, it was an excuse to throw a blanket in the car. I picked up Sheila in my parents' rusty, red '61 Chevy Impala that honked every other time I turned right.

She wore one of her many dark blue, amply-filled V-neck sweaters and plaid culottes. *Billy Jack* was the movie, but I missed the gist of it. Sheila and her sweater were the greater interest. She seemed to be fine with that, too.

The light was green, but I couldn't drive the stick, I didn't know what or how to do it. Third base for the first time was an event in and of itself. At least, I thought it was third. It was good enough to call it so. I was pretty sure I was past first, but not even sure what second base was or if I had passed it or not.

But I broke it off with her right before Christmas. We'd only had the one date. I couldn't figure out what to buy her as a Christmas gift or if I should buy her a gift at all. And what message would that send if I bought the wrong one? The one that said I wanted more of relationship when I didn't. I had a future to think of. So I opted for the cad route. Never mind at this point—too late.

Exhausting the list, I thought of horse-girl Barb. The plus was she attended Duchesne, the Catholic high school across town. Of course, we called them "douche bags." After our last and only date, she informed me she had little interest in boys and was more into horses. When we spoke on this occasion, I swore I would never darken her door again if she would grant me this one last and final date I just had to have. Stupidly, I expressed I was desperate. She said she was intrigued by the opportunity to dress up formal. I think she was more encouraged by keeping me away forever after.

Barb wore her long blonde locks done up on top, like guys hate, but it was impressive enough to put Pepe in his place. Pepe, the big college man, left Cameo alone at their table and hovered around ours to grace us with his collegiate presence. And Cameo—her hair was naturally full, crazy, and wavy, and it was charged, electrified, and would not stay in place. The only thing better than watching the spectacle with Barb, Pepe, and the fawning others who flocked around her was debunking my legendary lack of dating prowess. Cameo was voted queen of the ball, but Barb wore the crown that evening.

It was the only date Cameo and I didn't have.

* * * * *

Though not hip or hippie, I enjoyed life as a senior and did not want it to end. Playing football had been great. I had played my best yet, learning to play hurt, giving up worrying about getting hit, hitting the opponent harder first. Wrestling season was a first with a winning record, and I learned to put out closer to 100 percent. I never liked the term "giving a hundred and ten percent." If you gave a hundred and one, your heart would blow up. Being a jock, albeit a nerd jock, had its own perks.

The weekend evenings were filled with the cool-kid parties or those whose parents were out of town. I earned the right to tag along with the senior clique, even though I never smoked cigarettes or pot, did drugs, or drank. I was a hanger-on allowed to be "in" with the in-crowd. I did not want to leave for anything.

In February, the academy notifications were due. I told Mom not to pick up the mail, so I could when I got home. Oddly, one day Dad was home early from work, talking with Mom in the kitchen when I picked up the mail with the all-important envelope.

I had not been appointed by Vice President Agnew. I'd known my chances were slim. The letter went on to state that I wasn't selected for the Naval Academy, either. The letter confirmed I did have a congressional appointment to West Point and the Air Force Academy.

Racing up the short lawn, I screamed out with excitement as never before. I had the proof, in writing, I could accomplish what my parents said I couldn't. I burst through the door, waving the letter and yelling, taking Dad off guard. This time, one of the few times he talked, he snapped and told me to shut up. I was too loud for his house.

Shot in the face amid my exultation, I yelled back in a lesser voice, saying he didn't understand the impact of my outburst. I had been selected for the Air Force Academy and if that wasn't enough, I was also approved for West Point.

He told me to pipe down and wait. The bite of his bark stung, collapsing my sail. I stood dejected, having failed to impress the one I most wanted to impress, trying to get him to understand this importance. I wanted to be like him. That is what I wanted to say to him but didn't.

This was the longest conversation we never had.

Cameo congratulated me and hinted she might try for an appointment too. She would follow me to Colorado Springs the following year.

I feigned support but didn't tell her she shouldn't. That world of gladiators, warriors, airmen, Marines, and soldiers was the National Football League, ugly. Men learned to tear each other asunder. War was slaughter, not a place for girls.

On the night of graduation, my head was in the clouds. It was a comfortable June evening, and the air was filled with confidence and the scent of the honeysuckle that surrounded the football stadium, where the ceremony was to be held. The speaker, whose name I don't recall, said commencement was a beginning and not the ending I felt it was. I could not see how the rest of my life could be any better than the last four years had been. I dragged my feet, not wanting to move on, wanting to make time turn around.

In July, I left childhood behind.

CHAPTER 5

Galatyn Park

N odding off, I snapped to the right, trying to catch my head.
*I was with a company of Marines attacking a hill in South
Vietnam. It was supposed to be a surprise attack, but Cong was
rarely surprised. They had noticed a repositioning of forces into this sector
and moved an NVA regiment, in sandals, ten miles over an escarpment to
blunt our attack. We had been in the jungle three weeks. Dysentery and
diarrhea had taken its toll and forced us to leave a quarter of the company
behind. Those with the balls and the strength to stand up were slogging up
from the bottom of this canyon.*

*The objective was a Cong division headquarters on the military crest,
four miles ahead. Each of us carried a hundred pounds of gear; M-16s, 1911
Colt .45 Automatics, 5.56 ball ammo, tracers, 7.62 machine gun ammo,
claymore mines, grenades, pop-up flares, engineering stakes, e-tools, three
rounds each for the 60mm mortar, Ka-Bar knives, four canteens of water,
and minimal C-rats. Didn't need shit paper. The view ahead was mud,
roots, blanket-size leaves, and assholes, as jungle rot and the shits ate out
the ass end of our fatigue trousers. We would climb three, four, five feet up
and then slide back two until our ass planted on the guy behind us. It took
four hours to move a thousand yards.*

*We reached a small crest, and most of the company was over when
the first rounds came in by the dozens. We would have dove for cover, but
we were already eating mud from slinking on our bellies, and the cover*

was being shredded by ferrous shards. The HE (high explosive) rounds fortunately had little effect unless they were direct hits. The mud soaked up most of the explosion. There were enough of those, though. The lance corporal to my right was gone, except for a smoking boot with his part of a leg still in it, and I was covered with the rest of him.

Cong knew the HE was not having the effect he wanted, which was the complete annihilation of us. They must have ordered a switch to VT (variable time) as a rain of steel shards showered upon us. We had to get out of this kill zone.

The captain, a hundred yards back, called in fire support. My face was so far down in the mud, I could hear only the crescendos of explosions. I couldn't see for the mud, and I tasted blood. Private Adams was ahead of me twenty yards. I thought I heard him scream. I looked up briefly to see him begin to run, when a machine gun opened up with a slow rat-tat-tat-tat. A fountain of Adams sprayed over me.

I wondered how bad he was and if I should do something.

Our counter battery fires finally opened up from thousands of yards behind us, and they missed. It took the captain too long to realize he called in the suppression fire mission a klik too short of the suspected VC mortar position, and now we were getting killed by both sides. I would have run down the hill, but my legs wouldn't move. I wondered if I was hurt. If this shit storm ever stops, I will have to look.

Survival was the only option; giving up never was.

My mind never slept.

Slight of eyes, a flash, an image, droop.

Where do thoughts go when you're dead?

I struggled to look up. The DART swooshed on. I spied the Fox and Hound Restaurant, a Richardson pub. I needed to check it out sometime. Liked the hot wings and beer at Humperdink's, though. Every time we tried something new, we found out we should have gone back to the old stomping grounds. Wish they would stop dropping my favorite beverage, though. They had Bass when we started going there but then dropped it due to a dispute with a distributor. My new favorite became Smithwick's. They quit serving it and started offering their own microbrews. Now, it's a blond-something. Can never remember the name.

Who was Fox, and who was the Hound?

* * * * *

"Brick, hi, it's Cameo. How are you?" On the kitchen phone, the cord circuited the dining table and stretched to the basement steps. I hadn't talked to anyone outside family, especially not friends from high school.

"Brick?"

"Yes, I'm here."

"How are you? I heard. Do you want to talk about it?"

"No, not really." Nothing a quitter says matters. Nothing alters fact. "I can't explain it. Over my head, cold feet, lost. I don't know. Just didn't feel right, as dumb as that might sound. I knew it was going to be hard but to not feel right? I don't know what I expected. I'm sorry. I don't know what to say."

"It's all right. You don't have to say anything. I am here to listen if you do want to talk. What have you been doing?"

"A lot of nothing. More nothing than I have ever done. Watching the Watergate hearings on TV, mostly."

I understood suicide. A heavy-heart weightless, without the burden of blood; the brain is blocked from perpetual rewinds.

Cloistered in the basement, I couldn't hide from myself. Apparently, I couldn't hide from Cameo either. I finally realized what I had done. When in a horrible situation, you try to justify the actions your feet have already taken. In my mind, I felt I could go back to my previous life, but the cloud I had been on dissipated on the night of graduation, dispersed to the wispy memories in a lofty mind. I had not wanted to graduate from high school or even grow up, for that matter.

I wasn't ready to move on.

The first couple of days at the academy had been okay. Then we were lined up in front of a dorm when the upperclassmen ceremoniously changed. Good guys no more, the fire-breathing demons were unleashed upon us, consumed now with rage. The screaming, hollering, and push-ups were incessant. I looked around, and as I did, an upperclassman would pounce, telling me to get my ugly face locked up or he was going to skull fuck me. Eyes straight ahead. The meals offered no respite, barraged by constant, trivial questions, the answers to which we were to memorize. I lost fifteen pounds the first week, withdrawn and sick with myself, feeling I'd signed myself up for lifetime imprisonment. An awkwardness seeped in, reminiscent of Coach Scum. My brain overloaded, unaware of latent wounds that were unhealed. I had to get out.

"I was in a state of shock most of the time," I said to Cameo.

A battery of tests was given to retest what we had learned in high school, as if the ACT and SAT scores were not valid enough. I took the chemistry test and didn't know a single answer. I was the first in my family to go to college; it must have been a joke. *This college thing must be way over my head, how can I learn in this hostile environment?* I couldn't study with music on or with my brother in the room. Perhaps I was not cut out for this mess, to put up with this crap for four years when what I wanted to do was fly.

"Thanks for calling." I said. "Call again soon."

"Brick, wait," Cameo said. "I know you hurt. It will get better."

"They always say that." After a month, the genesis, what few friends I'd had, were not around anymore. Well, probably not. I wasn't trying to look them up; I didn't want them to know I was a failure, not worth their friendship. Life had moved on, and I hadn't. "Cameo, thanks. You don't know how much hearing your voice means to me," I said.

The home where I felt most comfortable didn't exist anymore. The formerly successful me was no longer there. Mom was just Mom, as she had always been. She loved me, thank God, but didn't understand I'd failed in being a man. I hadn't realized soon enough the great opportunity that the academy appointment had presented. I didn't want to go out or be seen by anyone, as if I had a "stupid" sign flashing on my forehead. I emerged from the basement at first light to start running, without knowing the direction, to find a new life. Otherwise, I watched TV, lying on the old couch, playing the game-show games and watching the non-stop Watergate coverage and the testimony of John Dean.

I hoped for supreme intercession, some hint or suggestion, a sign or signal to arrest me from personal disgrace, but that only happened in the movies. *How do I emerge from this disgusting place? Me and who I am.* I couldn't stand myself.

Cameo and I talked at length about the effect it had on me and that I had not been mentally ready. I began to realize it was only a game, a game I hadn't learned to play. I was never good at gamesmanship. Cameo's friendship, our special bond, a kind of love and support, drew me out of my pit.

* * * * *

Everyone knew Mom by name at the local Hedges & Hafer grocery store. She heard of an opening for a bagger. Heeding the hint for motility, I grizzled at the interview with the manager. A straight-A, honor-roll dud was a shoo-in to bag groceries, replacing the glory of soaring among angels.

Before long, it was standard 303 cans floating about as I slept, a ghost standing vigilant at the end of the checkout lane, putting soups, canned meats, and fruits in specific order on the bottom and the lighter bread or chips on top. Then I'd line and stack the cart to make sure it would hold everything without crushing the customers' products. Cases and bottled sodas deftly secured underneath the cart would complete the missions.

"Ma'am, would you like some assistance? Yes, no bother, of course I'll help." It went on 'til dawn.

Mom hollered down to the basement one random night and stated her usual, that it was late, and I should go to bed. I stormed upstairs, reminding her everything was different now. I could handle myself and didn't need to be told what to do. If I stayed up late, it was my problem. I was out of high school, not a kid, and over eighteen, and besides, who cared?

My friend 3-D enrolled at the University of Missouri–St. Louis (UMSL), a commuter college he would drive to daily. I'd reviewed schools to attend, but time had run out to apply, so I decided to go along with 3-D to UMSL to knock out some credits.

3-D bought a used commuter car, so we squeezed into his road-hugging Fiat. The shock-less foreign jobber held the road too well, never giving an inch; we felt every pebble and chipped every tooth, with the undercarriage six inches above the pavement.

The university was boring as hell. No camaraderie, or atmosphere, or friends with whom to relate I was comparing it to my former life as Captain America and in the senior clique. Classes filled the days; I'd signed up for a full eighteen credit-hour load. Evenings and every, single Saturday were booked solid, working at the grocery.

I left UMSL after the first semester, neither knowing nor caring whether it had been the school and the classes giving me the headaches or the exhaust fumes pouring through the Fiat's hole in the passenger side floorboard, as we charged through the highway traffic each morning and afternoon.

I talked to Cameo on occasion, wanting her but not the reminder of my high school self and the ROTC instructor's disgust for me, his recommendation becoming a washout. Cameo respected me more than I deserved. It was time to stand up, stand my ground amid the flaming arrows of lethally barbed comments. I asked Cameo to the high school's annual Sweetheart Dance in February. We had a nice time, and afterwards, we had a light dinner at a local landmark restaurant, Pio's. We didn't eat much, more interested in each other than in the food. She recommended we go back to her place, her home with her parents.

When we arrived, fortunately, her elderly parents were already upstairs in bed. Cameo's parents had been over forty when she was born. She left me sitting on the couch as she went up to tell them she was home and that I was downstairs. When she returned, we sat close, holding hands.

Cameo became apprehensive. "Brick, you have never come out and said it, but what do you think about women in the military? Because you know I am still going to apply for the academy."

"That is a loaded question; I'll have to handle it with care. I must resort to nothing but the truth. Several reasons why I think there are places women should not be. Have you read some of the articles in *Reader's Digest* about the soldiers and pilots coming back from the war?"

"I read the 'Humor in Uniform' but don't recall any specific articles of soldiers' accounts."

"I love 'Humor in Uniform,' some of my favorites, but some of the real personal account articles are quite disturbing. I read one where the Viet Cong, you know, the VC, burned a village leader at the stake because he failed to feed and hide them from the US military. Before they lit the fire, they slowly tortured him, cutting off pieces of him. When he was barely conscious, they cut off his genitals and sewed them to the inside of his mouth while his wife and children were forced to watch. Then they lit the fire, shot each of his children in the head, and raped the wife and then poked her with a bayonet until she died."

"Ew-w-w, that's horrible."

"Another account I read was about the USS *Pueblo* crew captured by the North Koreans. They tortured the officers and crew to reveal their true spy mission, as the North Koreans claimed they had been doing, and to denounce the United States. One borrowed technique from the Chinese was to bind the hands of the men behind their backs and force them to kneel on round wooden poles for hours on end, depriving them of sleep. They would do this until they passed out; then they'd wake them up and start over. Another technique the Chinese used was forcing glass rods up their penises and then breaking the glass."

"Oh, I cannot imagine…"

"When I think of the military, I consider it at its most base level, horror and murder; of two armed camps opposed in a battle for life, hand-to-hand. All soldiers are men, except for a finite few in the developed countries. I prize women too much. I don't like the thought of women being subjected to the horrors of the battlefield. Worse still, what happens to those captured and tortured? I don't think our country would want its daughters subjected to such abuse. What happens to the men is horrible enough. Even though I expect my sons to do their duty, if need be, I don't want my daughters anywhere near it. I wouldn't want my mother subjected to it or a wife. Call me a chauvinist if you want, but then don't ask me to step on spiders for you."

"But there are roles women can do in the military. What of those?"

"Okay, there are, if you can keep them in those roles, away from the bloody edge of conflict. There is now no requirement for women to sign up for the draft. If everything were equal and fair, then women should be drafted at the same rate as men. But in order to protect my daughters, I will always remain a chauvinist. I don't want my daughters to be drafted. Besides, did we run out of men? This is not about equal-opportunity training or social programs. This is about eviscerating the enemy before he does the same to us. Tear their hearts from their chests before they can do the same to us—whoever *they* are."

"Okay, okay, that's pretty much what I gathered you would say. Didn't mean to get you going. But what do you think about my getting an academy appointment?"

My skin crawled. "I support you 100 percent. Just leave the spiders to us."

Cameo's long, full yellow dress must have been stuffed with crumpled newspapers, considering the rustling it made when she walked and especially as we kissed and rolled around on the couch. I found her ticklish spots and learned she had a secret goal: she was a virgin and would not do *it* until she graduated. As we caressed each other, going nowhere, we respected each others' company, despite cotton, nylon, and moral boundaries.

The ROTC instructors urged Cameo to apply for the academy, because women were starting to break down the admission barriers. They wanted her to be the first woman in the country who was admitted.

She was aptly qualified academically, and though not in any sports, they would cover those bases with her multiple club participations.

She did not know whether to try, but she wanted to go to college. Her parents couldn't afford her tuition either. We spent hours talking pros and cons. Secretly opposed to her goal, I thought it better the powers deny her request instead of me.

Cameo called months later to say she had been nominated by the local congressman to attend the Air Force Academy. I said I would be right over. She thought I was nuts. Twelve inches of snow blanketed the ground, and it was three miles between our homes.

Mom denied my request to borrow the car. Layering running clothes, I put on my academy-issued combat boots and ran over to congratulate Cameo. I stood dripping and melting on her entrance rug inside as we discussed what she believed her chances were.

* * * * *

Spring coincided with Cameo's physical exam at Scott Air Force Base in Belleville, Illinois, an hour east of St. Charles. She took a whole day off from school for it, and when she returned, she called me and said we had to talk. I had to come over, she insisted. She couldn't talk over the phone.

With temperatures in the seventies, trees budding, the air was alive with competing scents of blossoms. We enjoyed the fresh air as we sat on her front porch. She described her physical in detail and how long she waited between different parts of the process. She did not go through with the fifteen other candidates, as I had. As the only female, the Air Force medical personnel made special arrangements to handle her alone. She spent most of her time sitting on an exam table, wearing a back-less gown.

Muffling her words, I struggled to hear her over the chorus of birds in the neighboring trees. I couldn't make out what she was saying was real. She told me how the medical technician performed the typical medical checks, then his tone changed, and he began to fondle her. A canary's call grew shriller as Cameo whispered. She hadn't known what to do. She was frightened. She wanted him to stop but didn't know how, for fear it would destroy any chance of passing the mandatory physical.

A ball from a street game of kickball careened into the bushes and spiked on a broken limb, gasping its last breath.

Then softer, Cameo confessed embarrassingly, she couldn't make him stop if she wanted to. She knew it was wrong but couldn't control herself. As I encouraged her to admit the feelings she felt, she said she had climaxed.

Colliding stun and reason, her words swirled about in midair. Loyalty and friendship were trampled in the overload. Having spent time getting her to open up so that I could comfort her as she had me, I could not control the rage or its vicious words.

The whole wrongness of it smacked me again and again, over and over. Incensed and overcome by the turn of events, everybody would agree this personal encroachment was scandalous—except Cameo.

"What the hell are you going to do about it?" I demanded. "You have to report it. You know damn well they would hang that tech." I took a step off the porch.

"I know, but why would anyone believe me? What can I do? What proof do I have?" she asked, her cheeks flushed.

"You have to do something. You can't let this guy get away with it."

"I know it's wrong, but who would I report it to? And if I did report it, I would never get the appointment. I could tell the colonel, if he would believe me."

Jumping back onto to the porch, I stared at her and said, "Who cares about this guy? You should have screamed and called for help."

"I couldn't; I froze. I didn't know what to do. Part of it was the exam, and then I couldn't tell anymore. By the time I figured it out, I couldn't stop it. It was too late. I feel it is my fault, and I can't do anything about it now."

Deadened, I knew this wasn't about me, but... I thought she cared, and to have her stop me from going further... This stranger who abused his power and position made her feel a spark she had not felt before. *I should have been the one to make her feel that special way.*

Stepping off, then stomping back up on the porch, we argued until intolerable words grew inaudible. With no words left, the only resolution was for me to leave before saying something I would regret. It wasn't her fault. I shouldn't dare think distrust. It wasn't her, I kept telling myself. It was the stench of the whole thing, the situation with me and with Cameo, with shattered goals and no visible, tangible future.

Cameo's senior prom was coming up, and I had wanted her to ask me to take her. It was her place to ask. I couldn't call her, and she never called me. A lump swelled my throat.

And then I married the next girl I met.

CHAPTER 6

Bush Turnpike

"The floors were ruined. Thankfully, my home warranty took care of it. The contractor is doing a good job. He has plastic draped all over the kitchen, but the sawdust is everywhere. You know you can't stop it when they are sawing all day long. They should be done in a couple of days. The new floor will look great, but they have to be done before I leave for Russia. You know, I just can't sit still."

Blue Hair was sitting at the window seat. I had the aisle, with the *Slick* opened on my lap, rustling.

"So the whole floor was approved to be replaced because of the leak from your ice machine in the fridge?" I said.

"Yes, the damndest thing; it never leaked until I left for that week in Singapore. My husband would have loved it. We traveled everywhere when he was alive, but he didn't really like leaving the country. Still called the Japs 'Nips,' you know. He hated the Japs. In the Army, he was captured in the Philippines. Survived the Bataan Death March. Saw many of his buddies shot and killed for not keeping up with the march. Some starved, some gave up, but he wouldn't. He had problems with his feet after that. He had a busted leg, but he forced himself to walk on it, or they would have shot him for straggling. Walked mostly sideways. He was a tough old bird. He wouldn't buy anything made in Japan or Korea either, for that matter. He must be rolling over in his grave but laughing because it leaked on the floor. The refrigerator is a Samsung. You can hardly find products made in America these days. We had a thirty-year-old Zenith TV when he passed. Refused to give up. Wouldn't die either, when it came time to."

"Was he in a lot of pain?" I asked.

"Hard to tell. He never said anything about it. He just kept working until he collapsed in a coma. Stayed alive in hospice for a few months, and then I sent them away. He lived another year. Damndest thing, that man. All that pain, and you never met a sweeter man." She stared through the reflections of the glass enclosure, past the lights as they raced behind. "I never saw him shed a tear until our daughter was sick with breast cancer twenty years ago," she said. "Once the dam in him broke, he shed a tear at the hint of another's pain or suffering. He hated it, he said."

"That must have been hard on you, too, caring for him all that time."

"He was there somewhere, just not with us. The day of 9-11, a tear appeared on his cheek. Odd, I thought, and then he was dead the next morning. He must have been listening from wherever he was, just unable to move or communicate. The Lord works in mysterious ways. I am glad I took care of him on my own and kept talking with him. I told him every day how much I loved him and missed his being able to talk to me. I know it sounds strange."

"No, it sounds beautiful."

After some time, she said, "Let's see where I was in this book. Seems I can never get through it."

I glanced down at the *Slick* ad of a movie with Jack Nicholson playing at the Emporium. My eyelids slipped south, deceiving me.

* * * * *

Full time at Hedges Grocery, I worked the day shift. I also worked evenings and Saturdays, working any and all overtime I could. The day would begin with an early morning run, then work, sleep, repeat—it filled the time and fed the dead in me. After six or seven months of work at this pace, I would cover most of the college tuition somewhere. Girls who came into the grocery store weren't enamored with a bagger's passion for dash and daring, so my dating chances became bleaker with each passing day. Work was all I had time for. For three or four months solid, sixty-hour weeks meant fifteen minutes of late night TV before dropping to sleep.

Mom struck up a conversation with anyone at the local Laundromat, next door to Hedges Grocery. She met another women and her daughter, who was my age. I can't imagine what they might have said back and forth, but Mom came home with a phone number and said the daughter was cute, and I might want to ask her out.

A mother's version of cute compared to that of her son's impression rarely matched. She offered the phone number later that evening. Wary, I accepted the phone number, not expecting anything more than the gal had a great personality. I was due for a diversion and had nothing to lose, so I took a chance on this possible blind date. Besides, she went to school at Francis Howell on the other side of the county. Chances were better that she wouldn't know me from Adam.

I called and introduced myself. Her name was Cheryl. I asked her if she was as apprehensive as I was about our mothers hooking us up. Her mother encouraged her that it could be interesting; it was how she had met Cheryl's father. Cheryl admitted it was a bit crazy but was willing to meet me and determine whether or not a date was in order. We set a time to meet, and I drove out to her house the next day. They lived down Highway 94 and then back along Chalk Hill Road onto the ridge that used to be the bank of the Missouri River. They were the third house up the ridge from the river bottom.

Cheryl was more beautiful than I could have imagined, since I was expecting the worst. She had sparkling blue eyes, an oval-shaped, pale face, flowing, shoulder-length black hair, her lips painted cherry red. Her personality was okay, I guess, but who cared, for now? Surprised at Mom's luck of running across a girl whose looks surpassed her personality, I sat across from her at her parents' dining table, mostly speechless.

We agreed to go to the movies. We drove to a local drive-in and struggled to decide on the movie, as we didn't know anything about any of them. We flipped a coin and picked one. *The Last Detail* was playing, with Jack Nicholson in his signature rude role as a foul-mouthed sailor. Fifteen minutes into the movie, with both of us silent and not knowing what to say or how to respond, I apologized, turned the speaker off, and hung it outside on its stand. We talked, searching for what we had in common. Cheryl planned to attend Southwest Missouri State College in the fall, and by the end of the evening, so was I.

My research into escaping my own hell had me considering Southwest. I could save on tuition, a hundred dollars less per semester than the more well-known, reputed Mizzou. Southwest did not have any degree I was interested in, but the specific degree was inconsequential. Getting away was primary; the girl, a bonus.

We dated the rest of the summer. I met some of her high school friends and found several of them were also going to Southwest. I met her old boyfriend, Wade, and we hit it off, so we decided to room together. Better the enemy, you know.

Wade and I were both putting ourselves through school and lived in a shared room at Freudenberger Hall, or Freddy, as it was called. The cheapest of the men's dorms and the oldest; it could boast no elevators or air conditioning. It suited us perfectly, saving us fifty dollars a month. Wade planned to become a dentist, thinking to obtain his pre-dental undergrad, which didn't exist. A biology major and chemistry minor would have to suffice to fill his dental school prerequisites.

"Why do you want to spend your life looking into dirty mouths and fixing rotten teeth?" I asked with my nose turned up.

"Have you seen the money they make?" he said.

"Money. I never considered money."

Sure, I needed it, but it was not an overriding goal. It could come in handy. We weren't poor; at least, not poor enough to qualify for any college loans or grants. Poorer would have made providing for college easier. No matter, I was eighteen and alone responsible.

What could I do, day in and day out, for the rest of my life that would make me happy? Wanted no 9-to-5, no rat race, no fighting off hoosiers (what we call hicks in Missouri) to get to Boresville every day, no lifetime in traffic backed up at the Blanchette Bridge like Dad had done. There was his back-and-forth from downtown city to suburbia, then rest, and then the cyclotron repeated. He would die the day he retired amid a properly manicured lawn with the mailbox as a grave marker. His plot, a quarter-acre home lot, subbed for a life. *That* was no way to run a life, but if only I could figure out what my *that* was.

No degree decision was needed for several years, so I shopped around, taking courses ranging from Population Studies to Macro-Economics. A degree itself was an adornment, a receipt for collegiate attendance; I had not lost the embers to fly. The military and flying billowed in my thought clouds. To deny I wanted it so, I sought interest in other fields. Any degree would suffice to prove post-high school aptitude. The military services did not require a specific degree; what was needed was the generic collegiate pedigree.

The dorm's racket didn't die down at night until after ten or eleven each night. To focus, I became accustomed to staying up late into the post-raucous stillness to enhance focus for studying. Pretending to be something I wasn't, I could not synch with the random throng. I was trying to ensure that every precious self-earned penny lasted, so I tabulated expenses on a calendar, down to the gnat's nose. On the twentieth of September, I scrawled, "Fifty-nine cents for a two-liter bottle of soda, a dollar for popcorn and movies at the student union," as the grand sum of week two.

Being a gaud-damned independent, or GDI, as they called it, and a nondrinking, nonsmoking, nonsnorting sort, with no fraternal associations or athletics other than track. I went through the college motions. Biding time, learning great quantities of irrelevant data that would be good for a master's in trivia or as a contestant on *Jeopardy*, but I learned little on how to survive a dogfight, firefight, a scruff, or a dust-up. An armed adversary would be sure to cower if I were to block his parry with a quote from *Beowulf.*

Biology, the study of life, was something of which I knew little. I took more courses in it and defaulted into a major. The dreaded chemistry later would be required as a minor, only because I had to take some for the biology major, and finishing the minor out with chemistry was the shortest route.

Cheryl and I were inseparable until the summer break. She went to work on a gubernatorial campaign, and I found a part-time job as a clerk in an antique store on Main Street, St. Charles. Too many opportunities presented themselves, and I fell for another girl, one who put out and turned my cherry to Jell-O. I tried to play the field and keep the balls in the air, but I never learned how to articulate to one or the other felines what I was doing when I was out of their atmosphere. So I broke it off with Cheryl, but it wasn't completely broken off until she got even by sucking off her candidate for governor. That's when she said we were really done. We men are knuckleheads, but women are crazy. Most men would agree; virtually no women will. There lies the void in gender equality.

Cheryl transferred the next year to Central Missouri State, which made our separation easier, especially when I started to date a gymnast. The only bad news was I had to buy a cheap car, as the one available in college was the one Cheryl's father had bought her.

A great-uncle of mine died and left me $2,500, which was just enough to buy a used '69 Camaro. I had it two weeks before I planted it under the chassis of three parked cars. I had been returning home from Johnson Shut-Ins State Park in southeast Missouri. The park is notable for visitors who swim the rapids, pools, and waterfalls created among elephant-size granite boulders in the middle of the river. The gymnast and I took in a lot of sun and stayed late, and I dropped her off at her home in St. Louis County. I hit the three cars a block from home, when I fell asleep at two o'clock in the morning.

Now I had to get another car, and in a rush, with the start of college nearing, I bought a broken-down panel van with shag carpet in the back. Cheryl showed up at the doorstep of Freddy a month after school started, and the van came in handy, as girls we not allowed in the male dorm after midnight. We didn't talk about the past. We consummated our separation, but for the life of me, I cannot remember any real communication. I assumed she liked the sex but never made a sound, like the shallow dialogue we never seemed to have.

A year later, I married that girl I had followed to college, because she asked me to. I hadn't thought about it, but I took what I could get, which became a problem a year later, when I ran into the hot chick I had met four years earlier.

Gerry was a dancer, dolled up in red, white, and blue and performing a routine at the Festival of the Little Hills, held every fall on Main Street in St. Charles. I was at Hedges Grocery, and the owner asked if I would like to work in their booth selling brats and soda at the festival. Gerry stopped by several times, and I was captivated by her look. During every break from their routine, Gerry would come back for some lemonade until the last of the festival, and then she asked me to drive her home.

We stopped several blocks away from her house, and I found her to be as interested in me as I was in her, but when, in random banter, she spoke about going to Duchesne, but in future tense, not present, I slammed on the brakes. She was only thirteen years old. I couldn't get her home fast enough and kept checking my rearview mirrors, as if it had been in a sting operation.

Several years later, and after marrying Cheryl and nearing graduation, I was back home, looking for future employment. Though I wanted to go into the military, I could not pull the trigger. I had lingering doubts about the Air Force and the stigma of having quit the academy. Cheryl was mute on the subject, but it was plain she did not want to leave the area.

So I applied at any civilian firm I could find by looking through want ads in the newspaper. As I walked into the nearest Hedges Grocery to pick up some bread and cigarettes for Mom, I ran into Gerry. We talked briefly, and I made a stupid comment about being shot down the last time I had seen her.

"No, you weren't," she replied, as my brain ceased to function and another organ filled with excitement and energy.

As I returned to Springfield, guilt ate me alive, and the only way I could relieve the pressure was to spit it out. I told Cheryl. I thought I was coming clean by being honest, but that was lunacy. Forgive-and-forget stories are fish tales. Residual guilt consumes practical sense. The best criminals never admit guilt.

She cried the rest of the night, and I couldn't do anything.

The next morning, she told me everything was fine—at least it would be fine, better. When I got home from school, she was preparing dinner and told me again that everything was fine. As she grilled dinner in the skillet, appearing to be as happy as a loon, she told me that she had gone to work crying, and the dentist she worked for wanted to console her. So she had him for lunch.

"Forgive and forget," she said, as she slapped burned loin on my dinner plate.

The ability to find work, much less a job or a career, is humbling. The only nug work I was able to find was by asking Cheryl's "gold-badge" father at McDonnell-Douglas for his assistance in landing a job. Within a week, a job appeared from executive thin air.

My immediate supervisor and his boss, both Navy veterans, didn't know exactly what it was I was supposed to do, but they did know of Cheryl's father and his position in the company. I settled at a desk, talked to a variety of people, and occasionally attended an engineering meeting to pass each day.

I had nothing to do.

Several months later, I was on a deer hunting trip with my brother when I received a phone call from Cheryl, informing me that she was leaving me. She didn't know or care what I was doing, but enough was enough.

I raced home and caught up with her as she was headed out the door. She didn't want anything from the house; she only wanted to be left alone. I pleaded with her that we should sit down and talk. I had been in school for four years and hadn't a chance to go deer hunting and that was what I'd been doing.

"Doesn't matter," she said. "I have been thinking about this for months. Join your air farts."

"Air Force."

"Oh, but I will tell you this much. It took little doing. I wore my white uniform to work like I always do but one day without anything underneath. I left a couple of buttons unbuttoned too. It only took about fifteen seconds to attract attention. You know, it doesn't take too much to turn on you guys. I bent over, the girls said their hellos, and I dropped to my knees with my mouth open. This fire-engine-red lipstick is magical. Now, I have a flight to catch to Vegas." "Oh," she said, "and that thing you keep asking to do that I won't let you do—Dr. Waters gave it a whirl, and he did quite well."

* * * * *

The drudgery at work amplified tenfold.

I recalled briefly an alcoholism film in high school health class, where a coroner was slicing the oozy brain of a worn-out alcoholic, much like Mom would slice a roast for Sunday lunch after church.

Then I never recalled it again.

I neither drank nor cussed, but I had to figure, there was no reason to preserve precious brain cells. I wasn't worn-out like the dead guy in the drunk film. I needed to begin my own social experiment, taste-testing concoctions never before imagined, seeing how the other half lived, and testing boundaries of reason and sense.

A bar seemed the perfect place to lift my spirits.

What the fuck.

"Whose floor is this?" I said aloud, squinting up at a toilet with a crusty rim of puke. The cold floor felt great to hold my thumping head. Somebody had shoved a dog's chew toy in my mouth or a squirrel had crawled down in there and shit itself, because I had this fuzzy, horrible taste. The chunks I pulled off my face had dried and were of something immediately unrecognizable. Week ten of the experiment.

Wait a minute, a birthday cake for the guy at work? How did that get there? Note to future self: never mix fruit drinks with tequila shots and six-packs and birthday cake. I staggered onto my feet, opened the bathroom door, and found myself in an apartment I did not recognize. I started to recall I had hooked up the night before with a girl I had gone to high school with. Through the haze, I saw pictures on the wall but none identified her. I found a door instead and my car was in the parking space.

Well, I like the way this turned out. Could have gone worse. The apartment was on Kingshighway across the street from Lindenwood College. *I recognize this place at least*, I thought. *Easy to find my way home. Happy Birthday to me.*

On my first weekend of trying things, I decided to go back on my deer hunting trip and taste everything that was sold in a convenience store that was packaged with a tax stamp over the cap. My brother had a bottle of peppermint schnapps, which made the cold days of hunting shorter and warmer. Later that evening, we went out to a bar called the Basement, and I acquired a natural liking for Jack Daniel's Black Label. So I bought a quart on the way home. It gave me the flu for three days.

The following weekend, I found my way to the bar closest to my folks' home. I had been released from the apartment lease and moved back home temporarily. I found the perfect establishment, O'Reilly's, three blocks away, with rock 'n' roll and cigarette smoke billowing from the front door.

I would like to say I started slow. I would like to say I initiated a deliberate pace. I would like to say I had patterned my analysis. I would like to say the plan was to try a beer of one type and then on to another, but I didn't know they had draft, or what draft was, or that it was nickel-beer night, and they had all these other drinks with cool names. So I had no particular order. I tried a Tom Collins and a gin and tonic. Because I liked sour stuff, it was, "On whiskey sour, on daiquiri, and on margarita!" Then Stag, Falstaff, Budweiser, and Blitzen.

R. M. A. Spears

The Army was never a consideration. I visited the other military recruiters and checked out each service as one would scan a bus schedule. I could apply to the Air Force but would have to wait until the following September to start training. The Marine Corps' training did not start until June. I would be required to attend their officer school and an additional six-month-long school called The Basic School, nine months to qualify for flight school. I could not wait. I had to get out of town quickly, or I was going to drink myself into a six-foot pit. The Navy had an opening for their version of officer school the following month, February. I could be in flight school by the end of the summer. Anchors aweigh, I went!

The applicants who qualified to train as aviation officers could fly commercially at the government's expense from their home of record, or they could drive, as a couple of us chose to do. We would receive reimbursement for mileage and hotels later. I met a guy at the Navy recruiting station who agreed to drive to Pensacola with me.

It was near my birthday. It took two days to recover from that personal commemoration. My new shipmate-to-be had to drive my car to training in Florida, except it wasn't my car. I had to switch with my parents. The new red Chevy Camaro I had purchased a month earlier was dead in the driveway.

The Pontiac Sunfire that Cheryl and I had agreed to purchase was one she favored but then left with me upon divorce. No self-respecting single guy with a future as a naval aviator could drive an economy car. I had no choice but to trade up. But the Camaro shorted out the day of my birthday, when I was installing the requisite CB radio. I couldn't fix it. Mechanics' shops were not open on Saturdays or Sundays, and to be in Pensacola on time, we had to leave on Sunday. I was forced to suffer a four-month long swap with Mom for her six-year-old Ford pickup.

Exquisite white sandy beaches, the most beautiful in Florida, were the temptress as the first several grueling weeks consisted of running in circles and pushing the ground until we were quite familiar with the sand's microscopic consistency. I now understood this military training *game* and smiled in my head, amused when the DIs barked and ran us around crazy.

"Just begin," barked the Marine drill instructor. Bends and thrusts, we knew it more affectionately as "bends and motherfuckers." The Navy used Marine drill instructors to make Aviation Officer Candidate School tougher than regular officer training. The DI commanded his herd of "poopies." We "began" until that particular set of muscles exhausted and most of the poopies pooped out, which even the best would do, eventually. The DI yelled to change to another muscle group, trying in vain to direct our bodies to do more.

"Push-ups. Ready... begin." Five minutes. "Leg lifts. Ready... begin." Ten minutes. "Jumping jacks. Ready-y-y... come on, ladies, begin." Whew, good, I can do jumping jacks all day. Fifteen minutes later... well, maybe not all day. "Look at me again, Cement, and I'll rip your fucking head off and shit down your neck cavity. Ten laps, go—get out of my fucking sight."

Gunnery Sergeant Daggs, the professional tormenter, had Staff Sergeant Toole, an apt henchman, and they tagged everyone with fitting names.

Sand floated, and I couldn't see. Sweat glued grit to me, rusting the joints. Ran over the chub in front of me, I had only to beat the girls, Seeger and Humboldt. Physical training, PT, was beyond grueling, and the DIs PT'd the dog shit out of us, until interrupted by scheduled events.

Each morning's wake-up call was an alarm clock of trash cans as they clanged down the corridors. We were four men to a room, except for the females at the end of the hall. The lids Frisbee'd against hatches.

"Get on line. Good fucking morning, pussies. That means you, too, C-gar and Hummer. Get your asses on line." The girls' names were Seeger and Ummer.

The prior day's requirements were met, we had a few hours of rest, and then torrents of rain pissed on the thirty mops of the class as they ran downstairs to stand on the yellow footprints on the unlit sidewalks in ninety seconds. We begged to hear "just begin" to stop our shivering at attention. It mattered not what time it was or whether it was hailing nails or mattresses.

Inside, a *hurricane* dislodged gear from unsecured lockers, racks were destroyed, the passageway clogged with gear, and bed parts flew out the windows.

"Incoming!" someone chuckled.

"Are you eyeballing me?" Staff Sergeant Toole snarled. He killed the perp behind me. Or so it seemed. Locked up, I was staring dead ahead at a fixed point, not budging, despite the bras slingshotted onto the shrubbery near the barracks entrance.

Poopies with last names starting with P through Z were dropped after ten days for the follow-on class. It was a failure of swim qualifications, they claimed at the time, except for C-gar and Hummer, who were left with the original class. The remainder of us spent the next two weeks at Training Tank Two, the swim tank, drown-proofing ourselves, until the next class formed. By then, candidate veterans knew the drill, and grinned internally as the new poopies arrived.

Aviation Officer Candidate School, AOCS, would last four months. Pensacola was alluring, splendid in the spring. We detoured off the well-traversed beach on one-, two-, and three-mile runs with our non-firing Springfield M-14 rifles at the port, through the streets of officer housing, with magnolia trees blossoming and azaleas expunging blasts of pink, scarlet, and violet. After two weeks more, we received off-base liberty. Better than doing hard time at the academy for four years.

Pensacola Beach beckoned, despite cooler early spring days. No stopping us from hitting the beach. The seasoned drown-proofers didn't venture into the water but instead sunned on the beaches on their liberated Saturdays and trolled for young teachers on break from Alabama and Tennessee.

Seville Quarter was the evening's haunt. A cobble of eclectic tastes, it was seven or eight bars and restaurants for one cover price, each with a distinguishing theme, look, and feel. Disco was in, and Donna Summers commandeered the airwaves of the disco at Phinneaus Phogg's. Nickel beer night on Wednesdays would be missed till the week of graduation. A small English pub, a steak house, a patio with a folksy guitar strummer, a Dixieland oompa-oompa place, and others rounded out the Quarter. Normally, it was alive with co-eds; when it was slow, we would saunter around the square, a block away, to check in at the world's leading unofficial officers club.

On Easter break weekend, we met a dozen young teachers from Alabama and Tennessee who were shopping for husbands. None of my friends were bought that weekend. Candidate Chase had already been bought on the flight in to begin training. I have pictures of him at graduation, with Glenna in the background.

One of the fine young hurricane mixologists who worked the open-air bar in the back was named Katherine, though she preferred to be called Kat. Her father was an Air Force colonel. After working up the nerve (or dumbing down the apprehension) with one or two of her infamous concoctions, I asked her out to dinner.

We went out to a Japanese restaurant in Ft. Walton Beach, another military town but to the east of Pensacola on I-10. Before picking her up, I tried to find landmarks to where we had lived in this town back in the '60s. Following dinner and drinks, I asked if I could sleep on her couch and not leave until the next morning. She hesitated but agreed as long as I stayed in the front part of her rented trailer.

The next morning, after kissing her good-bye, she asked why I hadn't made my move.

"You told me not to," I said, with a walleyed stare.

As I drove out of the trailer park, I could remember a few points from when I was six—this was the same trailer park where we had lived, the one where the grass field caught fire and I'd called the alarm.

When I stopped by months later to see how Kat was doing, she was five months' showing.

An establishment that AOCS candidates were all but required to visit was the strip club, Trader John's, or TJ's, the second home to generations of Navy and Marine aviators. TJ himself, the hirsute proprietor, had a bounty on his head—or more accurately, on his feet. If he was caught wearing matching socks, the pay-off was fifty thousand dollars. That was the wager he had put on himself. His marketing scheme worked as planned, and he was in a televised interview with Barbara Walters later that year.

Entering the time capsule of TJ's, walls ebbed with over forty years of naval aviation history: pictures, memorabilia, oxygen masks, flight suits, helmets, foreign war trinkets, hundreds of business cards, scrawled congrats on numerous dollar bills, autographed Blue Angels' pictures, a signed picture of General "Chappie" James (the first black four-star general), a variety of aircraft parts, and special license plates. Cargo netting made of thick ropes—the type you would see Marines climb down to board landing craft in the Pacific war movies undulated above the dingy barroom, holding flight flotsam and the spoils of training, as well as colorful bras, welcoming onlookers to the fantasyland. On a tiny stage, a squadron of young women invited the newest generation of aerial warriors to part with their wallets. Many a young woman's college education was fully funded by the kind-hearted contributions of the men in uniform. I had a date with one of the strippers for breakfast on a Sunday morning but gave up when I couldn't find the address she'd given me.

Training was culminating, with graduation and commissioning to ensign a few weeks away. A writer conducting research for a movie screenplay requested a tour of training and access to the trainees. The public relations officer of the Naval Education Command escorted the scribe to the swim tank, and our class demonstrated how the Dilbert Dunker worked. The dunker was a mock helicopter that simulated a water crash landing—each candidate learned to maneuver out from under it while submerged. The PR officer showed the guest the classrooms, run course, chow hall, barracks, and a smoker, where the candidates stepped in to the boxing ring.

The writer was handed off to Gunnery Sergeant Daggs, who handed him over to the graduating class. The writer requested to go on liberty with the senior candidates and get the rest of the story. The class was slow to share information with the writer, until word quickly spread he was picking up the bar tab. Greater still, the script was being written for one of Hollywood's biggest movie stars, John Denver.

The movie, *An Officer and a Gentleman*, would not come out for four years. I couldn't discern who played me in the movie, but I was not the one hanging. Lou Gossett Jr. did a great Daggs impression.

When we graduated, entry into flight school was backed up, and the newly commissioned officers were placed in a pool to wait for open slots. It would be six weeks before I started. Given the option, I could return home on orders to assist the downtown St. Louis officer recruiters.

* * * * *

Planets were aligning, the world smiled, and I smiled back. Traffic parted as I drove north. Summer suited me. It had been a long time since I'd felt good.

I wondered if Cameo was home from college. It had been four years.

Calling her house I spoke to her mother. Yes, she said, Cameo was home. Her mother, however, didn't appreciate my calling the week before Cameo was married. I pretended not to care. We were old friends, chums, I insisted.

After exchanging difficult niceties with her mother, I expected more of the same from Cameo.

"Brick?" Cameo said.

"Cameo?"

"Is it really you? How are you doing? I am so thrilled to hear from you."

"I am fine, in town for a couple of months. On a whim, I thought I would see if you were home."

"I'm getting married next weekend."

"I know. Your mother told me. She didn't want to tell you I was on the phone."

"She's overly protective. Trevor isn't in town yet."

"Can I come over? I would love to see you. It's been a long time."

"I dunno."

"Cameo, what would talk between friends hurt?"

"My mother..."

"I'll be over in fifteen minutes. We can talk outside. It won't hurt anything."

As I walked up the sidewalk to her house, the air hummed from the constancy of I-70 traffic, three miles away. Living there, you learned to forget it. An airliner adjusted its engines overhead, one every hundred twenty seconds. Faintly, I could make out the sounds of a baseball game at Blanchette Park, several blocks north, and summer band camp at the high school stadium, eight blocks the other way. 'Burb backdrop. Our white noise.

Maples trees swayed, pitching their helicopters onto the lawns. The peonies waved naked, reduced to shrubbery, the palette of petals missing. Kids chattered and laughed on the side street. Someone down the street was having fried chicken tonight. Everything was the same as before, except the two of us.

"You're beautiful. How have you been? So... you're getting married," I said, beaming at Cameo.

Maturity shone from her formerly virtuous pupils. Standing on the familiar front porch, Cameo was comfortable it was far enough away from her mother's watchful glance when we greeted. She sat where she had the last time, near the front corner, away from the open window. I sat and then shifted but couldn't sit still.

"I graduated last month from Southeast and received my commission," she said, and then she giggled. "You can address me as Lieutenant. Then, next week, you can call me Mrs. Wagner, I guess."

"Oh, I can, can I? Well, I guess you can address me as Ensign."

"Really? The Navy? I would not have expected that?"

I summarized the history of four years in fourteen seconds, including the divorce. "Enough about me. How did you end up at Southeast?"

"I didn't get the academy appointment, but I helped lay the groundwork for other women, two years later. The academies are taking women now. Well, Mom and Dad couldn't afford much, so I went to

Southeast in the hope of getting into the ROTC program and qualifying for a scholarship. And I did."

Slowly, we filled in the nice-to-see-you-again gaps, courteous and guarded, each putting a best foot forward. After pleasantries back and forth, we then got down to the grit each had wallowed in since we'd last seen each other. She was not the church lady her mother was. Being out from under her mother's thumb, she succumbed to things she had been unable to try. She had loved and lost.

"Do you remember my senior year prom?" she asked.

"Sure, I remember. You never called."

"I wanted to. I was going to, but Mom stopped me. She said it wasn't proper for a girl to call a guy for a date."

"No, it wasn't proper in your mom's day. Hell, they didn't have phones then. They had to use telegraph or Pony Express. It was your prom. I felt I was imposing if I asked you to your prom. That's why I waited for your call."

"I wish I had. Really, I wanted to call."

"When you never called, I thought we were done. That blind date I mentioned—I married her. She's the one I am now divorced from."

Cameo grinned. "I know. I understand. Mom has her ways. The only way is her way. It's why college was so great. I could get away from her but not far enough."

"What do you mean? You're in the Air Force and you're getting married. How can she be in the way?"

She glanced in the direction of the window and leaned over. "Mom found out I was living with Trevor, his mother told her when they came down to visit. I would say she ripped me a new one, if she talked that way, but she exploded in *her* way, quoting the preacher from church, scripture, Bible verses, and she wouldn't stop. I thought it would be over that evening but no. She woke up the next morning and started all over. She kept at it until finally, I blurted out it was okay, because we were getting married. I had to say something to make her stop. I just wish it hadn't been that. Now, I am stuck."

Cameo told me about the drill competitions around the Midwest and how she'd met Trevor, her reluctant fiancé. He had attended school in Minneapolis and transferred to her school so they could be together. They shared ambitions to be Air Force officers, but their other goals didn't jibe.

"Come on. You can't let your mother stand in your way. She already doesn't want you in the Air Force but you are doing that against her wishes, right?"

"I know, I know, but this is different," Cameo sighed. "I'm cornered. She is always on me every conversation, every phone call. I couldn't take it anymore. It was the only way. I have to get married to make it right, even though it will never be right."

Cameo drifted, sighed, and slowly tried to change the subject. She had more to say, but some issues were better left dead. Her marriage was doomed; we both felt it without saying it aloud. Cameo had bought a ticket on the *Titanic*, after reading the headlines it had already sunk.

"Why don't we disappear for the afternoon?" I suggested. "We are the ones that are supposed to be together, and it never seems we can time it right. Let's just get away from here."

Cameo grinned at me and thought about it. "I wish I could. It would be best. But the hell I would to go through with my mother, trying to explain that one… You're already on her shit list for being here now."

"Worth asking, I thought," I told her. The timing was not perfect, but better than before for me and definitely better than after for her. Symmetric lives in asymmetric orbits, our paths kept crossing but the stars would not align.

Again, I married the next girl I met.

CHAPTER 7

Park Lane Station

"I know. He said he loves me, but I don't think he is *in* love with me. I can't be *in* love with him, if he is not *in* love with me, do you think?" the blond chirped into her cell phone.

It was one of those fingernails-on-the-blackboard days. Who the hell was this bimbo talking to this time of the morning? More to the point, how long would I have to endure being part of her life?

There was a problem with the trains; they were backed up. Two scheduled trains ahead of mine had not arrived on time, in fact they hadn't arrived at all because they had been canceled. When a train pulled into the station, three loads of people crammed in as one. Standing near the back, I didn't have to hold on. I was so wedged in, I was going nowhere.

"Yeah, uh-huh, yeah, yup, I agree, but how would I know?" Standing packed in, back to back, Bimbo's butt was welded to the back of my legs, just as the cell phone glued to her head. She did not have to hold it. Couldn't turn, or budge, and couldn't choke the shit out of her if I wanted.

Discussions of love, does anyone know what it is? I get it with parents and children—that's blood. But the others are messed up. Men and women love differently, whatever "love" was. I needed someone to bring life into mine. Living alone was never an option, I'm boring. I didn't think consciously about love. Men don't. Consistency, a partner

71

I could tolerate having around day after day. And tolerate in a pleasant way, not "put up with." I put up with a lot with people at work. Love, to me, was not being in the way but complementary, supportive, and sharing.

Love is not prescient, controlled nor contained. No hiding or quelling it, regardless of whether you recognized or understood it. It just *was.* The rare confederation of love and a living arrangement is how a good marriage is sought; convenience, convention, chance, and availability is more likely occurrence for a nuptial arrangement. We tend to want what we cannot, and seek love to fill a void, whether it is the real thing or not. Men can only tell with time. We don't waste time on what we can't have; we take advantage of whatever is left. Love is leftovers.

As I wrestled with what it was, I tried to think what possessed me on several occasions. Thinking brought sleep. Easy while wedged upright. I've slept standing before. But sleep conjured more disputes than answers.

* * * * *

Once out of college and on my own, with a career of challenge and excitement to serve my country, it was time to merge convenience with convention and add coincidence, if necessary, to find someone with whom to spend my days and nights.

My brother Beve, so named from *Leave It to Beaver,* and because he did not like Bartholomew, invited me to a barbecue several weeks after I'd visited Cameo and the week I met the next Mrs. Me. The cookout was at my brother's friend's house, whose father was a doctor and was on his fourth wife. The home was near a small lake just east of I-270, the exit for Clayton. My brother's workmate was nicknamed Beve too, for some goofball reason. The confusion it caused at work forced the second Beve to become Wally, for fun's sake. Wally's girlfriend was Selma.

Missouri's hot and clammy summers made the lake inviting. We jumped in to cool off and horse around. The lake bottom was nothing but muck. Someone started slinging it, so everyone else had to sling it too, until Selma inadvertently used her face as a mitt, catching a glob in the nose.

Concerned about offending and potentially blinding someone else's girlfriend, I did what any mud-slinging officer and now congressionally-approved gentleman would do, and did my best to get the insoluble goop out of her nostrils.

Through the humid afternoon haze, insects, and grill smoke, we heard Wally holler that the food was ready. Selma was able to breathe unimpeded now, so we returned to the deck.

Wally asked if I wanted to check out a dance the following weekend. Given my especially light social calendar, I accepted. We met at a Legion Hall in Florissant the following Friday night. To my surprise, he brought Selma. We sat and had a couple of drinks, listening to the music. Wally didn't dance with Selma, so I asked if it would be all right if I did. We danced until the place closed. I had been up since 0400, run six miles. I should have slept in the car.

On the way home, I decided to take the back way into St. Charles, using the Old Bridge. I turned onto the unlit Rock Road. The Old Bridge was a long, extremely narrow, two-lane bridge with a bend in the middle, high above the Missouri River, which terminated at Second Street in downtown St. Charles.

Raining buckets, the route too dark on any given occasion, it was deep space now. Torrents of water mirrored oncoming traffic's headlamps and hampered the ability to see the road. One car passed, blinding me. I couldn't make out the center line and steered to where the center line should be.

One mile good. Two. Stay awake. I should pull over.

I closed my eyes.

Blam... thump.

My mouth bounced off the steering wheel as my body jammed under it.

Wedged under the steering wheel, I couldn't move. I felt water on the floor and realized that my pants were getting wet. Reaching above me, I strained to grab hold of anything. The turn signal was above me and I touched what felt like the door. There were the locks and the automatic window buttons. My left arm was cramping. I felt what must be the door handle. What else can I do? I have to pull it to get out.

A wall of water rushed in.

Jump! Shit! We're in the river.

Jump.

Fast, fast, hurry!

Wait… face first—not good.

Everything seemed in slow motion. My survival training was not wasted. Face first will kill me, *shit*, training *was* wasted. It had to be feet first—one leg wrapped around the other, one hand over my crotch, and the other over my face to protect me against the impact of the water and debris.

I choked on water, trying to swim. *Move, move. move.*

Not moving.

My leg was killing me. It was wrenched in the door, with my foot stuck under the brake pedal.

I closed my mouth and held my breath. Curling back and twisting, I dislodged my leg, pushed off, and started swimming. Then I was raking in handfuls of mud. I clawed through it, trying to register the bank and the river. Shaking loose the grass from my face and finally realizing I was in a ditch full of run-off. I got to the other side and looked back at the car. The warm rain was welcoming now, as it felt like I was in a shower, fully clothed. It was the washing away of my sins; I was being saved.

Waste of time washing the mud off and however much blood there is. I tasted for it and wiped my face. The rain was coming down so hard I could not make out if there was any blood in the mixture I was tasting. I looked to where the front of the car should be. Looking behind me, I was past the median. I turned to find the bridge and reached out with my left hand. Steel rivets, over an inch wide. Sliding the hand up, I felt another rivet and another, and to the left, it felt like an I-beam. There's the bridge.

Hard to breathe, without swallowing more water than air. I walked around the slough and looked at the front end of my car. No damage, but the front left tire was flat and the rim dented. I couldn't make out the back one.

A lone passerby pulled up to ask if I needed help. "No," I said, "I've used it all up."

He still offered to give me a lift home. My car would have to sit until I could get a wrecker out here.

On the way home, the driver put on his evangelist hat and tried to save me. *He could save me if he wouldn't talk*, my head was killing me. But I let him talk anyway.

Three days later, I receive a call at the recruiter's office. Selma had learned of the accident after the dance and asked if I was okay. She had called the house, talked to Mom, and extracted my work number. We talked a while. Her words and interest didn't register her being another man's girlfriend. I asked her what her relationship was with Wally. She said they hadn't been together for a while; they now were just friends.

I told her I was going to be passing by her home the next day. Could I pop in? She didn't get the joke. St. Charles was forty minutes west of downtown St. Louis, with no traffic backup, and she lived thirty minutes southeast, in Waterloo, Illinois. I stopped on the way later that evening. Beve was getting married the following week, and I needed a date. I asked if she would like to go along, and she said okay.

I drank too much at the reception, as was the rule, not the exception, in my first year of learning the drinker's ropes to happiness and bliss, but Selma drove me home this time. There was no room in the house, so several of us, including Selma and me, slept on the floor of the living room on top of layers of blankets. No covers were needed. Mom hated air conditioning, and we lay on the floor, sweltering. Without uttering a word, I rolled over and pulled Selma's shorts to the side and mounted.

We started dating. I hadn't had any stuff for months but was getting it regular now. My six weeks of home duty were quickly coming to an end. When it became apparent I would be losing a good carnal thing I didn't like being without, I remarked she should come live with me in Florida. Selma did not take kindly to this cavalier invitation.

I mumbled, "Okay then, let's get m-m-m-married."

To which she more quickly said "Huh, oh, huh? Yeah."

"But," I said, before her words hit my ears, "I am too busy with flight school, so you will have to set up the whole thing. Let me know what weekend I need to be back."

* * * * *

Three months later, we were married. She also bought her own engagement ring. I promised I would pay her back.

The newlyweds settled into a simple off-base apartment, south of Whiting Naval Air Station in Milton, Florida. Our love nest stank and seeped grease from the previous dwellers, the odor presumably matching the oil slick on the living room carpet. I had worked with the landlord before Selma arrived, cleaning the place the best I could. The smell improved marginally, from boiled road kill to a more nasal-friendly pine-garnished baked goat.

Some Iranians must have lived in our place before we moved in. My suspicions were based on the neighboring Iranians, whose apartment crammed ten or twelve family members into a two-bedroom apartment. Using the air conditioner's compressor fan under their back window to keep the flames on their hibachi glowing, they prepared each evening's dinner. Not so ironically, the lone Iranian in our class was named Hibachi.

An agreement with the Shah of Iran had the US Navy training Iranian pilots. The Iranian government paid the Navy ten million dollars for each student who qualified. There were marginal language barriers but more cultural ones. The flight students used the opportunity to bring their whole families to the United States. All Iranian flight students passed, regardless of actual skill or true qualifications. One Iranian flight student, not my class's Hibachi, purchased a new American van with all the features: air conditioning, cruise control, stereo speakers, automatic windows, and sunroof. He drove to Mobile, Alabama, to visit friends for the weekend. After he turned westbound onto I-10 and increased his speed to the limit, he set the cruise control and crawled in the back for a nap. He survived the crash, as did the joke I heard for years and years later.

A week's break for the wedding threw me behind in the flight schedule, as well as into winter, with poorer flying weather and a slower schedule. For the next three to four months, I ran three to four miles daily, ensured uniforms were squared away with military creases, studied ground school material, spent as much time with Selma as possible, and waited for my next flight. I averaged a flight a week instead of daily, as the summer weather permitted. It did not help matters there were five different instructors in the first thirteen training hops and daily changing NATOPs (Naval Aviation Training Operations and Procedures) for the brand new T-32 Charlie. The instructors could not agree on the newest change to the NATOPs, which complicated the flight students' chances of knowing what was correct and staying current.

Our landlord and a next-door neighbor were Marine first lieutenants, having been in the service for a couple of years each. My ensign's single gold butter bar was outranked by their single silver ones. The drill instructors I had endured at AOCS had been Marine DIs, and I felt more a Marine than naval officer. I had little respect for the stereo-typical slovenly, overweight Navy NCO (non-commissioned officer), but my chest swelled with pride with what the Marine Corps stood for, how they conducted themselves, and the proud history and tradition each Marine represented.

I approached the chain of command as required, seeking a transfer to the Marine Corps. My request was not very well received. Upbraided for daring to talk about leaving the Navy, I was informed to fulfill my initial four-year obligation. After I received my wings, I could then apply for an inter-service transfer if I wanted to, but few of them were ever accepted. The squadron lead flight instructor then said, "And take those military creases out of your shirt. We're the United States Navy."

All service branches were hurting to fill their goals with a recruitment pool of disaffected, pot-smoking, anti-Vietnam America. They loosened the contractual restraints and succumbed to political pressure to accept more women. They needed the numbers. Post-Vietnam recruiting shortfalls were more responsible for the increase in women in the military than the women's liberation movement or the Equal Rights Amendment. The basic flight officer agreement was a verbal one, not a written formal contract. Many of us were not obligated to stay in the Navy until flight school was completed and wings were pinned on. Even though I was more interested in the Marines than in the Navy, I was reluctant to pull the non-obligatory contract card.

Early the next year, a fellow flight student appeared on *60 Minutes* and broadcast the non-contractual obligation issue across the country. Immediately, a ruling came down from the Chief of Naval Operations (CNO), requiring non-obligors to decide within two weeks whether they were going to stay and sign a new contract or not sign the new formal arrangement and get out.

The Village People released their new hit single "In the Navy," which clinched it for me. I bailed out.

* * * * *

The now-pregnant Selma and I returned to Missouri to await my transition to the Marines. I quickly realized a flaw in my plan; I would have to be a civilian again. Interim employment was sought to take care of the new family. Working as a plumber during the days and clerking at a quickie-mart at night, I was thrashing myself. Plans to go into the Marine Corps were delayed with our firstborn on the way, due later in the year. I knew I should be there for Selma and the baby. I struggled in ordinary.

Despite the previous year's excitement with intense, invigorating training, my first child's birth was inexplicable awe. While Selma was pregnant, we decided the baby was a girl and chose a name. I would lie on Selma's belly at night and talk to the baby, calling out Haley's name, feeling her feet writhing about. Haley would reach out from the womb and caress my mouth.

We had two false alarms. As we were unable to extract fact from fiction with each bout of contractions, the next time was no different. I raced Selma to the hospital. This time, Selma continued to dilate. The next morning, Haley arrived. The doctors did whatever doctors do to check newborns and then laid her on a sterile tray table under a fry cook's lamp, still crying. I went to her and said, "Haley, don't cry, dear. I've been waiting for you."

Haley silenced. She turned and looked into me—calm, confident. My eyes clouded. A life zipped in a flash. I saw us dancing together at her wedding. Time would march forward, fast. Just born, she already was breaking my heart. My time would be short, and she would leave me. Too soon, this little one would be her own.

Between the Navy and the Corps, twenty months, we lived in four different places in three towns as I grappled jobs, from store clerk to plumber to lab assistant to chemist.

On a rotating shift as a lab assistant, I worked six days on, two days off on a regular eight-to-four o'clock schedule. Then I moved to the 4:00 p.m. to midnight shift and then midnight to eight in the morning. One evening, Selma had enough of the three-month-old's crying and handed Haley to me as I walked in the door. The neighbor girl in our trailer park was having friends over and had Selma asked to attend. She flew out of the house.

Haley and I talked and danced around the trailer for the next two hours. She would not stop crying. I changed her, but that was not the problem. I tried to feed her with the bottle, but she did not want it. I burped her anyway, and she cried. I sang to her, and she cried louder. I flexed her knees into her belly, trying to help her with gas, if that the problem. Nope. I plied her with the pacifier; she spit it out. I considered taping it her mouth but thought otherwise.

Exhausting methods to please her, I laid her on the floor in the middle of the room and waited. She cried. Fifteen minutes later, she stopped. I got down on all fours over her and looked at her. She smiled. I picked her up, hugged her, and put her to bed.

Haley never cried at length again. She was content being left alone.

The chemist's job involved my cutting up hundreds of pounds of beef heart to synthesize milligram vials of enzymes for resale or carrots for beta-carotene. The Marine Officer Selection Officer (OSO) said I was getting too old. Really? So I bolted for the next open officer candidate class, though Selma was pregnant again and due soon.

The OSO drove us to the airport when my report-in date was imminent, and he took Selma straight to the hospital once my flight had departed.

In OCS as in every boot camp, the DI is god. You followed the gods' orders to stay out of trouble, their trouble, the type of trouble only a god can bring on you. On my second night in the barracks, I was poked and awakened by the senior god to come and see him in his office. Gods do not have to let you do anything. The gods want you to think you have no rights whatsoever. Quick and cordial, he told me to get on the phone. Selma told me the new baby was a girl, and everything was fine. We talked briefly and said our good-byes.

I hated leaving Selma in the position of caring for Haley and now the new one, but guilt and feelings had kept me from my goals before, so I boxed it away. Guilt had to be contained.

Those first moments at birth, those critical early months, I didn't get to share with number two daughter. Izzy was four months old when we met. Her first words directed toward me would not be heard until I returned from Okinawa, two years later.

The Marines were established by an act of Congress in 1775, two battalions of landing forces required to support and protect the naval fleet. The Marine Corps' size, roles, and missions increased over time; it was the smallest but most determined of the military services. As an institution steeped in history and tradition, it does not let one Marine forget he is part of something greater than himself. It is a service devoted to defending the country to the death, if needed—the ultimate sacrifice when called upon by the nation. The motto *Semper Fidelis* ("Always Faithful") means that a Marine will do what he must to protect freedom. The mission comes first in the Corps. Marines are indoctrinated and understand they are to make a stand anywhere, in any clime and place. We stand and fight united—Spartans of the modern age.

The Corps consumed me. I lived and breathed it. We each were required to spend over two thousand dollars on uniforms, and tailoring sessions took three separate visits for each Marine officer. Marines do not carry umbrellas, chew gum in uniform, or carry babies while in uniform, so I didn't. Upon completion of OCS, the candidates were commissioned second lieutenants. The Corps' distinction from the other services in officer training was an additional six-month school. Regardless of future jobs and skills, all new Marine officers were to attend. Called The Basic School, or TBS, it had a myriad of alternate names—The Big Suck or The Bad Summer, as two examples. A desk in one of the required classes had a hundred such derivatives written on it. I preferred the school environment and prospered in it. I studied late into the night to come out on top. The graduation order determined military occupational specialty, additional training as required, and assignment to the Fleet Marine Forces that guarded the globe.

Flight school was what I wanted, but I wanted to go back as a Marine. This might have been wishful thinking. In the absence of an aviation flight contract, I trained as a grunt. I had to be a fighter and knew nothing could match Marine infantry in a firefight. I could handle the stress, but Izzy, at four months old, couldn't. With the lack of a set schedule, she cried for six months.

Mess Night was a formal dinner, a private, formal Marine celebration. Wives and girlfriends did not attend. It was a time of camaraderie to toast fellow Marines, traditions, and history. The Marine uniform was dress blues or dress whites. Specific instructions governed the conduct of a Mess Night—with port wine, cigars, permission to speak required from the president of the Mess, fines for any infraction of the rules, and a Marine band parading in the beef while the assembled stood at attention.

Following the formal Mess, I talked to a lieutenant general, who had been the invited guest and speaker. He was an aviator, and I relayed my story about leaving the Navy and giving up flight school to be a Marine. He listened attentively, offered to assist, and tasked our company commander, Major Light Pack, to talk with him later in the week.

The major received his name while we were unloading a truck relocating bivouacs at the Three-Day War training evolution. A pack was shifted and found lighter than it should have been. The officers thought it belonged to one of their TBS classmates who was cheating by slacking. They quickly examined it and discovered the major's name on the inside. We were taken aback that our recon ranger commander, our fearless leader, not leading by example, thus tossing the morale of the class clumped in the shitter. Light Pack never knew what he had done to lose the vitality, vigor, and luster of his company or what his new name had become.

Two weeks later, I visited a bird colonel at Headquarters, Marine Corps, Aviation Selection branch. He said my wanting to become a Marine was no excuse for leaving flight school the first time. *Huh?* Flying was more important than the Marine Corps. *He didn't just say that. Am I hearing him right?* He said nothing in my flight records indicated promise. *No, normally everyone equally sucked, which is why it was called primary flight training.* He had once been the general's chief of staff, so he could easily persuade the general to ignore my request.

I uttered blah-blah-nothing, unable to speak coherently. As I walked out without seeing the general I was scheduled to see, I flipped the bird to the bird.

He didn't see it.

At Camp Lejeune, North Carolina, I was assigned as a rifle platoon commander to the newly arrived Second Battalion, Fourth Marines—the Magnificent Bastards. The unit was part of the Fourth Marine Regiment, which fought valiantly on Corregidor in the Pacific Theater but suffered surrender under orders from Major General Wainwright,

US Army. Here in North Carolina, they were part of the Second Marine Regiment. The only Marines ever having to surrender did so under orders while under Army command.

No wonder the Marines could provide 17 percent of the nation's defense on 10 percent of the budget. The platoon was half the strength of its assigned task organization, with no platoon sergeant. The platoon sergeant's Table of Organization (TO) rank was staff sergeant; the highest rank in my platoon was corporal. The M-16s, radios, and other communications equipment were Vietnam-era, H-style barracks, vintage World War II. The standard sidearm, Model 1911 .45 caliber automatic pistols, were last manufactured in 1945. The Marine Corps had stockpiles of .45s minted during the last year of production and preserved them. My .45 had a rear sight that would fall off if jostled, so I held it on with a piece of duct tape. It fired true for targets at arm's length. It was all I needed if I had to point it at one of my own—never necessary, but there, in case a Marine wouldn't charge into withering fire as ordered, or he thought too much, emotions getting the better of him.

Mission comes first. We don't do emotions. They get in the way of mayhem.

We trained with what we had and trained to accomplish the mission. We PT'd daily, ran five times a week, and marched with heavy packs, humped, weekly to build strength and endurance. The training tempo increased, starting with routine actions at the fire-team level, until such actions became reflex. The fire teams trained to coordinate as a squad and the squads as a platoon. The four platoons, led by the four newest lieutenants, trained as a company in the attack and in defense. Companies, commanded by captains, trained together for battalion exercises, and so on.

Joining a couple of months after the Bastards were reassigned to the United States for the first time since war's end in the Pacific, our new battalion commander was a lieutenant colonel we named "the Baron." A tall, dark, imposing figure, his father had been a Nazi SS commander, posthumously awarded the Iron Cross for actions against the Allies in France. After the war, the Baron's mother brought him to the United States, and he grew up in South Carolina. After joining the Marines when he was seventeen, he served as a reconnaissance sergeant in Vietnam.

The Baron changed the Corps from the bottom. His officers started reading military books and analyzing battles. He put the daily routine back in the hands of the enlisted. "Read more, run less" was the Bastards' new motto, and it was emblazoned on the back of the battalion's PT shirts.

The general in command of the division, "Big Al" Gray, often stopped in, as he was impressed with this refreshing reading program and enhancement to officer development. The reading program later became the professional standard for the Corps when Big Al became Commandant. The general also took with him the seeds of another now central Marine concept. Maneuver warfare, or hitting the enemy where he is weakest instead of into his strength, was a maxim from the Baron, moving the Corps from the blunt-force trauma, in-your-face days of the past.

The impact of this is lost on neophytes. The post-Vietnam era not only brought on the aforementioned shortages of personnel and equipment but race riots, drug use, and undeserved shame on many veterans, who felt pissed on by their civilian countrymen. Before inspecting the barracks late at night, duty officers had to lock and load their sidearm for their own personal safety. Officers took more control, as there was a lack of seasoned, enlisted NCOs, many having been forced out of service in the subsequent drawdown. The seventies were unkind to the military—and this is what I walked into.

The decades' long battle between the Israelis and Palestinian Muslim forces, Syrians, Lebanese, and others boiled over in Beirut streets. The lead antagonist, Yassar Arafat, and the PLO (Palestine Liberation Organization) attacked villages in northern Israel from Lebanon's relative security. Israel responded by invading Lebanon. In June 1982, Marines who were positioned in the Mediterranean Sea, just off the coast, were ordered in by President Reagan to evacuate Americans trapped in Beirut—part of an international peacekeeping effort.

The Bastards were on schedule for participation in a NATO operation in the North Sea. Northern Wedding/Bold Guard was a NATO operation designed to test the operations plan, the US military response to a Soviet invasion of northern Europe. My platoon was plussed up to 59 percent strength with the temporary assignment of four cooks.

The Commandant, General P. X. Kelley, visited the Bastards in a Danish defensive position and spoke with the Baron. Impressed by the commander and the Bastards' strength and agility, the commandant wanted the Bastards to relieve the unit in Beirut.

The mission in Beirut was muddy, and the rules of engagement were overly restrictive. Marines carried loaded weapons but with no rounds chambered. They could fire but only if directly fired upon. The Marines were to make a presence, not restore peace or order. The PLO and Israeli forces were battling throughout the countryside. Several incidents reported the Marine battalion currently on the ground was being fired upon by both. The Marines were not to return random fire in kind. Orders were to occupy a static position at the Beirut International Airport. The Marines were sitting ducks.

At hearing the Commandant's behest to deploy the Bastards to Beirut, the Baron, with his signature Southern drawl punctuated by a German accent, said, "If de Israelis fire upon us, ve vill be in Tel Aviv in twelve hours."

The Bastards were *not* deployed to Beirut. We returned stateside, as scheduled.

* * * * *

Marines slaughter on command, taking control of the chaos. Generals sell their testicles for politics and support of misguided diplomacy.

Our chance, my chance at redemption, to be in action was vanquished. Upon our return to Camp Lejeune, we prepared for the ritualistic deployment to Okinawa for six months.

We had a new lieutenant colonel in command by the time we deployed. This rotational cycle started the month before I was assigned to the Bastards to address personnel shortages globally. It continues still. Our training continued, adjusted for tropics, with forced marches, weapons training, rifle range, patrolling in triple-canopy jungle, setting in the defense, night attacks, and fire-support coordination. Fifty percent of Marine training is conducted in the dead of night.

Our training continued through additional deployments from Camp Schwab, Okinawa, to Fuji, Japan, and then to Hokkaido, the northernmost island of Japan. Deployed aboard ships as part of a US Pacific Fleet exercise, it was the largest such exercise held that far north since the end of World War II. Perhaps it was too far north, too provocative. The Soviets shot down Korean Air Lines 007. Declassified reports, years later, would say that the exercise in Europe and this deployment had the Soviet Union on edge and close to the brink, closest since the Cuban missile crisis.

Several ships broke from the flotilla to search for survivors. The remaining ships turned south to participate in a semiannual exercise off the coast of Chinhae, South Korea. The heliborne assault landed our company in the hilly countryside, several miles west of town, to establish a blocking position on a north/south highway. Fixed-wing aircraft broke overhead; noisy helicopters swooped in, offloading Marines. Racing to preassigned fighting positions, the company dug fighting holes, pockmarked their ancestral land, and established the block. The Marines must have seemed as peculiar as aliens as they patrolled the rolling hills, walked through the farms, and visited with locals in villages of thatched huts, with three-foot-tall jars of fermenting kimchi sitting along the outside of the hut walls. In three days—poof— they were gone for six months, until the next training exercise brought back the swarms. The locals were unperturbed, having been thirty years content. The good news to them was that we weren't North Koreans. I found a green hand-blown shot glass with air bubbles suspended in its shape, half buried in a riverbed while on patrol, a reminder of how far behind us the rest of the world was and how far they needed to come.

Monthly long-distance charges in the hundreds of dollars were common, in order to stay in touch with loved ones. When phones were available, I would talk with Selma for a half hour, giving her the highlights of each country in my international travels, ignoring the agonizing four weeks of cold and dreariness in which we operated at the base of Mt. Fuji. Haley would update me on play with the neighbor kids and on her sister. She would try to get Izzy to mutter something, anything, but Izzy didn't know me—her father, the stranger.

After being redeployed to Subic Bay for several weeks of jungle training, the company bivouacked at the lower MAU (Marine Amphibious Unit) Camp. One would think the entire company could receive training as valuable as jungle survival, but it wasn't how the Corps worked. Only a few seats were available in the prescheduled classes. Marines raised their hands, and we filled up to the miniscule limit with maybe seven Marines.

Upon completion of training, liberty call was sounded, and the Marines invaded Olongapo. The Cubi Point Officers' Club beckoned a trio of us officers. Dwoof, our company commander, didn't have fun in his Rolodex. He was rigged straight, bent backwards at attention. Captain Gumby, with nerd glasses. We were not sure he was straight. When back in the States, a girl stopped by the company headquarters to see him. He ran out the back door. The senior lieutenant was Mac, a health nut—he thought 6 percent body fat would make him a general. Rags was left behind in Okinawa on temporary duty. The island stronghold of Okinawa was held together with cadre forces and baling wire.

Hailing an on-base cab, two single officers, Folgers and Spaz, and I rode up the winding hill, passed by historical Korean and Vietnam-era pristine, white clapboard officers' houses and tropical gardens painted over with explosions of color. The cab dodged monkeys darting from tree to street, not to be confused with the barbecued skewer version we were warned not to eat.

Located on top of the world, the hill-crested club crowned an unimaginable view. Subic Bay lay at our feet, with every ship and port in full view, as well as the lower MAU camp we had come up from. Aircraft was doing touch-and-go's hundreds of feet below. The training area, White Beach, etched the distant shore, where I had purchased a well-crafted knife made from a derelict jeep's leaf spring.

The club's inside decor was as original as the exterior. The bar's ceiling and walls bristled with wooden depictions of Navy and Marine Corps aircraft, bombs, and rockets, which made for uniquely varied squadron plaques. Each was carved mahogany, painted, and lacquered, engraved with the commanding officers, execs, pilots, and navigators. The room breathed history and warrior life. The club pulsated, rivaling TJ's but more polished and proper. We stayed until closing and later, we visited often. Sunday brunch was the most delectable, delightful, and tasteful I ever encountered—and the first time I had fresh pineapple.

Heaven and hell resided next door to each other. Olongapo was out the base's main gate and across Shit River. One could get laid for a few pesos. Hundreds of young and not-so-young girls, thick as mosquitoes, scurried and darted around on little scooters.

"Hey, you sailor? No, you Marine, huh. You show me your hard core, okay?" The main drag was littered—girlies with miniskirts up to their navels clung to lampposts, luring men with their cheap provocative squawking.

"Hey, you like me. Pretty, huh. No? Why? You gay." Music quaked, hawking a party from each club's entrance—Club 69 or Ho-Down Heaven. By the hundreds, Marines and sailors marched into the blaring, darkened caves of decadence that sported Americanized names. One could get anything for a few dollars.

"Fuckie suckie two dolla'." Like lambs to the slaughter.

Intrigued by the circus, I spent my evenings observing from the balcony of the USO, sipping Red Horse or San Miguel Negra beer. I didn't know what love was, but I knew what it wasn't. "Hey, Marine, love you long time, ten peso."

It was sad, and I tried to wrap my head around it. How different was this spectacle from Copenhagen, Bangkok, Las Vegas, or back streets of major cities everywhere? Everybody sold themselves for something.

Fulfilling a need, wasn't that what they taught in business school? Free will—maybe that was the difference. Were they free or forced? All I knew for certain was that they were so young, not much older than I was when…

As we boarded our ship to depart, a corporal of mine said he wanted to get married, but by regulations, he needed my permission. Understanding purchased love's value, I told him he could, after a five-day waiting period. A few days later, the corporal returned and thanked me for my support of his previous decision, because he had purchased a newer girlfriend since.

The Philippines, notable for liberty call, was stellar for training—except for a married corporal who had a thing for the Asian delights—his delicacy and fatal flaw. He contracted a penicillin-resistant strain of syphilis. He was ordered by the Navy and State Department health officials to remain in the Philippines until they found an alternative medication.

We returned to the States two Marines short, the married corporal and a Marine busted by Okinawan authorities for possession. The Japanese were more stringent than the American judicial system. He was convicted and sentenced to serve eight years in prison, eating nothing but fish heads and rice. Shame—I liked the kid, a black kid, Lance Corporal Stringfield, from New York City. I'd positioned him in a dairy barn on an observation post during the exercise in Denmark. When we pulled out of that area, he expressed shock at what he'd discovered. Milk came from cows, he announced. I responded, "And the black ones produce the chocolate milk."

Selma and the girls met me at the new battalion headquarters upon arrival at Camp Lejeune. When Marines rotated stateside, they rotated headquarters buildings, too. President Reagan had pumped up the Defense Department budget for the first time since Vietnam, providing much-needed funding for upgrading housing and infrastructure. Construction moved at a breakneck pace, demolishing the iconic H-style barracks and building apartment-style living quarters in their place, in case Congress changed its mind about the money. Money ebbed and flowed into the services not based on any grand long-term national stratagems but on political leanings, so when the services received funding they spent as much as they could as fast as possible before someone changed their national minds. The new barracks were another touchy-feely guise to boost recruiting and attract and keep servicemen. And women screwed up the older open-squad bay arrangement.

To include the family in my Far East adventures, I bought colorful Oriental gifts for Selma and kids. I gave Selma a necklace and earrings I'd found in Kadena, but she deferred. Then I offered bright ginger jars, soapstone-carved horse statues, and other typical Oriental trinkets. To all three I handed bright red-silk robes. Selma didn't bother to put hers on saying she did not know what to do with it. After cajoling her for a picture of her wearing it, she put it on for the first and last time. The offerings to the goddess were meaningless. Not knowing to what to make of her reaction, I ignored it.

Izzy had not spoken to me since she was born. After hearing another Marine call me lieutenant, she mouthed out "Gaga"—her name for me for next four years. For everything else she said, Haley translated.

Rotated units immediately went into a stand-down to rest, recuperate, and reacquaint with their families. Training resumed on a loose, restrained schedule. The Bastards were assigned as the Air Alert Contingency battalion, with no thoughts to its actual employment. In assuming this role, the Bastards were to train to new techniques and tactics and have packed bags at the ready in the unlikely event we would be called out. We were ready to launch for parts unknown in twenty-four hours.

Three weeks later, disturbing news and images hit the airwaves. The Marine Headquarters in Beirut had been blown up by a suicide bomber that crashed through the front main gate, killing 241 servicemen, of which 220 were Marines. It was the largest single-day loss of Marines since the Battle of Iwo Jima.

Deeply saddened and pissed, our unit energized. We were that unit's backup, reinforcement, and support— the go-to guys. For the next six hours, we called in Marines and spun up preparations to leave and for aid to the beleaguered battalion in Beirut. We were ready, but then the chain of command realized the fallacy in having the most recently returned unit ordered away again. They halted our preparations as the backup unit and sent our backup instead.

As horrible as the bombing was, every Marine wanted to answer the call. Marines race to the sound of battle. Only for us, our hope of being those Marines was quashed. We were back on the bench after being so close to going, we could smell sulfur. Most of the infantry battalions stationed at Camp Lejeune were part of the multiyear peacekeeping effort in Beirut. Ours never was.

The unit en route to Beirut was additionally called upon by the president to invade the island of Grenada, restore order, and rescue American medical students held captive. Wish we had been there. Wish we had been anywhere. An Army battalion pinned down was relieved by a single Marine liaison attacking the hill and taking out the solitary sniper. Grenada should have been a Navy/Marine-only operation; it's what we did.

Military politics is as disturbing as civilian politics. Every service wanted a piece of action regardless the best suited. Even the Chairman of the Joint Chiefs of Staff, Army General John W. Vessey Jr., commented, "We have two companies of Marines running rampant all over the northern half of this island, and three Army regiments pinned down in the southwestern corner doing nothing. What the hell is going on?"

This thrown-together joint operation displayed chinks in the armor similar to the botched operation at Desert One in 1978, when a taxiing helicopter collided with a C-130 on the ground. When I first heard of the '78 fiasco, I was in Hannibal, Missouri, working with compounds and concoctions made up of mercaptans, a sulfur-based chemical compound that had the odor of skunk. As a lab assistant, I analyzed its composition as a precursor for a pesticide. The dichotomy of the situations kicked me in the gut, and that was when I could not wait any longer and the next day drove to St. Louis to join the Marines.

Tours of duty were normally two years long. Mine was almost up, so I volunteered for assignment to Parris Island, South Carolina. Marines do not get to design their career. Their tours of duty start in the Fleet Marine Force, then a tour of duty away, maybe a school, and then repeat. My family had as little to say about my next assignment as I did, which was West Coast or East Coast. I picked the West Coast and was planning to go to Marine Corps Recruit Depot (MCRD) San Diego, but the coding on the orders was wrong, then clarified, and then I was driving down the road to Beaufort, South Carolina.

Parris Island had been in military use since it was captured by Union forces in 1861 and converted to a Navy coaling station. Marines, who have occupied the island since 1891, turned it into a training station in 1915. At Parris Island, I trained to be a Series Commander, one of the two officers assigned to each group of two hundred. The series further broken down into four platoons of fifty recruits, each led by a pair of drill instructors.

The Series Commander was required by law to ensure adequate supervision and oversight of the DIs, a law instituted after the Ribbon Creek incident in 1956. In that incident, Sgt. McKeon had awakened his platoon late one night for a march into Ribbon Creek. Six recruits accidentally drowned. Sgt. McKeon was court-martialed, busted to private, fined, and served prison time. The Marine Corps instituted additional measures to ensure such incidents would never happen again. Two drill instructors per platoon were increased to three, and the Series Commander position was added. As more requirements and restrictions were added to Standard Operating Procedures, or SOPs, listed orders for what one could and could not do with recruits in training filled a three-inch binder. Due to various challenges and problems over the years, the Series Commander position was given an Assistant Series Commander. The additional role was to ensure the training schedule was maintained, not stopping or getting in the way of the other twelve series, each on its own schedule and training day. With fresh recruits offloading daily, one foul-up would gum up the works.

Early in the training cycle, officers had to be on deck from fifteen minutes before recruits wakened at reveille until fifteen minutes after taps. Days in common were from 0445 to 2015, seven days a week. Drill instructors' and series officers' workweeks could easily reach one hundred hours. Series officers' interaction was mainly supervising the drill instructors. Little direct contact was made with recruits. The DI maintained the platoon leadership position, and the officers oversaw the DIs from a comfortable enough distance that the DIs maintained the authority.

Still the days and weeks got long and then longer after several months. The schedule was a day off every two weeks, working four hundred-plus hours each month.

My brother came to visit and took Selma and the kids to the beach. I got to enjoy it by viewing the pictures he sent back a month later. The kids' youth was invigorating as they ran and played around the windbreak fence. I wished I could have been with them more. Images played through my mind—the toothless smiles on their faces, grinning ear to ear; Haley's blonde curly hair, like the young Shirley Temple; and Izzy, with her blonde Dorothy Hamill haircut, wearing sandals and a dress in her favorite purple. The most time I had with them was an occasional Sunday and maybe a dinner right before putting them to bed. I did get the chance to craft their Halloween costumes that year. Haley was a in a large box I made as a jack-in-the-box, and a tube of construction paper and an old costume witch's hat turned Izzy into a walking, talking purple crayon.

There was so little time for family, I almost didn't get the night off when my son was born. My new assistant series commander had yet to check onboard. A full series was ready to graduate and another was forming. Four hundred recruits were on deck as I scrambled to reach the hospital. I hoped Selma was quick to pump this one out, because I had a graduation of the senior series in twelve hours.

Noah arrived in the early morning, allowing barely enough time to see him and kiss Selma congratulations before I raced back to the base for the series' formal graduation. The ceremonies took place on the large asphalt grinder. The Series Commander led a graduate ceremony and then marched the new Marines in review before the assembled proud parents, the battalion commander, the regimental commander, and the base commanding general.

Never-ending days, PT twice a day, heat, thick humidity, and the flying teeth known to others as sand fleas were no real bother compared to the monotony. Repeating the same cycle, with little or no mental invigoration, wore on me more than the five to ten miles a day I ran. Having to be present here or there to keep an eye on the DIs was numbing. After a year, I signed up for college evening classes. Sleep deprivation pushed into ethereal overdrive as I ground out courses for a master's in business administration. I was reading more about money, finance, and the market, including a new and refreshing national newspaper called *USA Today*. Along with *Newsweek*, I started reading *Time* magazine, until they published a list of the nation's top leaders, with Michael Jackson on the list. I canceled my subscription.

Three alarm clocks hit a crescendo each morning—one next to the bed, a second across the room where I would have to get up to turn it off, and the last in the shower, where it clanged loudest. Each clock set fifteen minutes apart. Every day, I got up before 0400, which was really no problem. The factor was what time I crashed the evening prior. With no classes, I hit the rack at 2300—eleven o'clock. With the graduate program in full swing, lights out three nights a week was at 0100 or 0200—and I was comatose. If the kids cried out in the night, I never heard. Selma was busy taking care of the kids, full time, and didn't rise with me when I left for the day, thirteen days out of fourteen, for two years. I understood. Did she? I didn't have another inch to give.

In lieutenant-ship discussions, we talked about women, promotions, DIs, kids, next duty stations, our routines, and how much sleep we missed. Someone tabulated a tour of duty at Parris Island cost each of us four years of sleep.

Marines rest when they're dead.

CHAPTER 8

Walnut Hill Station

W*hen will this friggin' cattle car start moving?* The DART stopped halfway downtown due to a problem with the lines. Heat lightning, the conductor claimed, had hit a transformer.

Reading about entrepreneurship via an assortment of self-help books, I endeavored to grasp the concept of what made men great by reading biographies and listening to motivational speakers, such as Harvey Mackey, Zig Ziglar, Bob Proctor, Norman Vincent Peale, and others, who profited from preaching. There was money to be made in talking, but I was not a talker. Some good concepts, though.

I read *Think and Grow Rich*. Napoleon Hill interviewed hundreds of successful men in the early twentieth century, analyzed their comments, and crafted eleven basic concepts required to be a success. Of the eleven, I could remember only two. Men desired power (money) to get women (sex); women used their charms (their power) to get men's money (security/power). Sex and money was what drove the world. Life's questions could be answered with two words.

Why else would a seventy-two-year-old billionaire have a thirty-year-old gorgeous third or fourth wife? Wish it was that easy. Maybe it was, and I was making it harder than it should be. I tended to do that. But some seem to have it figured out, if you don't count divorces.

The car went dark, dead. *It should only take a few minutes.*
Ten minutes passed, then fifteen, then...

* * * * *

Having been away from home ten years and no longer wanting to disown my family by distance and absence, I was increasingly disturbed Dad might not have long to live. His grandfather Henry survived a gunpowder factory explosion in Quincy, Illinois, during the First World War. Twenty years later, he hit his head on the ice while skating and went crazy. He died in the state's mental institution at Fulton. Dad's father, Dad Sr., couldn't find his way back home in the micro town of Reading in '63. They found the brain tumor too late to do any good. Dad was quickly approaching the age of concern. Hoped brain turmoil was not genetic.

No more than eight when Bryson Sr. died, we visited the funeral home, where I touched my first dead body, a man I barely knew. He was cold and lifeless, dead or alive. I had no emotional connection to him. It appeared Dad didn't either. I never heard a sigh or witnessed a tear. Men didn't do tears. I wanted better. I wanted my children to weep at my funeral. They deserved to have better from me.

In joining the Marines for action, the glimmer had tarnished. Months in the field, dozens of weeklong exercises, mountains of books, miles run by the thousands, and training, training, and more training didn't bring me closer to the sound of the guns, my wanton destiny, or my spectral redemption. Marking time, doing nothing vital, and missing the challenge of danger, it appeared it would never happen. I wasn't born to be a staff weenie, ride a desk, or savor the smell of toner in the morning. It was time to move on and seek adventure elsewhere.

My young family needed to know more about my father, who he was, and how he could be. Hell, they needed to know about me, too.

Dad was different from the man I knew as a kid. He was good man, had a sense of humor, and we could relate man-to-man, some. I wasn't the best at following Cardinals baseball. He talked more now, even though neither of us was a talker. He communicated with me by being a welcoming grandfather to the kids. He had emerged from his shell, and I enjoyed his company, despite the shortage of words.

Leaving the Corps with a trusty MBA sidearm and more responsibility than most people my age could have hoped for in a lifetime, I was confident suitable civilian employment was waiting for me.

Alas, the funds expended on a graduate degree were wasted. I hadn't learned to read the business climate. The month I left the Marines was October '87.

Black Monday brought fresh, warp-speed realities to civilian life. World financial markets crashed, causing the largest one-day percentage drop in stock market history. Ten years of savings invested halved before the month ended. With no signs of near-term employment on the horizon, I requested an extension to my honorable departure and was granted such until the next year.

Companies in St. Louis, like IBM, Monsanto, and McDonnell-Douglas, held off hiring. Six months scrabbling for work, our savings vaporized. An open slot was found at a large, privately held company. I went to excruciating lengths to convince the hiring managers I wasn't violent. Sixteen interviews finally extracted the position of sector fulfillment database manager at a company called Schwadron. The job paid 30 percent less than I'd been making, with one-hundredth the responsibility. From a male-only world of warriors, I was thrown into a crocodile pit of near all-female administrative assistants.

Before long, my confidence meter pegged at zero. Assimilating into the civilian world, I had to learn a new language, one where every sentence did not start with *fuck*. I outfitted in the appropriate business garb to blend into this new, foreboding environment—corporate dark wool suits; the quintessential blue or white cotton button-down dress shirts; red or yellow power ties. lunch was *lunch*, instead of running. New dress shoes were shined so well, I could read the light bulb wattage over my head as I stared down into them.

I had plenty of time to sleep—at work, if I wanted. I worked half speed to keep pace with the job; the automation was geared with high-end, thirty-year-old mainframes. The first person I worked with was a guy named Leo. We had military service in common. He had been in the Army, a supply technician, and said he could have been a Marine, too, if he'd really wanted to.

"Me, too," I said.

Leo ran the fulfillment program for a client company named ComGraf, out of California. He hated the job and groused about it. He said the woman who ran the program from their end was calling daily with problems, changes, and updates—the bitch.

Two months in, they gave the bitch to me. Her real name was Cynthia.

Fulfillment programs were incentive promotional programs, assigning tangible luxury items and travel, instead of money, to reward attainment for sales milestones and goals. The biggest clients were large automotive manufacturers, but over time, ingenious new angles were introduced to attract different and smaller clients. Large or small, sales numbers changed monthly. There were continuous problems and disputes over who got what and for how many points.

The client visited St. Louis the following month. Her bosses had been here before, but she hadn't. She said, "I went to school in Kansas City, but I'm surprised to see you in suits and ties here."

Scuffing my toe into the carpet, I said, "My bib overalls were in the dry cleaners. Damn-nubbit, I tried real durn hard to get there before it closed yesterday, but the creek flooded, and that cuss of a mule of mine wouldn't budge it. Had to take one of them two-by-four boards to it, just to git him back home. Pissed on my good boots, too. Real pardun, ma'am." Her face blistered as she shrunk.

Cynthia and I had no problems thereafter. I addressed her concerns, called back when problems were solved, and ensured monthly statements were mailed on time, until an issue above my pay grade rose the following year.

In annual contract negotiations, the client had complaints about the price of the database program and found a company on the West Coast that could do it cheaper. They were walking out the door. I leaped from my rookie position and blurted that personal computers with a desktop database program would cost a tenth of the price that we had been charging them.

My shocked supervisor, a fifteen-year resident of mainframe land, apologized for my outburst but said he would research the potential. Upon personal discussions he held with staff programmers in the basement, he learned a program could be written for a mere sixty thousand dollars, instead the half million we were charging the client. Overnight, it seemed, the PC killed the mainframe biz.

Nobody said boo to the rookie, but the gig was mine to manage. I would have to hire an assistant to stay on top of it. Dozens of applications came in, and I couldn't tell one from another. Talking to Selma about the dilemma, she had a friend who knew someone who was looking. I interviewed and then hired Molly Sue Tyson, and she ran the program flawlessly. What qualified her was what qualifies most people for their jobs—I knew someone who knew her. That cut short the hiring process. The only downside was she coerced me into the intricacies, inner workings, and gossip of the *floor*.

Joining in the cubical foraging frenzy, I contributed obligatory snacks for the all-too-frequent celebratory excuse to commemorate anything and everything. I would bring whatever Molly Sue told me to bring. We toasted Gladys' carbuncle removal, Vicki's eighteen-pound baby with eleven toes, everybody's birthday, their kids' birthdays, marriages, anniversaries, semi-anniversaries, divorces, hirings, firings, C-sections, periods, and cramps—or so it seemed. We feasted on indiscernible delicatessen delights from bottomless Crock-Pots, bacon-wrapped beanie-weenies, mini-hamburgers, sliders, slingers, thirty-seven varieties of chips, Tanya's memorable and must-have spinach dip, seven-layer dip, taco salad dip, regular taco dip, pizza salad, bean salad, chocolate salad, Mandarin onions, Italian ice cream, fried Twinkies, pickled pigs' feet, and on and on. I could not see my weight on the scale anymore.

Molly Sue and the PC program gave me an idea. I labored to take the ComGraf example, multiply it, and overlay the success onto the rest of company. In so doing, a study resulted that reduced the company's size by 25 percent by employing more PCs and fire teams of Molly Sues to run them. When the work was submitted, the civilian chain of command yawned. I was offered a seat on a token corporate creative committee, brainstorming future productivity recommendations. The committee met to analyze current trends and work habits and then drafted recommendations for the president to disregard. After several meetings, I was ready to search for a more worthwhile use of my time. So I quit.

To me, politics was pretending to do the right things to stay in office or to move up the ladder to bigger and better—or should I say, to more popular and powerful—positions. It is the grandest popularity contest. Another better definition I'd picked up from a motivational speaker, Bob Proctor, was that "poly" meant many, and ticks were blood-suckers.

I abhor politics, so I changed jobs to facilitate running for the legislature, where I hoped to fight the beast itself and to do things for the right reason. I started a year early and met the party faithful. Weekends were expended by knocking on doors in the district. My inability to gain the support of my party's state senator, because of his fear of disaffecting the other party's members who supported him, didn't help my candidacy. I was on my own. With a few friends' assistance and Haley and Izzy, we handed out leaflets at local parades and fairs. My biggest official fund-raiser yielded little support. I lost money. Since I did not have the support needed, I used my own resources to print brochures and buttons, accumulating personal debt to cover the shortfalls. It didn't help.

The twit to whom I lost was an asshole wearing a smiley face—that's what Haley told me a few years later. She learned it from a girl she worked with at Steak 'n Shake, who used to be his secretary. He's now in jail for misusing campaign funds. Wonder if he has his smiley face now.

The average voter was an idiot. No wonder politics was idiotic as well. It was easy to see how much they knew by watching Leno or "Watters' World" on O'Reilly. Surprising to learn how little everyone knew of politics, government, the military, geography, and the world at large. I missed working with people who knew the stakes. I missed the edge.

Unable to make ends meet, I asked Selma if she could find a job. The ship was listing and taking on water and would go down without her assistance as a plug. I hated asking—I felt I'd failed to live up to my obligation as provider. The kids were better raised by a stay-at-home mother. Becoming a two-income family was a whole new experience, as Selma had not been employed during our dozen years of marriage. Haley and Izzy, already in school, would fare better than Noah, who would have to go to daycare.

I had left Schwadron's and become a sales representative and then a branch manager for a dying computer company. It imploded, along with other overly abundant, high-priced IBM-compatible personal computer companies at the end of that recession. The personal computer had become a commodity, following Moore's law of doubling processing speed every six months. Computer hardware companies could not get the product life they needed out of their systems to make a profit.

Perpetually on a quest for the purpose to my existence, it seemed like I was always running, to or from something, I didn't know, not slowing to think. Deep thoughts squandered time, and I kept busy to stop thinking. *Quit thinking, dammit. Have to have more action in my life—live*, I kept telling myself, thinking again. I needed to prove myself. The Corps should have done it but didn't. Spent all the time training to be one of the world's finest, but I missed the call. Doubtful they'd dialed a wrong number. They had the number. I'd never been tested under fire, if that was the answer to the abiding question. Something was missing in me.

The summer and fall of '90 brought a force buildup in Saudi Arabia to counter the Kuwaiti invasion by Saddam Hussein's Iraqi forces. The St. Louis reserve unit for which I had been responsible when I left active duty mobilized for the first time since Korea—*great*.

I immediately investigated how I could return to active duty. By the time the paperwork churned, like a gopher through a snake, through Marine headquarters' administrative guts, Desert Storm was over. My request surfaced months later, and I was denied active duty affiliation but offered a commission in the reserves. Though I did not like the prospect, I accepted the fate.

In the fifties, the reserves met monthly on an evening. It was where the World War and Korean War veterans reminisced over a couple of beers. Vietnam changed the routine, as it became more formal and required Marines to meet the same annual requirements as active-duty Marines. Drills for us on many weekends began on Friday afternoon. If travel to a training base was required, we often would not return home until so late on Sunday, it was Monday morning.

Annually, I applied to return to active duty. In addition to monthly drills and the annual two weeks of active duty training, I volunteered additional weekends and led several West Coast counter-drug joint task force missions. I drove to various reserves-required courses in Quantico, Virginia, over several summers and attended intelligence school another year. Finishing the copper cupolas on the chimneys of Roemer Originals jewelry store in another short-term job I held, I deployed from St. Louis with a twelve-hour notice, in support of Gitmo operations—guarding encampments of Cuban and Haitian boat refugees.

Selma, the kids, and I, had a version of "QOL" for once. QOL was "quality of life," a term and program adopted by the other services but not widely accepted by the Corps. We were around her family and mine, vacationing in a way that did not involve hours of highway travel crammed in a car, and settled in our first home purchase. We learned of crab grass, weeds, trimming, fertilizer, mulch, and landscaping, common issues of suburbanites.

Haley and Izzy were my hunting buddies early on; Noah was still a bit too young. We would spend the weekend up in the country, where Mom and Dad had retired. They would occasionally go out in the fields and walk with me. When it became too cold in the deer stand or walking around, we would make our way back to Mom's house, a stone house with a cabin attached, where she had fixed biscuits and gravy or scrambled eggs and chili. The kids enjoyed spending time with her more than the hunting but that was part of the appeal. What we all liked about being in the country was Mom and her country cooking. In time, the girls were less interested, but Noah grew older and able and took their place. The girls would sometime go but take a book, and they might not leave the stone house. On the way home, we would stop at a convenience store and pick up some gummy worms and soda, a treat that in time became a requirement.

When not working or at a soccer game with the kids, I was improving and remodeling the house. Our home had common ground behind it, a creek serving as a storm sewer. During spring rains, the creek swelled from its usual trickle to become a torrent, fifteen feet deep, frothing at the brim. The embankment, a precipice, was the backyard's terminus. Upon moving in the first winter, with temps in the low thirties, I built a white picket fence to keep the kids from running out of the yard and off the cliff. The need for a fence overrode the fact the post holes weren't as deep as they should have been—the ground was too frozen to dig them deeper.

Wade, my former college roommate, hadn't been accepted into dental school right away. He spent a year rehabbing houses, skills he'd acquired from leafing through a bunch of *Time/Life* books on construction. I took up the cause and, with the help of Wade and 3-D, tore down my first wall. *Refreshing.* I never stopped and spent the rest of my life tearing apart and rebuilding. I could see progress and improvement in something.

Over time, Selma and I wallpapered a couple of bedrooms, the living room, dining room, and hall. The linoleum was ripped up in the bathrooms and tile was laid. In the basement, a bedroom was built for the girls by walling in a section underneath the basement steps. New carpet was installed in the basement. Beve, 3-D, and friends from church helped put on a new roof. A brick walkway was built and the front yard landscaped. The small kitchen was enlarged by removing another wall. The cabinets were painted, new appliances and a new countertop was bought, and the original, ugly harvest-gold tile backsplash was painted. Despite the litany of improvements, repairs could not remodel our marriage.

When I left active duty, I anticipated things would improve, certainly. It was not how things happened. Nothing seemed right. The relationship between Selma and me, assumed as a given, slipped and yawed and stalled. Stress and strain was expected with transition, but a merry-go-round of jobs was unsettling. Selma resented me for her needing to work outside the home. She bounced between jobs herself. She understood her personal struggle but couldn't understand mine.

In bed one night, she commented a coworker earned more than she did. The coworker had a college degree. I tried to blow it off, as I'd been here. *Don't reply; she'll fade.* Time to sleep for me was talkie-time for her. Talk between us was generally more like sparring anyway. The limited chatter she wished to conduct was in the dark, when I was asleep, which was normally the second my head hit the pillow. Besides, for me, the bed was for one of two things—and the other one was becoming the rare exception. Selma never opened up to discuss real issues at the table or while sitting on the couch, where I could look at her. She could not debate and analyze while looking me in the face. She reserved open-air discussions for rage, venting her bile and disgust. The dark—her shroud of security—must have hidden fissures in her crust.

Selma babbled something, the same as before, but twisted the words and context, pretending to make it different. This topic had come up too often and disturbed too many nights' sleep. Placating her would not do.

Did she want to be a nurse or a hygienist? She couldn't choose. Around and around we sashayed to nail down which one would make her dream come true. *A nurse? Okay, you sure?* The money would be tight, but maybe she could ease in, taking a class at a time. She was afraid I would not support her or that I'd expect too much around the house with her traditional duties. "Picking up the slack is easy enough," I told her, *How hard could it be?* What mattered most was she would be doing what she had wanted to do for years, and I wanted it for her, too. *Agreed—so sleep.*

* * * * *

Selma quit her likewise, unfulfilling job and enrolled in school. I understood.

She never blinked, looked back, or slowed down; she virtually left. When Selma wanted something, she got it, and everyone stay out of the way. It was her way or no way. The classes started slowly at first, all prerequisites. Originally, she'd signed up for the first open semester three years out, but she completed her required classes early and a nursing program slot opened up.

Selma had a grueling schedule: classes, labs, homework, and study groups, but why was she was out until two or three in the morning? Who she was with? It never occurred to me to ask; she was doing what she needed to do. She worked all weekends, every weekend, at a friend's, many times dragging in between 0130 and 0200.

In the tumult of those long four years, I met the guys and girls from her study group once, except for Mary Jane, whom I saw regularly. She would stop by anytime, with a pack of wine coolers under her arm. The others I knew by names and voices, as they constantly called the house, especially Gaylord. He was an airline mechanic, married with two kids, who was looking to change career fields. If Selma was not at school or asleep, she was on the phone, talking to one of them. Giving her flexibility, love, and the support she needed, I didn't intrude; I stayed out of her way. Our limited talking grew quieter.

During infrequent, polite conversation, Selma would relate the horrible lives others in her group were leading, how their husbands had done this or that.

My common response was, "Aren't you glad I am not like that?"

Selma's study group seemed more devoted to gossip than anything else. Mary Jane's husband worked two jobs to support her going to school and had no time or energy for her. She complained about that when she finally had time to spare for him. *How peculiar*, I thought when I overheard the conversation, *for the wife to gripe about a husband's working* too *hard to make ends meet but never being there.* What the hell did Mary Jane want, the working man or the lazy one? A man couldn't be around if he was at work. The money had to come from someone's working. She couldn't have it both ways.

To Selma, I said, "Aren't you glad I am not like that?"

Selma later told me Mary Jane was screwing an Arab car dealer she'd met. It was so heated she met him at his dealership after her evening class, where they would do it in the parking lot in a car of her choosing. She would pick a different convertible each time, and they would do it with the top down, hers and the car's, under the security camera. The Arab would enjoy the security tapes when they were apart. As owner, he was also in charge of security.

The tension in the house elevated the moment Selma woke. The clean dishes were not in the right place, and too many were dirty again. I was not doing enough around the house to suit her, or I'd fixed dinner wrong for the kids. When I went to the grocery store, I didn't buy the right brand at the right place from the right, cheaper food store. Lucky Charms were bought at Aldi's and the bologna was cheaper at IGA. I tried to assist her studies but seemed to hinder her more than helped. My reserves weekend obligation fell at the worst time of the month, she said; plus, I liked the Marines too much.

The kids needed help with homework each evening, and if they had to ask her a question, that meant I was not helping them right. She was upset with my lack of contentment in myself, for not liking the job I had, whatever it was that week. Her venting was caused by the stress of her school and not really because of me. That was what I kept telling myself. Life's ankle biters were getting to her, and she was never happy around me. To justify it and continue the daily pursuit without reaching out and rubbing her out, I chalked it up to my being the easy target, the lowest hanging fruit.

During the time Selma was in school, I'd been let go three times and was working on my fourth job. The first two companies had collapsed. At the third, I wasn't the slick talker or liar I needed to be to sell the volume of stocks and mutual funds for meeting the multi-million dollar sales goals. In the current one, I was selling crappy alarm systems to small businesses at ninety-nine bucks a whack. My personal goal was to do well enough for a promotion to higher-end corporate systems, where the big money was made.

It was not what I wanted to do, but I had to do something and aspire for something better. My desire to escape my downward spiral was incidental with my greatest skill, which was poor timing. I couldn't apply to the CIA or FBI—their hiring was frozen by President Clinton. By the time it thawed, I was too old.

Married but alone, I stayed busy working on the house. I would think myself to death. Physical labor was therapeutic. A project done by my own hands was real and more satisfying than efforts applied in making a living. Whatever the office job I had, it didn't seem like real work. It was a way to make ends meet. The Monday-to-Friday world I lived in was played by someone else. It must have been my avatar, because I couldn't recall being there.

The kids were not alien to the constriction, sure. They were inhabitants of their worlds, doing kid things in going to school or the mall, watching TV, playing with friends, and participating in soccer and baseball or softball. Unspoiled to me, they were the true joy in my life and kept me sane. Their weekly assigned chores were dishes, laundry, cleaning their rooms, and helping out as needed on other things. We watched *The Cosby Show* together or Tim "the Toolman" Taylor but never *The Simpsons* or *Married with Children*. The lack of parental respect displayed was inappropriate for my children to watch.

Haley and Izzy, now in their teens, didn't like to be seen with Dad too much. My trust in them was complete, I explained, but sometimes the world was an ugly place. I would stay to the side, keeping my eye on them in case they realized they needed me. Noah and I went to the movies. He was young enough still to let me clasp his hand, which meant more to me than it did to him. We would watch the latest action flick, fans in common. He was my bud, my hunting partner since the age of six, when I taught him how to shoot and the safe handling of weapons.

Haley had no problems with learning and school. It all came to her naturally. She crashed head-on into teenhood and thrashed about the house, wearing her "I've arrived, and I am in charge" attitude. I had to sit her down and adjust her compass, redirecting her enthusiasm. I spelled it out, expressed my heartfelt regret that she was growing up, and explained I wasn't ready to let her go. I would, little by little, whether I liked it or not. I had to slow her down and let her gradually assume a little responsibility to prepare her for being in charge of herself when that dreaded time came, when adulthood unfortunately commenced.

With the older two reaching the age of having problems with authority, I pointed to the frayed shag carpet on the living room floor.

"What color is the carpet?"

Izzy looked down and said, "It is green."

"Haley?" I said.

"I would say it is green, too." Haley said.

"What if I told you the carpet was purple?" I asked.

Both girls' eyes crossed. "No, it's not," they said in unison.

"Yes, it is," I said. "And I will tell you why. Because I said so. What you will learn in life, as you are beginning to understand with expected confusion, is that the one in charge gets to determine what is right and what is wrong. It may appear to you to be one thing, but your teacher, or a parent, my boss—whoever the authority is, normally the one paying you or paying the bills—determines what is and isn't the *truth*. It is an unfortunate but important fact: he who is king makes the rules."

Simmering, they thought they understood. The carpet was now purple, because I said so.

Izzy was never a bother and did as she was told, sliding into her teens without a whimper. Not the best student initially, she bucked and strained against the odds and with herself, until eventually, self-taught and composed, she became one of the best and brightest around, stepping out of her sister's shadow.

Noah was Noah; boys are easy.

Noah's toughest time was with reading, and he really didn't want to learn how to ride a two-wheeled bike. We spent hours painfully reading his books, and I eventually convinced him to give the bike a test. We started at McNair Park, a couple of blocks away, where falling would not be as painful, if and when he fell off.

As we returned, I expressed to him a lesson I wished I could have taught myself. As we slowly went down the hill from the park's entrance, on the sidewalk toward our house, a light pole loomed large—a hundred yards ahead—in the middle of his path. The sidewalk was built around its base on both sides.

"Don't focus on where you don't want to go by looking at the light pole," I told him. "Concentrate on the narrow path on either side—the path you *do* want to take."

"I can't," he said and hit the pole. He refused to try riding his bike for the next couple of weeks. But when he tried again, he rode better and never hit another pole. The lesson he demonstrated taught more to me than him—to concentrate on what you want instead of what you don't. It is the hardest lesson to learn.

The kids and I had mature conversations. I treated them as if they were older than they were. Didn't teach them right from wrong, as much as how to analyze the reasons for both, to better prepare them to stand alone on principles. They heard more than their share of my personal opinions on socialists, Communists, and evil Democrats and their contribution to the demise of self-reliance and democracy. We talked of life, family history, and American history—as it really was instead of as misplayed by the media. We discussed politics, responsibility, the meaning of money, what was real, and what was phony. Anything and everything under the sun was up for discussion, except the most nebulous and vaporous unconstrained human emotion. We never spoke of love outside the natural love that parents had for their children. The other love's meaning and understanding was completely lost on me. I didn't know how to contribute.

I could not broach it—it was too caustic, too cold. How could a man and woman live together and have nothing in common but children.

* * * * *

"Brick, the phone." Selma had answered the phone, expecting it to be for her, since ninety out a hundred calls were for her and the rest for Haley. She hollered downstairs to the basement family room, where the kids and I were watching TV. I went upstairs and pulled the fifteen-foot cord over to a chair in the living room.

"Hello," I said.

"Hi, Brick. How are you doing?" the voice said.

"Who is this?"

"I moved back for a year temporarily and thought I would see if you were around. I looked you up in the phone book and found your phone number."

"Cameo, is that really you? Well, I'll be! I couldn't place the voice. I never talk on the phone except to clients and Marines. You sound good. How long has it been? I have to rattle my brain to figure out when the last time was that we talked."

Her voice was soft and caressing, a tone foreign to me. It had been at least seventeen years.

"I'm on the Inspector General team over at Scott Air Force Base. I am staying in my old room. I moved back home, but I left the family in Texas. I was going to be gone so much, and the girls did not want to leave their school. I am staying in my old room. What are you doing?"

I hated to tell her. "What rank are you these days?" I said instead.

"I'm a lieutenant colonel, the inspector for fiscal administration. And you?"

"I am in sales. I sell security systems, and I'm in the Marine reserves."

"Marines? How did you end up there? Weren't you in the Navy last I saw you?"

"I got out after two years and joined the Marines. Did it for about eight years and then out again. I went in the reserves a couple of years ago for something worthwhile to do. Do you have kids?"

"Oh, yes, I have two. Darlene is on the flag team at her school, and Margie is very good on the piano. They are both good students."

"I have three kids, Haley, Izzy, and Noah. The girls are both teens, and you know what that means. My buddy is Noah. We do everything together." We talked about her Air Force and its differences from my Marine Corps. I admitted how great her career was and my lack of one, putting as much of a whitewash as I could on this civilian thing. "My wife is in the nursing program right now. I didn't expect the phone to be for me. She is usually fielding calls from her study group most of the time." I expressed my hectic life and the trials and tribulations of Selma's nursing degree program. We prattled to each other for an hour, as one might with any old acquaintance unseen for a half life.

"We should get together sometime for lunch." Cameo said. "It would be good to see you."

"That would be great," I agreed, while shaking my head no. "We'll have to do that sometime while you're still in town." I hung up the phone and shared the whole conversation with Selma.

CHAPTER 9

Lovers Lane Station

I have come to consider dysfunctional, normal.

"What did you say?" I mumbled. I realized the voices were coming from behind me. One ding-dong talking to another.

Ding said, "Are you one of those guys that just goes about his business, working hard every day to make a living, and then finds out his old lady is banging his ugly jackass neighbor, the one with the schlong peeking out of his too-short '70s shorts? If it is your problem, hell, no, you don't have a smile, and you have an innie instead of an outie by now. If this unfortunate episode has made your face a tomato, because you know in your groin it's your life, then you need to call 1-800-GET-EVEN for a confidential investigation. All matters handled delicately."

"Ya kiddin', right? After that blast, you used the word 'delicately.' Who'd buy it?" Dong, the lesser idiot, said to the first.

"You never know what they will print. I wrote it. Original, huh? Definitely gets your attention. And how can you forget the phone number? An ad for *Cheaters*, written for the *Slick*—that didn't quite make it past the censors. But I got it into another rag."

"Really?"

"Yeah, there's another trade paper down where the strip clubs are. Small circulation, but they'll print anything."

"What is your job, public relations or sales?"

"At a place as small as ours, it blurs. Mostly PR. It's crazy interesting. Every year, we have a client that opens a club for just six weeks at Christmastime."

"What's the place called?"

"Ho-Ho-Heaven. Using the Santa Claus theme doesn't work well past New Year's. Said he saw the name in the Philippines."

I was the idiot for listening.

* * * * *

Affection was not an affliction Selma had; I can't recall if she ever did. It would have required emotional attachment beyond the desire for cohabitation. Dating gave way to lust, lust to marriage, marriage to I don't know. I never sought compassion—never thought about it much, but when I needed it, it was not to be found.

Selma was the type, at least with her friends, who became impassioned during a telephone intercourse with one of her fellow talkers. It allowed her to stand off and remain disconnected from reality. If they who categorize and study these things have a malady on their list, Selma was the type who was unaffectionate and asexual, except once a month. She never said she loved, never said sorry. Words were meaningless; feelings were emoted through actions. Surprises and gift giving excused the need for verbal pronouncements—the action alone spoke.

If I took that at face value, I would think she hated my guts and was too much the coward to say so, using us, mostly me, to get what she wanted.

Out of the blue, years earlier, before her student stint, Selma announced she was never ironing my shirts again. Who knows why—she must have seen something on *Oprah*.

Selma slept mornings. I was up and waiting for the girls to come and kiss me good-bye. Haley and Izzy never ate much for breakfast but were busy ironing their clothes and in the bathroom, doing the makeup thing. I heard footsteps head to the front door. The door opened and then closed. I waited. It was in the thirties outside; they must be warming the car.

I waited.

"No. They didn't," I said.

I hurried to the front window and saw them backing out of the driveway. I ran to the door, threw it open, and stood at the glass storm door with my hands on my hips, wearing only green Marine nylon running shorts that doubled as skivvies. They did not see me motion them back.

The car was half in the street when they looked up and saw me, waving them back for my good-bye kisses. They both grinned and shook their heads.

With shaving cream still on my face, I ran after the car. Both girls burst out laughing, twisting their heads about as they looked down the street, hoping none of their friends had seen me charging at them. I opened Haley's driver's side door and planted a big kiss on her cheek, smearing shaving cream everywhere. By the time I went on to the other side, Izzy already had locked the door. "You'd better open it, or I'll crawl over Haley to get to you!" I told her. Struggling to buckle her seat belt while laughing, she yelled "Okay, okay, but hurry!" She opened the door and stuck out her cheek, getting her deserving shaving-cream smooch.

I shook my finger playfully, but they knew I was serious when I said, "Don't ever do that again."

The kids knew they had to kiss me good night every night. When the girls started this teenage habit of ignoring of me, I would hunt them down. But that is what they wanted, I think—to see if I loved them enough to come downstairs and pounce on them in bed and kiss them good night.

Haley and Izzy fought over the covers and who was on whose side. They complained of sleeping in the same bed. I explained over and over that they might hate it now, but it would make them closer as adult sisters, as it had for my brother and me.

I needed their laughter, their affection, and their love. It was all I was getting. One night, I admitted it was not for their benefit but mine. Being a father seemed the only thing I was good at, if that. I had nothing to tell me one way or the other.

Having come to expect Selma's distance, I could not bear the fact she behaved the same way toward the kids. She let them go to school without getting up or even calling them into the bedroom for a hug and a kiss good-bye. I chided her for it, and in time, she slowly warmed to the idea—they needed it more than she did. They needed the reminder, as they walked out the door, that their mother loved them. It took years to finally get through to her, before she could say "I love you" to them.

I was not as fortunate.

Our inconsistent coexistence troubled me. I wondered from time to time what problems were making her so distant. What should I do to help? Ask her what was wrong. Brushing me off or outright ignoring me for weeks. Selma let thorns fester, build up pus, until the sore had to be poked to relieve the inflammation.

Invariably, it was a wrong I'd committed, the latent infraction corkscrewing in her memory. Weeks or months had passed, and I could not recall or relate to her allegation as portrayed. After the toxic cloud settled from her atomic outburst, she might explain it away as a "pity party for Selma." I glowed in radioactive dust.

It was my fault. Whatever *it* was that week or the new *it* on sale that month—unless Selma recalled and connoted this *it* to other discrepancies in the past, and then *it* was a character flaw or illness I suffered since we first met. Whenever I was near, her Geiger counter chirped *it*.

In trying to figure out the current *it* as the *its* copulated and multiplied, I pondered where we were headed and expressed as much out loud. We needed to set goals to drive our actions to get us to whatever blank future we shared. Were we to live in the country? Travel or stay in St. Charles? What were we trying to accomplish?

She surrendered her inability to conjure even a skimpy impression of a conjoined future, when she couldn't see past the end of the week. With the current helter-skelter we had, I could take the hint, but this was how it had always been—this repast already tasted. To me, a dream or goal had to be set, or I'd go nowhere. Because we were nowhere now, anywhere seemed nirvana.

When she had the available time and money, Selma enjoyed collecting. Her main interest was finding inexpensive, colorful, baked-enamel-clad turn-of-the-century cookware called Granite Ware. As time allowed, she retreated with friends, had lunch, and visited various antique shops and malls. I didn't want to buy her Granite Ware as gifts; I was afraid it would look like I was encroaching. If she wanted a hobby, she could keep it. Besides, I didn't know a good one from a bad one.

I offered to go with her just to spend time together exploring. "No, thanks," she said. "Meeting friends." More often than not, however, she said, "I don't care."

Having become bilingual and learning to decipher native woman-speak, saying she didn't care translated to no. Woman-speak, an imperfect study of the ever-changing and evolving female dialect, professed only by female interlocutors, had not been my first choice for a second language. I needed it to study it more intently, though, to circumnavigate this remote and foreign culture.

Selma withdrew completely. Constantly, at school or studying, when she was home, life was better for the rest of us when she was asleep. Awake, she was angry and hostile. The kids would say or do something trivial, and Selma would scream at them. They'd ask me what they had done. I would tell them they'd had a glimpse of hell. Then I would tell them they had done nothing; whatever it was, probably *it* was something I'd done, though I hadn't a prayer what *it* was yet. "Come back in a month or two." I'd say. "I should know by then." At church, they spoke of Satan. I couldn't help the image I saw of him was their mother, sitting beside me.

To confront the Beast, I let things pile up. As one particular mountain of *its* stewed pockets of volatile, wretched gases so large I couldn't open the front door, I lit the match.

"I don't want to hear it again," I said. "I am not the terror of the world and certainly, the kids aren't. Leave them alone." The explosion registered throughout the state.

"I'm late. Get the hell out of my way," she thundered, splitting her tongue as she spoke.

"Hell—funny you should say hell, because this is it; this is where you belong. We are all dead, stuck here in the hell you have created. Enough of this horseshit. Quit dumping your problems on the kids. I am always the bad guy. Find some reason to pierce me like you do most of the time, but leave the kids out of it, whatever the flying fuck *it* is this time."

She slugged me and then quaked the house with the door. Woman-speak translation: your guess.

The kids played sports, but if one of them had a game, Selma came only half the time, and if she did show up, it wasn't until half-time. She received phone calls from study partners and talked for two, three, four hours without stopping, never acknowledging our presence or existence, day after day, night after night. A new roof over her head, freshly painted walls, a warm bed, food, phone, car, financial support—she visited the house but didn't dwell there, cutting herself off from the rest of us. We were the nuisance, spoiling her career enhancement. I could no longer remember the good wife and mother, beautiful and caring once upon a time. Her liberated scent was pungent, but to her, it was springtime.

Though I didn't care for how she treated the kids, she treated them better than the troll—me. We put up with it. We had no alternative but to grin and bear it. Without money to spare, I spent too much trying to find a key, a hint, a code, a clue by purchasing some trinket, bauble, or notion as an appeal for appeasement—a parole. Several hundred dollars for a ring wasn't much, but when the acquired investment plan was accumulating debt, using credit cards as my savings account, every dollar counted, plus interest.

The new job was short-lived. I was helping out an old acquaintance, Bud Reinhold, doing maintenance and odd jobs at his small jewelry store across from Lindenwood College. He had been a dental tech in the Navy and had learned how to do castings and work with gold. With creative talent, he had turned dental training into one where he designed and built his own line of jewelry.

It was a handout more than a job, but I appreciated the work while I sought my next employment dead-ender. I admired Bud's creative collection. I couldn't afford one of the more glamorous of his original creations, but I bought a small, simple tanzanite ring, fashioned similar to the one worn by Princess Di. Selma had lost the original ring I'd given her, claiming she took it off and misplaced it at a cleaning job she'd had years before, when she worked. Bud offered to sell the Di knockoff at a good discount, so I called my financial partner, Mr. MasterCard, and bought the ring to give Selma for Christmas.

But she didn't appreciate it. In fact, you'd have thought it was a turd. How could I give her something so *not* her? Had I really known her, I would have done better. This disaster was proof I had no knowledge of what she stood for or what she was after.

My only redemption would be returning the ring to the store. I... couldn't do it, though. I didn't know her. I knew nothing. She would have to do it. A month passed, and Selma picked up her personally designed bejeweled construction. She didn't like this latest cast either. It would have to be redone a third time. Apparently, she didn't know who she was either.

Personal birthday celebrations and Christmas gifts were unimportant to me, and I preferred dispensing with the annual reminders. I especially disliked surprises, and Selma knew that. On a day that coincided with my birthday, she kept me busy and hidden in the master bedroom. She knew I hated surprises, but I played along in anticipation that the kids were busily putting their version of a birthday party together. I could understand, tolerate, and appreciate their surprise.

When Selma allowed my escape, she led me to an odd assortment of a dozen random acquaintances to fake a happy-birthday testament to me. What an idiot.

Me.

Red-faced and embarrassed, she had gathered blank faces off the street in the last ten minutes and bribed them with cake to show up and help me look foolish. I should have known better but went along with the ruse. The past ten years were wasted, no better than deadwood. She did the same stupid thing on my thirtieth.

I may not have known her, but she did not know me any better.

* * * * *

Selma's unfurled, seesawing schedule eased its flailing as she entered her last semester. White space emerged on her calendar. In an unusual conversation, we actually talked and decided to take in a movie, something we had not done in years.

Couples clash over movies and shows to watch—no secret there. Men respond to high adventure and superhuman action with guns a-blazing, the heroes posed with scantily clad enticements. Women prefer a film that brings them to tears over absurd romantic abstractions.

We discussed which movies to see. I deferred to her selection. She could not choose. Oh, hell, another insipid test. We stood in the rain, each waiting out the other. We could be there until the next year.

The movies weren't familiar to either of us, but I recalled a trailer for *Showgirls*, a Vegas film starring a young woman from a show the kids used to watch. We decided to give it a viewing.

Selma didn't rustle or move a hair or a muscle—until she headed for the exit, not halfway through the show. I said she got what she deserved for leaving it up to me, but I pleaded forgiveness nonetheless.

How could we salvage this calamity, wandering the halls of the mall? She spurned my urging her to select another movie. Her ongoing dissent forced my hand. I searched for the most obviously boring title I could find. Blindfolded, I pinned the tail on *The Bridges of Madison County*.

The movie wasn't half bad—interesting historical perspective on Iowa farm life and picturesque wooden timber bridges of a bygone era. The storyline troubled me, as I watched myself on the big screen, duped by the lackluster farmer wife's deliverance from an unfulfilled life. To women, the movie was heartwarming, a tale of true love, rising from the ashes and the drudge of family. And how to have both.

To the farmer and me, it was a tragedy.

CHAPTER 10

Akard Station

To perfect, practice. To hero, chance. To laugh, smile. To write, read. To live, love. To run, run. To sleep, work. To rest, stop. To conform, submit. To walk, step. To critique, speak. To confront, fight. To run... *No, that's not it. Try again.* To live, love. To love, feel. To feel, hurt. To hurt, dare. To dare, risk. To risk, let go. To let go, fear not. To fear not... To fear not... live, *that's it.*

I jotted notes as I did in high school. I scribbled quotes about which I felt strongly, profound thoughts from another's genius, curious bits of interest in dozens of log books, spiral-backed notebooks, Post-its, or discarded envelopes. The microcassette tape players were inconvenient and lacked poetry. Besides, I didn't like the sound of my own voice. After an epiphany, I'd wake from the daze, wave at the webs that clutched errant clouds and clusters of thoughts and notions, and use my gel pen for notable foci.

"A gentleman sits with the utmost discomfort on a train, its destination the same for eternal. Working diligently on the day's crossword puzzle, facing from the curled newspaper he holds, he scrawls a few letters in boxes to correct vertical rights with horizontal wrongs. Lost in attending, putting preprogrammed letters into their juggled order, making the best fit, he cannot see the future, or reason the collision racing toward him. Another train hurls in his direction on the same track. Everyday passengers don't contemplate disaster. They

just ride and play their games, unsuspecting. Train wrecks happen…
to good people." No choice—they're ignorant of the train's true course.

I slapped the frayed notebook shut and set it back in the helmet
bag. I stole a drink of coffee and tucked the cup next to the notebook.
No recourse, no good options. Some schools of thought say the simplest
solution was the most probable—Occam's razor.

I had learned the hardest option was more likely the best… though
I took the easier course.

* * * * *

When Selma graduated, I was thankful, hoping hell on earth was
wintering. Three long military officer schools, eight cycles of boot camp,
and two deployments were nothing compared to this tortuous existence.

St. Charles County Community College held its degree ceremony
at O'Fallon South High School's football field on a Friday night, with
the nursing program's ceremony at a local church the next day.

Selma graduated with honors. My parents drove down from
Reading, a round trip of more than a hundred miles, on Friday night
and would return the next day for the church ceremony. Selma's own
mother did not make the closer drive from South St. Louis County.
She didn't like to drive at night and especially did not like crossing
Blanchette Bridge, the eight-lane highway over the Missouri River.
My parents, kids, and I met Selma's study partners and their families.
I had to be reintroduced to everyone she studied with for the past four
years, except for Mary Jane, of course. Following the ceremony were
customary group photos as they hugged and bid each other congrats.

The next day marked a candle ceremony, where they addressed
future nurses directly, including three men in the class of a hundred
graduates. Selma's mother, her family, and mine attended. My parents
had not wanted to make the circuit again, but I had something special
planned for Selma after the program.

It was a tight fit for the church to accommodate the new nurses
with their well-wishing family members. The collection of hundreds

on a hot, humid Missouri June day overloaded the ability of the air conditioner to compensate. It was 95 degrees inside the building, with what had to be 90 percent humidity. Tougher still, squeezing into the aisle to take pictures in the dimly lit room was like trying to get the last dollop of toothpaste out of the tube. Noah wanted to take the pictures, so I showed him how to operate the camera and pointed where to stand to take his shots.

When the program was over, the nurses mingled in the crowded basement where refreshments were served. Selma elevated the mugginess with her fuming. I kept waiting for the overhead sprinklers to douse us. She didn't say anything but her face clearly sent a message: how dare I ruin her special day. I had blown it again. She forced smiles while posing for each snapshot with her friends and then proceeded to grind me to atoms. Noah shouldn't have taken pictures; that was my *duty* and crystal-clear proof that I didn't care.

On the drive home, she let me have more. Her particle accelerator had discovered the god particle, and she was it. Her unofficial celebration was staged and ready. I could tolerate her proton barrage for another hour. *I can take it*, I thought, as I chewed a finger off.

Selma's friend Rachel hosted for me, and her not-yet-ex-husband prepared food at my request. Rachel and her husband separated after Selma felt duty bound to blab to Rachel what I told her in confidence— that a gal in the jewelry store was dressing provocatively and flirting with Rachel's husband at his store.

Selma's vitriol abated to shock the instant we arrived at Rachel's house. The shrimp-boil party in her honor bustled in the shade of the double-car garage's open bay. Selma beamed at the banner, offering her congratulations. Tears welled in her eyes when she saw herself as a three-year-old, dressed up, playing nurse—a picture I found in the basement, growing moldy. From it, I'd made a three-by-five-foot poster. The perfect centerpiece, it showcased in front of her closest friends and family that sometimes a dream does come true. A crowning moment after endless nights of study, challenging labs and patient visits, hard work, sacrifice, and having endured—this was what love was.

During graduation month, Selma's friend Mary Jane filed for divorce and went to court to split everything down the middle. Mr. Mary Jane didn't know what hit him. The Arab-banger and her husband had been married twenty years and had teenage kids—and the wheels came off their ride.

Poor Mary Jane Rottencrotch,
For hours, for days and four years of nursing school,
She toiled, she toyed, she went,
While clawing two jobs, her hubby's life was spent.
To her friends in the belfry, the outrage, the insult,
The how dare he do what he did, she'd vent.
As she went on and on, her life was a wreck,
Complaining without relent.
To the Arab she preened and snaked,
Offering herself naked, she leaned over and bent,
While crying foul in the throes of ecstasy,
From a Mercedes, whose condition no longer mint,
My marriage has cratered, oh woe is me,
How do I survive this ignoble dent.
My husband's money I pilfered for schooling,
It is used up, and almost all spent.
Then she recalled, and she chuckled,
The payment for the last mortgage bill had been sent.
Mary Jane just laughed and laughed,
Her half, half of his,
For she knew just how divorce court went.

Bitch.

With Selma's graduation, the tension could be eased, built-up pressure released, and a return to normalcy in the offing. That summer, I had several courses to attend in Quantico. I was home for two weeks and then left again to be the mission commander of a counter-drug joint task force in the Upper Los Padres National Forest for over a month. Not too much to ask, I didn't think, as Selma had graduated and would not be in school. Plus, we needed the money.

Things did change; they sped out of control. Selma had to study for her state boards. When I talked to her weekly by phone from California, the pressure of the kids off for summer and her board preparatory studies were killing her. Instead of complaining to me at length, her time would have been better spent studying. I held the phone, rarely talking. Each successive call was worse than the one before. I let her rail about why her life was a mess and why I should be ashamed for living. Her anxiety and woe was so extreme, I wondered if she was suicidal.

The counter-drug mission was south of Carmel in the vast oak forests on federal land. Changes to laws had forced marijuana growers to start using public land instead of their own. The federal government was seizing land if they located pot farms on private property.

The teams were assembled from reserve units throughout the Midwest. A week's training preceded each patrol. Marines trained on the rifle ranges and for patrol coordination, fledgling squad-based GPS device usage, rules of engagement, indicators to find grow sites, primary and secondary communications plans, medical triage, and rappelling. In the operations center, patrols mapped in advance and were displayed on a large tactical map, with different colored lines laid over several thousand square miles of forest. Long hours were spent monitoring communications traffic, ensuring all Marines safe. Patrols started at two days at a time, gradually advancing to seven.

Army reserve helicopters transited separate, squad-size patrols to their routes. The warrant officers in charge were Vietnam veterans. Each had over five thousand hours of flying time in the UH-1 Hueys.

After twenty days, we received a visit from the national commander, an Army lieutenant colonel, accompanied by his Army sergeant major. The commander expressed approval and commended the operation. The sergeant major pulled me aside and expressed concern the Marine patrols were exhausting—too many days in the field. I said, "These are Marines, not soldiers, Sergeant Major." And I changed nothing.

Our mission yielded some old sites, drip lines, empty fertilizer bags, booby traps, abandoned meth labs, and ten-year-old human remains— probably the homicide of a rival drug dealer, the sheriff said.

On my way to another regrettable call for my telephonic bloodletting, I told Vulture, my operations officer, "I guess I better go and get this over with. It doesn't get easier with time. I've got to call the Mrs. and find out how horrible I am this week." When I returned from the phone call, I said to him in jest, "You know, I need a life… Maybe what I need is to have an affair. Ha-ha. Fat chance." I was *not* reminded of the preacher's sermon to not tempt fate, but a seed was planted, where the fertile subconscious took over.

The day I arrived home and dropped my bags, the phone rang. A helicopter in support of my counter-drug mission had crashed. A crew that had supported my mission had volunteered for the follow-on mission as well. Their tail rotor smacked the wall of a canyon. The lead pilot survived but broke his back; the co-pilot was banged up, with a broken leg. The Marines onboard also survived. They were part of the mission that relieved mine. I didn't know them. A good leader would have returned to California to check on the pilots he knew well and respected. Phone calls to the hospital and flowers would have to do. Selma needed her lightning rod handy. The kids needed it more.

Selma successfully passed her state nursing boards, but we were never the same. Haley's boyfriend mentioned a motorcycle in the driveway at two o'clock in the morning while I was gone. Selma said Gaylord, her nursing study buddy, had stopped by after work. It wasn't anything; I shouldn't worry. I had no reason to doubt her. I shoved the event into my mind's bottomless recesses.

The standard welcome-home roll in the hay was in order. I was lucky to get that. She didn't want sex again that week or the next month. Hadn't had it for four months, and it would be another six months until the next.

Mom was proud that her father was still having sex with her mother several times a week when they were in their seventies. I wished. If it weren't for sex, men wouldn't marry in the first place. Or as Mom often commented about mores of the younger generations, "Why buy the cow, if you can get the milk for free?"

I must have bought a horse.

Our routine had eroded to once a month. Selma wanted no part of sex—at least not with me. We attained the level of hallway sex. The first stage was kitchen sex, in years long gone, when a glance at your partner caused cosmic flashes and hormonal overload, leading to wild, hot, crazy passion on the floor, the dining table, or with her against the kitchen sink. The second stage was bedroom sex, where discretion was employed due to the kids. The third stage was hallway sex, passing each other in the hallway and yelling, "Fuck you!" I was in full receive mode of her hallway foreplay.

Selma rarely talked anymore. When Selma studied, days would dial by with no words spoken. When upset or the rest of time, she would not talk for two to four weeks, the quiet interrupted only with crunches on my neck bone as she bit my head off. I preferred the sound of silence.

That summer and fall were a kick in the head, a seasons-long root canal with my role as the cavity. When not deployed over a weekend, the kids and I were alone each night, as I helped them with homework, supervised their cleaning the house, put them to bed, readied for the next morning, and kissed them as they departed for school. Then off to the salt mine I would go. Hi-ho, hi-ho.

After passing her boards, Selma was hired immediately at St. Robert's Hospital in St. Louis' West County. She announced the money from her job would be placed in a separate account. Her schedule had her coming home late. With each passing week, late became later. Pretending to be asleep, I could wake to a whisper. Selma changed her clothes in the bathroom, which she had never done before, and then tip-toed into the bedroom, crawled in bed, and faced the wall 'til morning. My suspicions rose, despite the lack of evidence. When she was in school, she was marginally immersed in the family. Now, even when she was home, her head was elsewhere.

It was increasingly difficult to watch TV. I couldn't sleep. Confrontation was not my strong suit, but this skill was dulled even more in the presence of the master of disputation. Selma could pother better than a Clinton. Convinced her views were justified, her rationalized distortions became facts. She refused to accept other's viewpoints. Yet I was required to accept her pronouncements. I would argue that we could differ but still respect each other's opinions and agree to disagree. She disagreed with that option.

I convinced myself that I should look for tangibles, so I checked the closets, under the bed, in the basement, in dresser drawers. I pushed aside drab clothes and the convenient tracksuits she wore (that I hated). I'd suggested better, brighter clothes were in order. In her dresser drawer, I flicked aside the detested granny panties—and what did I find hidden underneath but new, clean, elegant, stylish bras and panties, neatly folded.

Another drawer kept a notebook. She was cataloguing her feelings about life—mine, not hers. It was a compilation of my problems. Everything in her life was screwed up because of the likes of me. One passage addressed my desire to investigate different small business ventures and not succeed—my pipe dreams, she called them. She knew nothing about getting ahead, thinking one did so by taking a job. Hadn't she heard of never giving up? Try, try, and try again.

Giving up was the failure, not starting and stopping a business. Businesses were opportunities to succeed big and yes, there was the possibility of faltering, but wasn't I already there? So, what was wrong with moving up from the bottom? She'd rather direct my life, not let me live it, suggesting once that I take a job on a highway crew, which I applied for but was not hired, as I was over-qualified. In her world, anything was better than dreaming, except in the world where I supported her dream come true.

I picked up the phone and called her at work. The nurse on the other end said Selma wasn't scheduled to work. I excused my stupidity and hung up.

Validated yet deflated, I did not know what to do. Who could I talk with? Not with any guys I knew, because I did not want anyone to know my fears or suspicions. It had been so long since I'd talked with 3-D, Beve, or anyone other than the kids, reservists, or people at work. I longed for a warm conversation, to talk with a woman without ducking for cover.

Going to bed was worse, as I wondered when Selma might show up. The motorcycle-in-the-driveway comment hung in the dark closet of the back of my mind. I tried to leave it alone and let it collect more dust. Selma's genius was lying, I'd come to accept and tolerate and at times, I'd even enabled it by returning money to the kids that Selma had borrowed but never seemed to repay.

Was I wrong for trusting her? There were other closeted cloaks acquired, but I had never found the occasion to wear. Was there more to the talk about her boss when she worked at MetLife? Bosses have lunch with their secretaries all the time.

Did the Arab bang Mary Jane, or was it really Selma?

Images grew wilder. Was she really a lesbian? That would explain a hell of a lot.

What about that story she told me about one of my buddies, a dozen years ago? The buddy's wife got pregnant by this captain, who was not her husband, who remained behind in the States while we were in Okinawa. What was his name? Selma and she had both partied with the derelict captain when they went out. What *was* his name? Sturdevant, a former Chicago cop. I dug deeper.

Shit, was Noah my son—or his?

I stopped and tabulated my son's gestation period, which coincidentally was within a month. Was that the real story? What other things had Selma said that were not as she stated? How would I know?

I no longer knew her, thought I had. The good or bad her—which was which? Was one the same as the other? This had been going on a long time.

Confronting the adept liar where reality was crafted made resolution impossible, lopsided. Girding for battle, with my armor of glass, she knew who I was and used it to kick the stump out from under that which kept my dangling life from hanging. Liars as artists created new worlds from vapor and were exquisite at perpetuating their own good, building around them walled cities of denied denials and unfailing failures. Whatever the eye of the liar saw was true; a liar's eye cannot lie. The craft perfected, practiced, nurtured perfect recall of the lie or dodged by carving another. When the liar hated you, it gloried in its feast. The liar enjoyed nothing more than the taste of honesty, slaying those confined to the truth, savoring nothing sweeter than eating them all. Her tongue slew me every time it whipped, drawing blood with each syllable, her words leaving gouges.

It was better that she didn't speak, lest the acid etch my heart.

* * * * *

Our wedding anniversary approached. Selma hadn't said anything to me, and I hadn't said anything back. Demanding control, I figured she'd let me know if she cared to embrace the nuptial remembrance.

The Republicans were holding a fund-raising barbecue at McNair Park on our anniversary. I had volunteered to assist. It was Saturday, and Noah had a soccer game, so I said I would come over and watch a little bit, even though the location of the fund-raiser had changed to Blanchette Park, on the other side of town.

Humidity stagnated the air, clouding the otherwise clear blue skies. It was unseasonably warm for a fall day, and the fund-raiser boiled the elected officials and those who paid in support. The sheriff's father, who had made his political debut barbecuing for his son across the county to raise funds, was grilling hot dogs and pork steaks. I helped him, working over the hot fire. I paid my twenty-five dollars and enjoyed a few beers to keep cool. I was unable to make the game back at the other park.

Back at home, I asked Noah how his game had been, and we started wrestling around, but I was too rough. Selma screamed. I was obviously out drinking instead of where I said I would be. She wanted to know why I wasn't at the game. She said she didn't know what the hell I had been doing, but she was going out to eat with the kids. It didn't matter if I came along.

It was just too much to take. I stormed out. But I didn't need to be driving. Three blocks away, I turned into a subdivision, drove to the end where a cul-de-sac trapped me, and parked. I sat there, overcome. What the hell had happened? I'd busted my ass to be there as much as possible for the last four years and the twelve before that. I was the one at every game—and now this? Where did she get off with her holier-than-thou bullshit? How the hell could I stop this train? With the burn of the day and my weakened state, I rocked my head back on the headrest and closed my eyes, trying to see what was not there. My vapid thoughts went nowhere.

* * * * *

Splinters of light pried one eye open. The sun was setting, its rays hit a window down the street, focused, and found me, the ant. Tapping sounds forced awake the other eye, although I was afraid to see what was there.

"Brick, come inside. Let's talk. You don't need to be out here." It was Rachel, one of the girls from Selma's coven. My car was parked a hundred yards from her house.

My mind was jumbled, I was a mess, and I didn't want to be around myself, much less anyone else—and especially not this one. "Rachel, thanks. That's all right. Let me sit here a while. Then I'll go home."

"No, Brick. Come inside and talk to me about it. I can help you. Come on in and talk."

The only way to shut her up was to placate her with a few moments and then get the hell out of there.

"Okay, okay, I'll come in, but I don't feel like talking."

We went inside. My nose was running, my eyes were swollen and red, and I felt like crap. It would have been better to have been pulled from a wreck than being the wreck myself. I felt stupid, looked stupid.

Rachel fumbled about, talking, and I let her babble while wiping the mucous out of my moustache. What could I say? I didn't make enough money, and Selma had to work—was that it? I could admit to being stupid from time to time, but how had it mushroomed?

I once had swept Selma off her feet. Now, she swept me under the rug. No longer could I linger as lint.

CHAPTER 11

Walnut Hill Station

"Yeah, man, how you doin'?"

"Excuse me, what did you say?" I mumbled.

"Yeah, man, you know what it is."

"You talking to me?" I asked, waking.

Eyes glanced down at me, telling me to go away.

Crowded. Burns had bettered me somehow and was seated to my right. I was stuck on the aisle part of the seat, with a butt getting jiggy with my shoulder.

A black kid four rows ahead of mine held onto the handrail overhead as the DART whistled along. Fro Bro had one of those obnoxious blue-eared devices, I think they call them, and he was talking on. It was a great phone technology that made everyone other than the person to whom he was speaking think he was talking to them. The trainload was part of his conversation.

"Yeah, man, I can meet you there. I am heading that way now," Fro Bro said.

A pile-up on the mix-master early in the morning had backed up traffic over the greater Dallas area. Rain and gas prices added to the road entanglement. The morning TV and radio news had advised commuters to take extra precaution and add an hour to their travels. Many chose to can the drive and jump on the DART at the last minute.

"D'ya meet up with the honey I told you about? Fine, huh?" Fro Bro ignores the lot.

"Mona, I had my hair done at the Pink Mare as you recommended. I couldn't believe the customer service there. They were so great. They knew my name and asked if they could help me. It was clean and refreshing. I will definitely go back. They had free snacks and soda everywhere," said the fat girl with half her head shaved, as she munched her cell phone. The other half of her head was in purple spikes. I was pretty sure she wasn't heading to her corporate job as a tax accountant.

A splashy, crashing sound came from behind me. Sounded like someone dropped his Big Gulp. "Shit. I am sorry," said someone, confirming it, and I reached down to pick up my bags before they became the sponge.

The windows fogged. Female perfumes and male deodorants mated with sweaty pits, swamp ass, smokers' breath, and the homeless guy standing in the front. We breathed in each other's exhalations. The ventilation screeched to filter the contents of this sausage. An open flame would have char-broiled this picnic. Burns and I sighed in unison, trying to do so without breathing. Water ran off the sleeve of jiggy-butt's raincoat and into my collar.

"Tell Larry I will be in thirty minutes late," said a guy behind me on his cell. "I have the Haines account with me, and we will go over it when I get in. Things look better than I thought."

Rarely were things better than one thought. We tended to have a positive outlook, trying to be glass-half-full people when drowning. Instead of being confident, we needed to be paddling like crazy. No time for thinking at such a time. Let survival mode kick in.

Forget reading.

Can I hold my breath for forty-five minutes?

* * * * *

"How about the couple in the corner? The girl with the Cardinals T-shirt on? What is their story?" Cameo said. It took a month for us to match schedules with her Inspector General trips to bases across the country. I'd called Cameo's house, unclear if she was still stationed at Scott and living in town. Talked to the venerable Medusa, her mother, and left a message. I had to call back two more times before Cameo answered. Her mother had not given her the messages I'd left.

"Well, let's see here. She is smiling, eating her lobster, not talking while she eats, commenting occasionally, and letting him talk. They generally seem to be enjoying each other's company. It must be a date. They seem too happy to be married," I said. My perspective was jaded, distorting views and those in it.

"Okay, what do you think their story is? That other couple over in the booth near the window," Cameo said. The middle-aged man in the booth had his head bent over his surf-and-turf platter. He seemed to find it inedible and couldn't add fuel to his churning stomach. His balding head nodded; his lips clenched his teeth and words. He collected bristles from the open-mouthed woman sitting opposite him. The woman, obviously his wife, could have been fairly attractive, but her flesh matched the tone of her tongue—blood. Her unfortunate husband was the reason that her salmon filet was cooling and was wasted. A waitress in a red-and-white striped uniform hesitated near their cluttered table and then reasoned the table of six rowdy children throwing hush puppies was in greater need of deep-fried ammunition.

"She is saying 'Oh, how I love that we finally get to go out. Isn't this so much fun, my dearest wonderful husband? I love you so much. I will make love to you all night, and tomorrow, I'll serve breakfast in bed. As a special thank you, I think you need to spend the weekend with your buddies, watching football games at Hooters.'"

"I think he forgot to take the trash out," Cameo observed.

"He is the trash."

"What color would you say her face is?"

"The color of run-n-n!" I said. "Don't stop at go, do not collect two hundred dollars; forget your stuff—its hers now. Run as far away and as fast as you can." We both laughed heartily, slipping into a nervous chuckle. I gazed at the woman I had not seen in nearly twenty years.

Had to see what Cameo looked like, I told myself. Men became distinguished with age but time was less gracious to women, especially if they'd pumped out a couple of kids. I wasn't sure what to expect. Ugly would deter the course I was on. I didn't adhere to the GUE principle espoused by boastful fellow Marines on the prowl. "Go Ugly Early" was a proven pick-up trick. She might be more beautiful now, like the high school classmate I bumped into downtown a year ago, memorable. What was her name? Katy Maxedon. She looked great—better after fifteen years.

Cameo had agreed to meet for lunch a couple of weeks back at the Cracker Barrel on the east side of the river, in Illinois. A sales rep's lunch hours were flexible; I could drive anywhere in the metro area without no one knowing or caring. Maintaining monthly sales were critical to the luxury of infrequent monitoring. The location was closer for Cameo to get back and forth in the little time allotted to dine. I arrived early and looked around the place to see if she was there. *Not yet.* I sat facing the window to watch her approach from the parking lot, as I sipped a cup of coffee.

Though I wasn't a talker, all I wanted to do was talk—to hear another voice, tone, and story different from the same trampled tale of my starring role as villain. *Cameo should be dumpy*, I thought. Frumpy I hoped, extinguish any latent embers. *Perhaps she'll arrive as a Guernsey.* It's a friendly lunch between two old friends, I told myself. Nothing else. What would the harm be?

"Have you been here a while?" Cameo had purred as she strode behind me. I must have been daydreaming, missing her grand entrance. And she wasn't bovine.

"Hello, Cameo, how are you doing? It is great to see you. You look fabulous," I said. I would have said it regardless, but she glowed. Her hair was shorter, but she was as beautiful as ever, with her crystalline eyes and smirk. "Let me help you with your coat."

Cameo ordered soup and a sandwich. I was hungry for a bowl of hot anything but food.

We shared similar lies of the greatness of the time we had spent separately. The wonderment of our own children was the only salvation we shared. For me, lunch was over the instant she sat down.

She had to leave, and I walked her out. As I leaned back from kissing her on the cheek, she said we needed to get together again in a couple of weeks. To emphasize the point, she lightly tapped my forearm, slid into in her car, and left.

A live wire had grounded me. There had been no touch, caress, or embrace for five years. The world was not stark or dead. Possibilities hinted in tandem. Perhaps aging did not mean distant, destitute, and unforgiving. Warmth existed in the unexplored world. My thoughts took wing—I was unable to grasp them but was exulted as the shackles of convention loosened and the tonnage slaked off my shoulders as I stood welded to the asphalt.

Awakened eyes traced her until she was out of sight.

Cameo and I met a couple of weeks later on her Tuesday class night. I hadn't really liked the fact we were meeting in a Red Lobster, as that was Selma's favorite place. It never had been my choice for seafood. Real seafood was better on the coasts, where the catch of the day meant *that day*. We met in the lounge, but I didn't recognize Cameo in civilian clothes. Dressed in a very conservative patterned dress, she still had no fashion sense, dressing more like the Church Lady from *Saturday Night Live* or Archie Bunker's wife, Edith, from *All in the Family*. The dress went down to her knees, and the lace pasted on her neckline seemed to declare she was tired, stiff, stuck in the mud, and old. It served as my mental justification to get the hell out of there, which I should have.

We called the bartender over. I ordered a beer, and Cameo bore down on the guy for ten minutes, trying to figure out which particular umbrella-drink she had ordered a couple of weeks prior. After coming to a mutual agreement with the bartender, he brought her a sweet fruit-frothed strawberry daiquiri.

We chattered back and forth about nothing and then decried to have dinner at the bar, even though I wasn't hungry. I hadn't been eating much the last several months; my belly distended from anger and poison, unable to grip the current veneer I lived. But now, drinking—how better to dilute the buildup of acid in the bowels and stomach than to water it down with doses of cold barley soup and aspirin? Drinking, I was doing—*doing too much*, whispered the angelic animator hanging on my lobe. *Sit down and shut up. Who cares, anyway?* careened another blacker voice from the back row of the gallery, as I ordered another beer, siding with the devilish lesser of me.

"Where Friedens Church is, near the intersection of Zumbehl and Highway 94—that was my grandfather's farm at the turn of the century," Cameo said.

"I didn't know that. A lot of farms succumbed to development. St. Charles had to grow on top of someone's family history," I said. We rehashed old topics, making them new.

Cameo slipped into a confessional tone. "Remember the afternoon you came over, the week before I was to marry Trevor?" she said. "I wished I had taken you up on your offer."

"Offer? What offer?"

"You don't remember? I told you I shouldn't get married but felt trapped by Mother. You suggested we should have a pre-wedding fling. I should have taken you up on it."

"Why do you say that now?"

"I really left Darlene and Margie with their father in Texas because I could not stand it anymore."

"Oh, I'm sorry. I didn't know. Every marriage goes through some rough patches. I know Selma and I have."

"I should never have married him. Did I tell you about Francois? You always called him Pepe Le Pew?"

I nodded.

"Did I tell you we got together while Trevor was out of town?"

"No, I don't think so. I don't recall specifics. Was it a big deal?"

"I would say. He later bragged to Trevor, not knowing Trevor and I were dating at that time. Trevor and I had a huge fight. He slapped me, and we split up. I don't know why I ever went back."

"Okay."

"There was this competition between the men in ROTC, throughout the Midwest. Francois scored me low and shared the results with Trevor."

"What? Really? That's not right."

"Trevor was out of town one time, and I was alone in the apartment we shared. I started rummaging around and found this little black notebook with the names of the girls in every unit throughout the district's seven states. Scores were kept on all the girls the men bedded, with Trevor keeping the master scorecard. You can imagine—dozens, perhaps a hundred scorings by the different guys, to include the instructors."

"Why on earth did you marry this guy?"

"I don't know." Cameo stared into the past for several minutes. With a deep sigh, a sly confidence camouflaged the beleaguered face Cameo had previously mapped. She grinned and said, "Our senior enlisted advisor said my friend Sharon and I could make five hundred dollars a night, if he set it up."

"What? You're kidding, right? He's supposed to be a professional, and he said that?"

"It wasn't the first time. Remember Sergeant Carlin, our instructor at high? He made a pass during my senior year, too. I stopped him, though. Caught him off guard. He started sobbing and asked me not to tell anyone, or he would lose his job."

"You should have turned him in anyway. Damn, I wouldn't have believed it. He was such a nice guy. Wow, I can't get over that. What ever happened with the advisor from college?"

"Sharon and I never took him up on the offer. It was nice to be appreciated though."

"Did you ever do it with him?" I asked hesitantly.

"No, I assumed it to be more bluster on his part… could have, sure. He was no different from any other guy we ran into in ROTC. Sex was all part of the game, everywhere we went. I fought it at every drill comp. Being Trevor's girlfriend kept it at bay. Probably why I married him, but then it never cleared up in the Air Force. Trevor got worse."

"How much worse?"

"Trevor failed flight school and had to find something else to do. He wound up in special operations. Never could say really what he did. He was hell to live with. He would throw tantrums, depending on what had happened on this day or that. He threw a chair out our plateglass window of the apartment in California. His parents were there, too. They told me later they were sorry, that the good son had been killed in Vietnam. They apologized over and over for what they saw him put me through."

"Did you ever think of divorcing him?"

"I did, over and over, but we had the two girls. I was going to leave him in '83, but then he found a letter."

"What letter?"

Cameo shook her head, deciding on whether to reveal too much or little; it was as entangling and sad as the guts of a baseball once the cover flies off and the exposed ball of string quickly unravels. "I ran into the senior advisor from college. He was stationed at Travis when we were. I knew he had expressed interest in me before, so I found a way we could hook up, and we fell in love. Trevor found a love letter from him on my lap after I had fallen asleep. Now, he keeps it as evidence."

"Evidence?"

"I have to keep him living in the manner to which he is accustomed, I overheard him laugh about it to a buddy of his at a party. Infuriating—I can't divorce Trevor, or I go to jail. He has the letter and says he will use it against me. He will turn me in, since Tim was a master sergeant. Even though it goes on all the time, fraternization is a court-martial offense if it becomes a problem to the Air Force. I lived with this threat for five years and then things only got worse. Trevor could not get promoted because his evaluations were classified, due to his being in special ops. They could never really say what he had done. He got passed over for major—up or out, you know—so his career was over. He blames me— says it's my fault, because my job took us to different bases—lesser ones for special operations, in his opinion." Cameo sighed heavily. "He was a good man, once."

Breathing deeply, she seemed to be turning words over in her head, rethinking what she had just said. "I like your face, clean," she said abruptly. "When Trevor left the Air Force, he grew his hair long and didn't shave. He says he keeps the beard for playing Santa Claus at Christmas. The house is a disaster; the carpet is nasty, but he won't spend any money on new. The kitchen needs remodeling; the plumbing works half the time. All the money is tied up in his business, and he has no time to take care of the house, he says. He wanted to buy this stupid lawn-care business. We went round and round about it. I kept telling him, why buy into something you could easily start from scratch? That's if he has to get into that business at all, you know? Plus, he wasn't working except for umpiring baseball games. He hasn't had real job since '88. I think he might gross ten thousand dollars a year from the lawn care, if that. I don't even know if there is a profit."

"I thought I had it bad," I said, as I explained the gore of my marital calamity. I fidgeted in my seat, staring at the female version of me. How was it that each of us had to suffer a spouse who sliced open our veins, supped on our blood, and slowly drained our lives? "Thank God for the kids, or…"

"Yeah, the kids are great," Cameo agreed. "I don't get to see them enough. Last time I was home, Trevor and I were arguing over the carpets, cars, the kids. He is tired of putting up with them and driving them everywhere they need to go. He lost it and started choking me and kicked me. My oldest, Darlene, grabbed a butcher knife to protect me and told him to stop. He threatened to call the police if she didn't drop it. Trevor slapped her to get the knife back, dragged her into her room, and locked the door. Then he came back into the kitchen and slugged me in the stomach. When I doubled over, I hit my head on the edge of the counter." Cameo pulled back the hair from her hairline to reveal a healing gash an inch long.

"There's a man I want to kill, too," I said. "I don't think about it very often. I hope someone else has killed him by now."

"Brick, what are talking about?"

"It has become easier for me to talk about it now, where before it was buried. I was raped several times by a baseball coach that lived on my street when I was eleven. I quit playing baseball. I buried the incident and forgot about it. I tried to change who I was. Then I returned to St. Charles, and I saw him again."

"I am so sorry. What did your parents do?"

"I never told anyone for the first fifteen years. Then, I finally got around to telling Mom about it." I did not care what women thought anymore. I was myself, no holds barred. I never knew what to make of the man in my mirror.

"That's horrible," Cameo said. "I think you recovered well, though."

"Maybe physically, but mentally, it's a quagmire of questions, confusion, hatred, disgust—you know. A local thirteen-year-old went missing a few years ago, and I called the police to make sure they knew about this monster. They said they knew about him and had questioned him. When I found out he was coaching the eighth-grade basketball team at St. Peter's Church, I let one of the program directors know about his past, and they fired him. I called the St. Charles Parks Department and told them the story, but they didn't fire him. The girl I spoke to on the phone acted more disgusted with me. That's the dilemma."

"I'm sorry."

I looked down at the barely touched food and ordered another brew. I confided to Cameo that I had been searching for the elusive reasons why things happened. Was there a subconscious cause and effect to future personality traits or flaws? Was I good or bad *because*? Was I weaker or stronger than I should be? Since it happened to me, I could never, ever allow anyone else to be subjected to that. I didn't want to torture the bastard that did it to me, because that would require looking at him. I did want him dead—the only sure-fire way he could not do it again—to prevent other boys from suffering the same torment. Was it the reason I was comfortable as a Marine and wished for the opportunity to go to war? I didn't have a problem with dying for my country. It was living that was difficult.

Failure of not staying at the academy had compelled me to the Marines and Parris Island. I had to help young men understand that they should not take boot camp so seriously and not give up. I wanted to help them understand the game of wills. If they wanted to be a Marine before they came to Parris Island, the dream was still alive. I wanted to prevent those kids at Parris Island from quitting.

There had been a recruit in the first phase of boot camp who told me, during our SOP-mandatory counseling sessions, that he was homosexual. I asked him what made him think so. After much mental struggling on his part, he told me he had been sexually molested by an uncle when he was fourteen-years-old. It had been his only sexual experience, so he must be gay. I took the recruit outside, away from the prying ears, and we talked at length for over two hours. I told him my experience and how I had been violated. I charged him to energize his free will, his power of choice, and use his time at boot camp to build himself into someone he would be proud to be.

Weeks later, at the rifle range, a recruit on crutches hobbled toward me, calling out my name. He begged forgiveness for hailing me down like a cab and reintroduced himself as the one I had counseled. He thanked me for giving him the time and boost he needed. Reborn, he declared, he was unstoppable.

Cameo and I conversed comfortably, talking both personally and professionally. She could understand and relate, but on the other hand, I thought I might be giving up too much information.

The nibbled, half-eaten food was cold; the restaurant empty. We'd been busy talking, and neither of us wished to stop. The airing of errors was refreshing and forgiving.

After dinner, I walked Cameo to her car. She turned on the radio to a country western station. I wasn't too crazy about the music selection—that was Selma's preference. A woman thing, I gathered. More romance from the country and western stations. I didn't like the same old clunky beat and the country boys singing about being losers with women, drinking, and divorce. You never heard the women muck up.

Busted lives and broken dreams attested to exhaustion. The air thickened with silence.

"What should we do now?" Cameo asked.

"I don't know. What would you like to do?" I said.

"Well… I'd like to do something I haven't done with you in a long time." She put her hand on the back of my neck and pulled my lips toward hers. We kissed passionately for some time.

"If we are going to keep this up," I said. "We need to find a place more discreet than here along the main drag."

"You're right. Let's defog these windows and go somewhere else."

We drove north over Highway 64 and cruised the Drury Inn. We honed in on an empty parking space between two semi-trailer trucks. Perfect. She squeezed the car between the two and shifted into park. Kissing her sweetly, she responded in kind. This was what I missed from Selma. Cameo took the lead, and I let her. I needed to be warmed by the fire, not fried.

Her tender caresses drugged me; I'd been too long numb. Misted windows harkened the lateness. We opened the windows to the chill.

A week later, we were back at the Drury. The story to her mother was the need to stay late for school. My justification was going out with Tony, a coworker, even though we never got together for other than work events. We were grabbing a couple of drinks downtown, as my story would go.

Cameo lay on the bed facing me, as I sat in a stiff chair across from her. We needed each other. I was unconvincing, trying to talk myself out of it. I deserved it for what Selma put me through. What I wanted, I couldn't have. It was this or nothing. I needed leverage on Selma, to play her game by her rules. I had to go Old Testament on her—an eye for an eye.

After awkwardly fumbling and chattering, I shut it off. I crawled onto the bed, closer to Cameo, so I wouldn't appear as distant and removed from the situation as I felt. I leaned forward and kissed Cameo.

I was a good man, once.

CHAPTER 12

Spring Valley Station

Normally, if not nodding off, I could peruse the *Slick* in fifteen seconds to see if there was anything worth notice. A fish wrapper was too good a use for it; better for Big Gulp blotting. An article in the *Slick* reported a story of a soldier home on leave. While visiting his parents, he took off one beautiful Sunday morning for a drive on his motorcycle and never returned. The authorities spent the next several days looking for him, concerned he might have been suffering from post-traumatic stress disorder. A searcher found his body and motorcycle at the bottom of a ravine. The sheriff's department conducted an investigation into the accident and discovered it might not have been an accident. The soldier had not applied the brakes as he approached the edge of the canyon; he had accelerated and intentionally rocketed off. The suicide rate for returning Iraq War veterans was on the rise.

A colonel of mine, then a corporal, received a Purple Heart for standing in a chow line in Vietnam. His unit had just returned from the shit engaging Cong in the jungle. Rotated to a rear area for needed R&R, the Marines were still required to wear helmets and flak jackets. A mortar barrage forced the lunch line to run for cover. A piece of shrapnel tore through his flak jacket flap and into his shoulder. His buddy, who shunned the flak-jacket order, was killed. The colonel sheepishly admitted he was elated and grateful, no doubt glad for not having been killed, but felt horrible and guilty. The immediate feeling of contentment was that he wasn't the other guy.

I shuttered my eyes and tried to wriggle past the exposed nerve. Sins and omissions, slips and derelictions, moral dilemmas, innocence questioned, and chunks of guilt—the waxy substances plied our guts— broken, non-repairable chunks of protein fibers that no longer serve the body with their intended purpose. They crowd, they clutch, chunk up and clatter, and clog organs and tissues from supping on vital good, shutting us down in slow motion. Like the amyloids that killed my father.

I felt responsible for the first friendly fire casualty in the Iraq War.

Last-minute intelligence changed the division's initial attack across the Kuwaiti border with Iraq to launch the war. The change altered the "Opening Gambit" strategy we had written and trained to for months. I was asked to confirm or deny some new information. I told the colonel, and he told the general, that I couldn't rely on the higher headquarters position on what the enemy disposition was, because they were too political and had not provided us with the clear intelligence support we needed with immediacy. The change in our course of action at the nth hour caused a Cobra gunship to launch a Hellfire missile on one of our own tanks during the midnight border crossing. Marines were injured; thankfully, not killed.

"I am happy, I am rich, and I am successful," I said doggedly, reminding myself, and I shoved the *Slick* onto the floor of the train. *It's not littering if someone else wants to read it.*

I picked it back up, folded it neatly, and tucked it in the seat against the wall.

One sin fixed.

* * * * *

Mom recalled that her mother, "Momma Honey," grew no older than thirty-nine—each successive birthday was the same age proclamation. Momma Honey remained thirty-nine for thirty-nine years.

I hadn't expected to live that long. Thirty-nine—the bridge too far, past the halfway point, now at falling speeds into death's abyss. For the countless toil and precise planning, waiting to be burned out or burned up, sacrificed on the fields of slaughter in service to my country, but the request wasn't honored. I was a trapped spectator with no life chapter to declare worthy.

Had I made it to age forty-two with twenty years of service, I should have retired, brimming with memories of far-off travels and worldly pursuits, as did Commander McBragg of the *Tennessee Tuxedo* cartoons. Any leftover sense of purpose spilled over to watching the kids play sports and seeing whether a part of me—my spirit—was in them. This age was to be set aside for coasting. Sex did not even come close. Baseball and soccer games lasted longer.

Men learn early to sacrifice. To want or expect to have everything was unreal. You make choices and settle. You cannot have a great career, be the best parent, earn the most money, have ample quality time, and have a great marriage. Choices must be made. Settle on the spread to focus on one and a lesser. Regardless of best efforts, the others wither.

When I came home from work or from seeing Cameo, I tried to get home before the kids went to bed. I could not see her every night. Too much attention would come of it. I hated to leave the kids home alone, too, as I did love being with them. It was extremely difficult, however, to be home when Selma plodded the same floorboards.

We went through the pretense of dinner together and then helped the kids with homework. The girls were supposed to alternate weeks for chores, but the nightly procession needed close attention, or they conveniently forgot. The delegating of chores was a sore spot with Selma. I would delegate and coordinate the kids' actions. Selma would dismiss them upon their dereliction, and do them herself.

Cameo's job on the IG team kept her on the road for most of November. The inspections would stop in December for the holidays and pick up again in January. Voicemail at work was invaluable for keeping in touch.

Invariably and unfortunately, I saw Cameo on the nights when Selma worked late. Who had a clue when she was going to show up anyway? Cameo and I overlaid our tediums to arrange something on a Tuesday or Thursday night, to match her classes against Selma's planned work.

Cameo's mother expected her home on weekends. I spirited the kids around to friends, movies, and the mall; I cared for the yard and carted the kids to soccer games.

Cameo hid the flotsam of her bad marriage; unrepressed, she had to express herself somehow to survive. A unique softness and caring held Cameo to me; it was foreign to both of us separately.

The opportunity turned up she would be in town when my December drill was scheduled, so I urged her to get a room for Friday night. Whatever hour I would get off, I could meet her after. On this occasion, we selected the Drury nearest the drill center.

Arriving late, I called from the front desk to see what room she occupied. As I walked in, she greeted me with a big kiss. Lit candles traced opaque figures about the room. Flowery silhouettes flitted on the walls from floor to ceiling. Their images made us ants amid a moonlit grass, soldiering on to a forbidden picnic banquet. The scent of strawberries were behind her. Laid out on the end of the bed was a bouquet centerpiece and the elements to eat, essential to fuel the evening of our needs. Packages of food were set out, packed by her mother—so much of it that most would be left over. Cameo confessed she couldn't understand how her mother could complain about her weight then pack this bounty.

Massaging my shoulders, to loosen the tension of the typical fourteen-hour days for drill, brought the scent of peach from her flesh. The aromatic medley confused and entangled my enlightened senses, an invitation to taste. As shadows danced lightly upon the walls, images billowed, swept the room, and fell in tandem with our impassioned embrace, as the dozen wax eyes fell asleep. We woke. We made love for as long as we could. Cameo was insatiable and more so than I, but I undeniably was willing to meet her desire. When we were both exhausted, she lay in my arms as we talked briefly. I had grown to detest talking in bed. When my head hit the pillow, I was normally out. When Selma's head hit the pillow, it engaged her mouth.

"George was telling me about his girlfriend at Wright-Pat. I guess she's a captain," Cameo said.

"Don't you find it difficult? I mean, you know these guys' spouses by first name, don't you?"

"Oh, Francine, yes, I know her. I don't think of it that way. I know the guys don't either. Most of it is recreational anyway, like golf."

"How *Cosmo* of you."

"I am looking forward to Christmas and seeing the girls. It's been five months. But I really don't want to have to deal with Trevor. I know the house is a disaster. I can't stand living there."

"Prefer living like this, do you?"

"Sure. I can't afford it much, but it would be nice. With continental breakfast, and I don't have to clean it."

Playing around again, we warmed up to restart with desire I hadn't felt in many years, if ever. As I caressed the bottom of her feet to the back of her neck, we drifted into a nether land. Sex, it wasn't; we were healing each other's wounds with our hands, our lips. Having never felt so much force, we could not stop, enough was not enough. We continued late into the night and as we culminated in exhaustion, I released then slunk onto her and nuzzled her neck. I whispered softly, the words escaping before my lips could arrest the vowels. "I love you."

Shit.

The last spark of illumination hushed out on a nearby table, and the darkness echoed my words in the silence.

Sonovabitch. I had uttered a guttural response to the act as much as to her, having missed both for so long.

Damn. How to back out intact?

Fuck. I should know the right things to say, having learned tactics of escaping a few verbal clutches of the female persuasion. But I balked at this talking and emotional back-and-forth stuff. I wanted sleep, now and fast. With the silence and this elephant in the room—fortunately, too dark to be seen—I rolled over to vanish... *shit, shit, shit.*

Cameo lay her head on my shoulder. Not knowing when to shut up, I should have quickly filled the air with snoring, but sputtered, "We need to go to sleep. It's late, and I've got to get up early. Please set the alarm for 0500. We're different from the other services. The Marines start drill at 0700, as you might guess. The air guard and the Navy don't show up until 0800. Ha, ha... just in time for doughnut break. They get off drill at 1600, and we're there until 1700, 1800, 2200, or 0200—it depends on training. It's a joke we get paid the same."

Kissing her goodnight, I held her, my chest as her pillow. Selma couldn't or wouldn't ever sleep like this. The faint fragrance of peach filled my senses with satisfaction. Her warmth melded with mine; the dove cooed. I thought for a second of the other one elsewhere, the rusted buzz saw rip-cutting me in half. Tick, one-Mississippi, tock, two-Mississippi... asleep.

When we rose the next morning, I told her I did not know what I was thinking. I didn't mean to mess up whatever we had between us. Cameo nodded, pulled on her sweater and pants, and went downstairs to the complimentary breakfast. Returning, she nibbled a Danish as I made her tea. We shared the joy of simple—the aroma of hot tea, the first sip from a cup of coffee, a pastel dawn, the float of snow.

On Monday, I called Cameo at the office. She had to be out of town on a short operational readiness inspection (ORI), so we coordinated her return.

Fumbling to explain the hapless utterance of Saturday night, I wanted her to know I did not want or expect anything back. I was out of line. We had a lot to deal with, our kids being first and foremost.

Cameo said she did not know what to think, she had forgotten what love was. She appreciated and respected I might love her. She was touched, but she didn't want to blend me in her toxic amalgam. I didn't know what I was getting myself into, she insisted. She needed time to think over things. She finished by saying she would leave a contact phone number on my voicemail. If I wanted to and had the chance, I could call her.

The day after she returned, we met for lunch at Shoney's, adjacent to the Drury in Fairview Heights—cheaper and less trafficked. I handed her a letter I'd written and told her I'd missed her. I told her to read the letter later and let it sink in. "He-he," she giggled. I reminded her to keep an open mind when she read it.

Charcoal skies lugged overhead. On wintery days in Missouri, you couldn't tell the difference between 0800 and 1600, except for the direction of traffic. If not for the holiday season, such days would be intolerable. Cancel January and February altogether.

An Air Force base's amenities and accommodations are plentiful. A standing Marine joke was that Air Force base planners built the golf courses and clubs first and runways last, to ensure the former's inclusion if the project went over budget. Congress was obligated to approve additional funding for the essential runway completion. Air Force staffers considered temporary association with Marines on a Marine Corps air base or station as a hardship, and they granted their pilots and crews spurious automatic authority to incur recoverable, out-of-pocket expenses to stay in town at a fancy hotel of choice.

I parked and looked around to ensure no one was paying attention. Even in the dark, a guy in a suit has a tendency to stand out on a military base. I pulled off my tie, tossed it, and walked up to the door of the Scott's Inn like I had a room there. With no one in the lobby, I continued to Cameo's room, feeling like an intruder in the Air Force's polished, clean world of excess.

I smiled and handed her the red, yellow, and white roses I'd bought at the Amoco station up the road. "A bit rough, trying to hide long-stemmed roses in a coat pocket. I hope they still look okay. They still smell nice, but not as nice as you do."

Taking off my coat, I threw it down on the chair. A small living room was adjacent to the bedroom, with a kitchenette in between. Pretty nice for eight bucks a night. Budget cuts hadn't hurt the Air

Force. I dropped into an open chair, and we small-talked against the background of a female singer, crooning of boots and beds. My lips touched hers. We kissed longingly, and then we danced slowly around the room as she rested her head on my shoulder. She smelled warm and beautiful; the touch of her skin was comforting. The mood should have been more daring or raucous or scintillating, but we danced clumsily around the room, natural and comfortable, as it should have always been.

Making love seems a stupid term. It is filled with confusing contradictions, taking the most intimate personal event and trivializing it or having absolutely nothing to do with it. When I first heard the term and had to ask someone else what it meant, it didn't seem to fit. I'd had sex when love had nothing to do with it. One did not mean the other. In my world, making war meant peace.

Cameo was a challenge and a game. I had never known her power. Willing to please her, I did not want to let her down. If her power waned, mine increased, only to reverse again.

I couldn't stay, though Selma had worked late. I did not know if she would come home at two or four in the morning. It was a sixty-minute drive back across the rivers to where my other life died.

After last Christmas's ring fiasco, I was in no mood tiptoeing through the bouncing betties of the minefield, where the Grinch Selma stole any spirit from it. The whole meaning of Christmas was misunderstood and lost in commerce, peoples, and perceptions—too fake and misguided, too much pressure on everyone to give something special.

Thanksgiving is what Christmas is all about, and the two got twisted around. No gift requirement for honor and gratitude. Christmas without money, gifts, wrappings and trappings would be the way the real Christmas should be. The Whos from Whoville in Dr. Seuss's *The Grinch Who Stole Christmas* had it right—celebrate life and each other. It's not the battle between the Haves and Have-Nots or the Whos and What Nots. Christmas was dumbed down and sold out. Liable trifles were bought, and we indebted ourselves triple, having forgotten its significance.

I'd never seen *It's a Wonderful Life*, didn't know one existed. Shame so many watched the movie and failed to heed the message.

Caught in the tanglefoot of Christmas, I could not help the kids pick out an appropriate gift for them to give their mother. I didn't care anymore what she liked or disliked. Game over; I'd given up the ghost. I gathered her nursing awards and parchment degree with other mementos and neatly displayed them in a large, two-inch-deep shadow box. It was something she would never have considered doing but something she deserved. Maybe she would appreciate it.

What else would I give her to fill up the typical Christmas bounty? Clueless. Now that she had her own money, she could buy whatever she wanted without uttering a syllable to me.

The kids were fairly easy to buy for. For Noah, it was supposed to be the bike he wanted, with some effort on his part by saving his allowance. Teach him the need and power of saving, and then reward him for studying. That was the thought.

Then Selma, two months prior—outta nowhere—had bought Noah his bike and presented it to him.

"I wanted to do something with *my* money for the kids for a change," she said. I looked at her, dumbfounded.

"Do you have any idea what you have done? I have been telling him for months I wanted his grades up and then we would consider this bike. He already has a bike and doesn't really *need* another one. This is frivolous. This was between him and me. How can I teach the kids anything if you are going to zoom around behind me and screw it all up? What the hell were you thinking?"

"Well, I just wanted to do something for them with the extra money I'm bringing in."

"Extra? Since when do we have extra money? Ten years ago! *Your* money is *not* extra. Have you seen the bills? We have over fifteen thousand dollars in debt borrowed for your school and ten thousand from the campaign, mortgage, cars, and sundry expenses when you were not working."

"I did, too, work. Dammit, I worked cleaning houses the whole time I was in school, and then I started part time at St. Joseph's."

"The St. Joseph's money helped out some, but a hundred bucks a week from your cleaning houses five years ago that I never saw, didn't do squat."

"Well, it was money we wouldn't have otherwise had. It helped to buy groceries and—"

"Why don't we worry about the big bills before we buy a bike he does not need?" I said. "But that is not the main issue. He and I had a deal. He would save and study, and now you have made me look pretty stupid. Why do what Dad says? Mom will buy it. Why study? Why save? Besides, why the hell didn't you say something to me before you did it? You're the one always harping about making the money decisions together, remember? Then you go and pull shit like this!"

So enraged, I could have lunged like a cornered lion, gouging out her eyes with my clawed thumbs. I could have crushed her face against the wall before the screaming of the kids, covered in blood and slimy eyeball splooge, brought me back to reality. I walked away. It didn't matter what I said; Selma lived in a snow globe of floating kittens and fairy dust. Forget the past fifteen years. She had her own personal, private money, and that made all the difference. She was special now.

New rules applied for her.

Christmas' jingles lost their peal. Cameo boarded a plane and went back to see her kids—and Trevor—for the holidays.

Turning to take care of my funk and to grasp some tinsel of enjoyment of the season. I immersed myself with family in the maelstrom of the mall, to soak in the pulsating artificial cheer among giant gold and red orbs and plastic garlands choked with electric fireflies, twinkling and blinking. While walking between stores, my thoughts were with Cameo. I imagined how nice it would be to be with her, with someone who actually enjoyed my company. Noah still let me hold his hand. I savored his need for me and his innocence. Without thinking, I reached out, but it was Selma's hand I grasped, startling us both, but I held tight. It struck her as odd, sure. It had been so infrequent in the past that we were out of the habit, as are many couples, too busy holding the hand of a child.

As I held Selma's hand, my heart sank. I whispered in my own head, *I loved you, dear. I am so, so sorry you can't love me back. Why couldn't we be friends, like Cameo and me? Where did we go wrong, or where did I wrong you? Whatever we had is gone, and I have tried so hard for too long, and now it hurts too much. Why did you do these things to me? What did I ever, ever do to you? You're drowning me, and I must save myself. I am terribly afraid this is the last season of us.*

January's gloom arrived too soon. With the dark cloud Selma, the pallor of holiday dissatisfaction hung. Selma had a lousy Christmas. As usual, my gifts were stupid, and she declared the obvious—that I knew nothing about her. Gifts were spurned, despite the money squandered. Saved receipts allowed her to salvage a pittance of seasonal joy, but I might as well have put mine in the toilet.

Selma had a degree in grade-A "assery," with a minor in rejection and indignation. How had I expected anything else for this Christmas, one no different from the past half dozen? She was the life of the party; I was her hangover.

I chucked the despair and wondered how much of a disaster Cameo's Christmas had been. I felt satisfied that her return would be in short order.

The imprudent desire to spend time with Cameo called for exponential expansion of the truth for being out of the house. I could no longer use the holiday shopping tale. Addicted, I needed my Cameo fix. I couldn't stand the deadness of Selma anymore. Her charms had drawn me to Cameo, but gentleness bound me to her. She was okay with my being the man. We didn't have a problem deciding who needed to do what; no controversy between us. She didn't want the dirty work, to fight as Marines fought. She was comfortable in the supporting role, and she let me do what I had to do.

On the days when I could not see Cameo, I was compelled to call her. On the days she was out of town or I couldn't see or call her, I wrote letters. Slow at first, I eventually called her every morning she was in town and every evening she stayed at Scott for a class.

When she scheduled a legitimate night out with her coworkers, I drove by Cameo's house on the way home. The front porch on Park, where we used to sit, brought back the zestful feeling we had in high school. Seeing her car gave me an idea. At the Quik-Trip convenience store on the corner of Kingshighway and Elm Street, I selected the least-wilted long-stem rose from a vase crowding the counter with the other impulse-buy products. I placed the rose under the wiper blade of her car.

Later the next morning, Cameo left a message on my voicemail. Yes, she had found the rose and really liked it, but she wanted to make it clear that her mother had grilled her about who had left it. Cameo giggled and said her car must have been mistaken for another's.

The only peace of mind I could grasp was asleep, alone across town. Selma worked the midnight to 8:00 a.m. shift, and I was spending too much sleep time thinking, not sleeping. The notion struck me to surprise Cameo by driving over to her house and seeing her before she left for work. Setting the alarm for 4:00 a.m., I put on my PT gear—sweatshirt and warm-up pants—shaved (because an unshaven face reminded her of Trevor), and drove over and parked a hundred feet down the street from her house.

With a convenience-store coffee in hand, I watched the window as Cameo and her mother scurried about the kitchen. When Cameo's silhouette appeared in the backdoor porch light, I blinked my headlights. She looked up and nodded.

A second later, her mother appeared. As was their routine, Cameo and her mother made two trips to the car every morning. Cameo started the engine to warm it and if the windows were icy, her mother helped her scrap them off. Cameo carried her books for her classes, and her mother would carry a bag of sundries.

Since Cameo stayed over at Scott so much, her car was never completely unpacked; she stored clothes, blankets, food, uniforms, toiletries, and other odd items in it, like a traveling salesman.

Bolder and more daring, or stupid and stupider—one or the other or both—I wasn't myself anymore. Obsessed to see more of Cameo, I bought this potion she was selling. Concocting stories a feckless foray, nonetheless, I needed a cover. I whipped up excuses to stay out late with Tony, the friend from work, allegedly crashing at his place in the city. No story seemed too big of whopper for a junkie, but for me, it was too out of character.

Another way to see Cameo was by rising earlier and driving to Scott before work. At 0300 in St. Louis, the roads were empty, and I could drive at warp speed, especially in January. Starting off my day with a big smile took my mind off the road. As I took the exit at Scott, I braked late and went too slow into the ramp, having forgotten temperatures outside were near ten degrees.

As soon as my foot hit the brakes, the car's back end spun left as I tried to turn right. I pumped the brake and concentrated on steering, unsure where I was headed, but it looked like over the edge into the snow-covered median. Fortunately, the back end stopped slipping, and as my speed reduced, I was able to regain control.

When I got to Cameo's room, I told her what had happened and said she was lucky to see me alive. She blew me a big kiss. "I'm just glad you're okay. Now, come over here and show me just how lucky I am."

"Cameo, what is it? I have noticed this change, and I've seen it before, but you don't seem yourself. Have I done something? You're wearing a mask of someone else, not the Cameo I know."

I had noticed a sea change in Cameo after I had been with her a while. On the occasion when I stayed over, while lying in bed, I would watch through the open door of the bathroom while she dressed for work. While putting on makeup, she drifted off, as if painting someone else's face on her body. I would stand behind her, and as we talked, emotion was gone—she was icy and foreign. She was removed from the conversation, as if talking to her mother.

"Huh, no, I'm fine. You haven't done anything."

"There is something different here from what I felt from you not twenty minutes ago. Do you want me to leave?"

"No, don't go. I was thinking about Trevor. I should really give this marriage another chance, but every time I am with you… I realize how bad my marriage is, and I do not even know how to start over. Ever since I found his black book in college, with names of the women he had been with, I felt like I'd missed out on something and have tried to catch up and get even for all these years."

"I can understand the confusion you're going through," I said. "I love you very much, but I don't want to make you do anything you don't want to do or may regret. What am I supposed to say? That I don't want you? Will that make it easier for you? I can't say that, but I would understand. I don't have a real say, but you shouldn't be with him."

"I know. I want you, too. I was thinking about the girls. He has that letter, the one that he said he would use against me, my career, and everything. I love you, but just understand how difficult all of this is in my head. I'm sorry for the mask. You're right; that is what I have been doing—trying to hide the feelings, like I have for so many years."

"Well, you don't have to hide from me. I want you to be able to tell me anything and everything."

The next time we were together, Cameo suggested a dalliance with Tootsie Roll Pops. A couple of them together, doing what I was doing, would add a little flavor.

Not completely weirded out and still curious, I asked how she came up with an adult use for a favorite childhood treat. She scoffed and batted it away as something she must have read somewhere.

Not sold on the source and a bit hesitant, I pressed her to reveal more details, and how she had come across this new, randy use, to put the lolli- in the pop.

After a bit of stammering, she sheepishly divulged a situation that had started with Craig.

My eyes went wide as I fought to contain myself from caring. "Huh? Who is this Craig?" I said, as I sat up. *How stupid of me*, I thought as I swallowed the boulder-size thought that I was not the only one. Of course I wasn't. *Idiot*. "Who is this guy? How long have you... I thought..." Again, how puerile it would sound to actually enunciate my thoughts that I was not the only one. I was the latest.

I knew Cameo. She was no floozy. I tried to retain my composure and told myself it didn't matter. I had her now. Besides, it was different this time, because this time it was me. I couldn't judge her, not after saying she could tell me anything. I hadn't expected, however, to be shot at in the wrong place so soon.

I had to get out of there. I needed time to think, I told her. Time to digest and synthesize this revelation. We would talk about it later, if I dared to bring it up again.

Cameo happened to pull right in front of me as Highway 64 merged with Highway 70 in downtown St. Louis. I wondered what the odds were, as the entangling traffic rush merged. I blinked my lights and waved. I could see her laughing as she waved back at me, and we stayed together all the way into St. Charles. Every time we drove back to St. Charles in the future, we carried out this little ritual, the closest thing to walking her to her front door.

When I missed her on the weekends, and I would feel my heart ache, I would drive by to see if she was in her yard or in one of the windows. Depending on the time of day or night, I might leave a rose under her windshield, to spite her mother. Cameo eventually bought me a set of keys so I could leave letters, cards, and the roses in the car and out of sight.

Realizing how expensive our stays at the Drury Inns had become, we looked for alternatives when the Scott Inn wasn't available. Leaving the base one day and driving west back to St. Charles, I chose to skip driving through downtown St. Louis and took the north outer loop of

I-270. As I crossed the Chain of Rocks Bridge, coming from Illinois into Missouri, I noticed a sign for the Econo Lodge—only $29.95 a night. *Doesn't look too bad*, I thought. It would work sometimes, so I told Cameo. It was better than the sixty bucks at the Drury in Illinois, and we didn't have to drive so far.

Late January daytime temperatures dropped drastically, and thermometers froze, stuck at zero. Multiple snows smothered the Midwest. A layer melted by traffic action and another by salt, and the muck mixture refroze and caked the asphalt ice. A third and fourth snow encrusted the city in dingy frosting.

When I arrived at the Econo Lodge late, the parking lot was the mogul event for the winter Olympics. I tried to make out her car but could not find it. We had decided to meet at ten, and my slow driving in circles had killed a half hour. I'd already had a few and was trying to hurry up to keep the buzz on, hoping Cameo had a bottle of wine. I was in need of another drink of her, too.

I started to worry that she thought I meant another place. I drove the north outer road to see if she had mistaken the rendezvous place for another.

Back at the motel, I decided I must have missed her and needed to check the front desk. As I pulled in the parking lot for the sixth circuit, my beeper went off. I didn't recognize the number. I drove to the service station next door, pulled up to use the phone, and turned the heater on high. "Damn phone companies," I cussed out loud, making these hand receivers so short I had to lean half out the window. Cameo answered and said she'd wondered where I was. "Looking for your car for the last hour," I told her. She said to forget it and hurry up. The room number was 219.

Gingerly pulling the phone away from my ear for fear it might have stuck, I hung up, then drove back to the parking lot, and pulled into the same space I had been. As I got out, I dropped the keys. Glancing through a window of the car next to me, I noticed the clothes in the backseat were hers. Obscured by snow, melt, and salt, I had not recognized her car.

Cameo did not like the feel of place—too seedy for what we were up to. Our situation was nothing like that, we harmoniously lied to each other, so all we did was talk. Having spent so much time carving pirouettes around the motel's snow munch, I had to leave. We agreed to look for better alternatives in the future.

Our willful catch-me-if-you-can cavorting schedule brought our next arrangement within spitting distance of my house. Stupid never takes a holiday. I had exited at Zumbehl, as always, but this time I took greater notice of the Red Roof Inn on the intersection's south side. I never understood how a motel was profitable there, but the St. Charles city council approved a gambling boat, docked at the riverfront, as a cure for community tax woes. With a full-fledged casino on the river, St. Charles could compete with St. Louis for tourism and draw business to their renowned Main Street area as well.

While watching TV later with the kids, during one of the too-numerous-to-count Dad-only nights, a commercial advertised that the Red Roof Inn charged twenty-nine dollars a night. Leaving no mint on the pillow was to make you feel no less important; they held their customers in greater appreciation by passing the savings on to them. Cameo and I didn't need the mints anyway; our treats were each other and the additional ones packed by her mother. The price was right, and though the location was too close to home, I was almost at the point of bringing Cameo home anyway and introducing her to my motherless children.

Cameo hinted several times about playing with whipped cream, as I glumly commented minor interest. Love was messy enough already, and I still wasn't doing the Tootsie Roll Pop thing, whatever the hell that was.

As was normal, Cameo was in the room before I got there. Candles whispered about the stage and altered the mood, making it all right, helping us to pretend what we were doing was okay and assigning guilt to another day. It was not about us anyway. We weren't the problem. The world around us was the problem, and its appearance was altered into dancing shadows, only seen by us and the candles tucking us out of sight.

She had brought in her personal bag but asked me to retrieve the last bag from her car, which contained the delights we would need for that night. I retrieved the items from her car, set it down, and began to kiss her passionately, pushing her down onto the bed so her arms and legs could warm me up from the still blizzard-like conditions outside. The room's heater churned, straining to get the room warmer than the inside of a refrigerator. We needed heat.

We were past slowly undressing and ripped the clothes off each other, throwing them all over, and quickly jumped beneath the covers to contemplate how to best utilize the supplies that Cameo had purchased at lunch.

Cameo gasped, "Ahhhh!" *What was that all about?* I thought, but her contorted face made me burst out laughing. Without thinking, I grabbed the whipped cream and started to spray it all over her. She screamed again, snatched the can back, and shot globs of creamy foam on my back, the effect catching me off guard.

"Aw-w-w, hey! Stop!" I exclaimed as the super-cooled cream stuck to my back. "What are you doing? Get back. I don't want any part of that. You're right; this is no fun at all." I jumped off the bed, turned, and pounced on her as we rolled about, trying to warm up the tasty torture. She had bought the whipped cream at lunch and had left it in the car all day. We hadn't an inkling it might be frozen.

More sticky than excited—and glad the room was a double, because this bed was now disgusting—we took a shower and switched beds.

Staying later than normal, because the drive was minimal, I asked Cameo how long she was going to stay the next morning. She wasn't going to return home too early, she said, because she didn't want her mother to suspect anything. She would probably stay until noon. I kissed her good night as I pondered how to sneak off to see her the next day.

Selma was not a quiet sleeper and not a pretty one either. She slept with her head cocked and her mouth wide open. I had a fleeting thought of shoving a sock into it. It would make my life so much easier.

Hating her is what I should be doing, but men don't turn love to hate; they plummet in confusion. Look for good, you find good. Look for problems, you find them. Focus on where you don't want to go, and you hit the lamp pole.

I loved Selma in some way, like a barnacle loves a boat's underbelly. I thought I loved her, the mother of my children. Ours was a struggle like others out there had, working out the good and the bad, but the struggles were supposed to be financial or physical, not the mental roller coaster of nebulous emotion, those intangibles of which men know so little. If you have love and a positive outlook on things, you could prevail and appreciate the journey you made together. Eventually, it was all supposed to work out in the end. You had to stay and think positive, though; something I had done, but then I had the will beat out of me.

Quit thinking about it. It was the quagmire of things, a theory of un-relativity, as hard to fathom as the thought of infinity. All those things she said I had failed in—I could not understand how she could think that way. To survive was to forget. I wished I could get up out of bed and bring her a cup of coffee, tea, or hot chocolate. Who could know, though, which, if any, she would want and whether or not she would even appreciate it? She would only complain that I woke her and brought the wrong beverage.

When Cameo woke up, I would wake up. We would appreciate the sight of each other and smile. She was easy to love. It was easy to be together.

As I lay there, I could not stand to think that Cameo was sleeping alone and only a mile away. Love definitely trumped loathing. I had to go see her. It would be simple. I had only recently started venturing out of the house in the morning to get a hoosier cappuccino, coffee with a squirt of French vanilla, and I could say I ran into and talked to an old friend.

Cameo was surprised when she answered the door and saw me with my hot cup of alibi in my hand. She was very glad to see me. She'd been working on some paperwork for her last class. Setting down my coffee, I made her some more of the tea that she had been drinking, and we chattered small talk. I could not be gone too long or it would arouse more suspicion. We laughed about the escapades of the night before, and she giggled.

We enjoyed sitting across from each other, dreaming of a new future. It was great to be able to share, to know what each other liked and didn't like. We were not separate people and often thought the same thoughts. It was nice to be appreciated for anything, even if it was only for serving a cup of tea.

Mr. Stupid, took a holiday, and I went along for the ride. Enough was not enough. I had to have more of Cameo. I called her every night she was not home with her parents.

On the mornings she was at Scott, and Selma was at work, I called Cameo from the house. Since it was long distance, and I didn't want the number to show on the phone bill, I used my company phone card. Everyone did it, and the young upshot sales manager wouldn't know the difference, as long as the sales numbers stayed up.

When Selma was home, it was trickier. Running my normal three-mile loop, I passed several gas stations with phone booths. The problem was not the phone but forcing my butt to run in a wind chill that was below freezing.

One miserable February morning, I crawled out of bed before 0500. The layering process started with nylon shorts, then long-john bottoms, running pants, several T-shirts and a sweatshirt, and an insulated Adidas jacket I received back from Haley when Nike became vogue. To complete the Rocky Balboa ensemble, I put a towel around my neck to keep out the wind and then put on a stocking cap, shoes, and gloves. It was a half mile to a mile before I warmed enough to unzip the jacket or pull off the gloves.

That morning it was five degrees outside, and the wind must have been blowing at twenty knots. I had trouble making it up the first hill due to the frozen road. I slipped and then jerked to remain upright. I stopped at three phones that didn't work. The starting and stopping chilled me. When I finally found a working phone, Cameo was delighted I had gone to such lengths to talk to her. "Length is the last thing I have in this weather," I kidded, "so I'd better hurry up and run again. Nothing hurts worse than defrosting."

I was getting tired of making excuses to the kids each night Selma was not home for why I needed to leave for a soda or something from the store. I started to call from the house in the evening. The girls were supposed to be asleep downstairs in their bedroom.

The kids weren't allowed on the phone after ten o'clock. Their friends were not to call after that time either. If they did, they heard only from me, not the one for whom the call was intended. I was more than happy to fill them in on the house rule.

One late night when I was on the phone, I heard someone pick up the extension. I told whoever it was to get off of the phone and that I was talking with someone. Over the course of the next week, it happened several times. I don't know whether I heard every time one of the girls picked up the phone or how much they might have heard of the conversation. In a sense, I didn't care. If Selma could talk to her male friend, Gaylord, for hours at a time with me sitting there, I guessed I could talk to a female friend. That would be my story, as the country song I'd been forced to hear said, and I was sticking to it.

Cameo and I arranged to be together for Valentine's Day, but I didn't know what to do with or for Selma. The best way to speak out without talking was putting pen to paper. I wrote that I didn't know what to do for Valentine's Day, so I expressed the feeling of hopelessness between us. I couldn't buy flowers, candy, or a gift. It would be wasted on feelings we no longer shared. I'd be wrong, regardless of what I did. She must feel the same way. She didn't want me. When Gaylord called, Izzy told her mother that her boyfriend was on the phone. The kids and I knew she had a boyfriend, Gaylord or another. What did she take me for? How long could she live this way? Why didn't she decide what she wanted and move on? She should leave.

The letter was placed on the dresser, along with another note saying I would be late that evening. *By the way, I will be late on Friday night too. Tony and I are going out.*

Cameo had a room at the Scott Inn. She had left the door ajar. I knocked once and went in. Directly in front of me was my Valentine's Day gift.

Cameo was wrapped in white gift paper, a bow attached to her shoulder. She admired the white, red, and yellow roses I brought and the bottle of wine. We discussed the meaning of the colors for roses: red was for love, white for friendship, and yellow for passion—or was it the other way around? We weren't sure. I massaged her feet, pretending I liked to do it, and listened to her carry on. She unwrapped a small gift box. Inside was a pair of small butterfly-shaped earrings I'd had custom-made, adorned with small topaz stones.

"Oh-h, what's the story behind these?" she said.

"The butterflies?"

"Yeah, they're so different. I have never seen anything like them. They're beautiful."

"Well, when do you see butterflies?"

"Spring, summer, I guess."

"And how easy is it to capture one?"

"Fairly easy with a net. If you use your hands, you're apt to smash them."

"Their delicate, then, you mean."

"Sure."

"This will probably sound sappy, but you girls like this kind of stuff. The butterflies represent what we have—beautiful and delicate to hold without damaging. The sight of one flitting about in the warm breeze can't help but bring a smile to your face. The stones on each wing are your eyes that I have loved gazing into—they're fresh and alive. Whenever you wear the earrings, it will always be spring."

"I love them. I love them. Thank you so much." She would have been happy with almost anything, where Selma was happy with nothing.

We talked the usual talk, oblivious to the world outside the door. When we could get married, who would be the first to file for divorce, and how to make our lives work together. The time was coming to pull the trigger on splitting up with Selma, but I hadn't been able to do it.

Thoughts about my children killed me. Why couldn't Selma leave, like I knew she wanted? It would be so much simpler, and she hated being around all of us anyway.

Living as Prince Charming in my own fairy tale, I ignored reality in my personal life, as it was becoming harder to justify my feelings and actions. Selma must suspect by now. She was too suspicious about everything.

The mask was on me now.

CHAPTER 13

Park Lane Station

What made me unique?

Unusually awake, I grabbed my spiral notebook to scribe random notions and doodle quantum-mechanical calculations.

How to empower myself… what details, facets, angles could I finagle to visualize a level of being important and useful?

The population of the United States was over 310 million. I jotted the number at the bottom of what would be my hierarchy.

One-tenth was thirty-one million. What would closely represent that? Midwesterners? No, too large. Veterans? No, too small—save it for later. Bachelor's degrees? Maybe, at least when I received mine. I'd go with it. I penciled it in.

One-tenth of that was three million. What population group represented a number similar to it? Gays? Forget that. Jews? Nope. Didn't matter anyway; I couldn't claim it. Master's degrees? Money? Homes? Cars? Households with four TVs? Officers? Current active duty? Population of Missouri? Number of retirees? Active duty? Okay, maybe I'll split that hair to one and a half million.

One hundred fifty thousand was too low a number, but round it up to be the general number of active-duty Marines.

One-tenth of that was the number of Marine officers. Another tenth. Fifteen hundred, hmm? The number crammed into this car last week? No, more. The number of emails in my inbox when I get to work? Close but doesn't count for anything.

I sliced demographics until I was left with me on top. Now what did it mean? American, Marine, with a degree in BS, too old for the field I was in, and special to no one but me.

Great.

"I am rich, I am happy, and I am successful." Is that the right order? Forget it. No wonder there was the consumption of sports by others. Why did I feel a need to be different, special, one of a kind?

* * * * *

When Friday morning came, I packed a bag for my stay with my newest presumed friend, the infamous Tony. It was 0830. Selma was due home from work and I was struggling to get the kids off to school before she arrived.

She bolted in the door with an air that said it was ass-kicking time. *Shit*, I thought, but I bleated a weak hello. *Damn. She's not supposed to be here, which means she is up to something.* This Pavlovian dog had learned his response. I was trying to get out of the house quicker. *Ignore her and she'll ignore me. It's worked for years.*

She hovered, doing a lousy job of appearing normal. I tried to grab my bag in the confusion of good-bye kisses and scurry out the door with the kids.

"What is this about where you are going to be tonight?" Selma said. A loud, vocal grappling hook latched onto me.

"I am spending the night out with Tony. You read it on the note the other day, didn't you?"

"You're drinking too much. You have to stop. You don't need to run around with Tony. He's nothing but trouble, if that is all you're going to do."

So typical of her to go on the offensive. It's Selma the savior, the doer of mighty deeds, using the worn-out, fake-concern-for-me ploy to ignore this had anything to do with her.

One question meant she was loaded with twenty in her ammo belt to machine-gun me. Once she started, she wouldn't cease firing.

"What did that note mean? What do you mean, I need to figure things out? I have things figured out. You never used to be out with Tony all night. Now, it seems you're out with him all the time. Why, now? Brick, what's going on?" The vulture with its red gnarly head and piss-yellow beak closed in with swooping circles toward the dead meat that was me.

I sat my bag and briefcase down. I knew this would be a session from perdition or all the circles of Dante's *Inferno* at once, subtracting breathes from my life I'd never get back.

"Really?" I said. "*You* have been in a different world. Don't act like you don't know things between us are a mess. I don't know what you want. You have been ripping the kids apart, and I have tried to get out of you what is wrong. I am always putting myself in the middle. The kids want to know why you are so mad at them all of time. I used to make excuses for you, that it was school. Now it's work." *A good catch,* I thought, *reverse the direction of the argument.* "You want a lengthy argument, you can wait. I have to take Noah to school. I'll be back." I left, wishing I didn't have to come back.

When I returned, I took my position in the chair opposite the couch, where she still sat on the flippin' phone—with a council witch bitch, no doubt, soliciting potions from her slithering clan.

"I am running late, Sherrie. You're still going to our weekly lunch, right?" Selma said.

"Oh, I wouldn't miss it for the world," I could hear Sherrie squawk from the other end of the phone. "How could I not? Couldn't live without you guys. You won't believe what my husband did yesterday. I will tell you when you get there. See you later."

Pushing the tab on the phone, Selma dialed another number while I sat there tapping my foot. "Hi, Rachel. I am going to be a little late for lunch. You want me to pick you up like always, or are you going to drive separately?" Selma said.

"I'll wait for you. You're not going to be too late are you?" Rachel said, speaking just as loudly as Sherrie had. Either Selma didn't know I could hear the other end of her conversation, or she didn't care. "You talk with Brick yet?" Rachel then asked.

"We will talk later," Selma answered, thinking she was being sly.

"You finally listened to us, huh. 'Bout time. Can't wait. Good luck."

Beware the council of wives. The sour-grapes coven Selma called friends had deluded what used to be my wife. Friends were more important than spouses. What you tell them in private becomes common knowledge—a teachable moment for the others. They embellished and enlarged their woe-is-me status, digging deeper into their troubles to win some elevated stature in their female cluster, to win the award for greatest victim.

"Well, what do want to talk about?" I asked, taking the elevated, noncommittal position. The best defense was to do like her and pretend nothing ever happened, never happened, never would.

"The kids are concerned about your drinking," she said.

A tug on the heartstrings was good to break down the opposition's defense. Even though this clearly had nothing to do with the kids, except living with the aftermath. The D-word—drinking—had emphasis, unless it involved hers.

"When you're here, you have to go out and get something to drink. What is going on? Why have you started drinking so much?"

I sure could use a drink.

"So what?" I said. "Tony and I are bar-hopping tonight downtown. I don't want to drink and drive, so I am staying over. How is it different from your late nights?"

"My late nights are work," she said, quick on the comeback, as only a liar could. The truth needn't be checked or recalled. A liar could recant anything and cover a lie with another, changing hues, painting whitewash. "Sometimes they ask me to stay late. Since I am already there, I might as well get more hours in, if I can. Your late nights aren't work. Does this have anything to do with the phone call the girls heard the other night? What is that all about, huh? Are you seeing someone else?"

"No, I am not seeing anybody." My skin crawled. I hated to lie and never wanted to be good at it. I told Selma everything about any trip I had been on—escapades of the people I worked with, the exploits of this colonel or that, good or bad. I had always tried to include her in my life, to be an open book—until a few months back, that is.

The guilt smothered me. "I was talking to someone from work. So what? You do the same all of the time. When you're here, you're always talking to Mary Jane or Gaylord or Rachel or Bill or Bob or your sister or Faye or Crosby or Stills or Nash or Ernie and Elmo—name it. It doesn't matter if I am here. You're on the phone for hours on end, and I am not supposed to be concerned about any of that, now am I? And all of your late nights are work, right? You haven't been your normal self, even when you're here." "What does it matter, anyway?"

Any sense of normal had vanished like feathers in a tornado. Was the constant grating of past years normal or the current absence and ignoring? Both sucked. "The only way I can handle things is to stay busy, here or at work. And by the way, when did you start wearing colorful, silky underwear and changing in the bathroom with the door closed? Why don't you want me to see it? You're obviously hiding something yourself, because I haven't seen you in that! What the hell is up with that?"

"I bought it months ago. I needed new ones. It doesn't mean anything. I have been buying a few at a time, now that I can finally afford it."

"That doesn't make any difference. I have been trying to get you to buy nicer clothes for years. It is not like we couldn't afford it. Why is now different? It wouldn't have anything to do with the motorcycle parked in the driveway last summer at three in the morning, would it?"

"Brick, I've told you and told you. It wasn't anything for you to worry about. Gaylord stopped by after work, and we ..."

"...talked, yeah, yeah. At three in the morning, he happened to come by, and you just happened to be awake, if you want to keep that story going. You keep saying it, but I am not eating the half-baked shit you are calling casserole and the Kool-Aid that tastes like piss. I don't believe you. I have to go to work"

There was a pause in the hostilities as I tried to escape the inevitable. The air was thick with distrust on both our parts. She was bound to keep lying, regardless, only caring to be the winner. I was crumbling.

"Brick, I don't want you to go out tonight. Come home, and we can talk about things."

Yeah, that is what I wanted to look forward to, I thought. *Hours of loud denial on her part as she shovels manure entrees into me.*

"I don't want you out drinking. You can drink here at home," Selma said defiantly.

"Why should I stay? You are seeing someone. We could talk about this to the death, and you would never admit to the truth. We both know how skilled you are at hiding the truth. I don't have anything to prove you're seeing someone. I know it. Until you admit it, I don't see any reason to keep going over this."

We went back and forth for an hour and a half. My head smoked and hair singed, as I battled her and her silent co-conspirators who were allied in my downfall. They supported her no matter what she did. Moral support was a misnomer, having nothing to do with morals but creating whatever platitude they needed to justify.

Poisonous silence seeped in. I could detect the wail of my conscience, trapped with the inevitable truth. "To thine own self, be true," the Bible said, and my lies convicted me.

Sales courses teach to wait out the pregnant pause in closing. The first to break the awkward impasse psychologically gives in. Salesmen are trained to wait this out, and they make the sale. I sucked at sales.

"Yeah, I am seeing someone else. No different from you." My words were flung out, naked in the quiet.

"*What?*" She leaped off of the couch in a panic. Tears burst from her eyes. "*What?*" she screamed. "You're seeing someone else?" Stamping, she paced back and forth, yelping in disbelief.

Her outbursts shocked me. She liked to go for the shock effect, and though I knew it, it caught me off guard. I didn't think she cared enough to be this great an actor. Now, this was really going to be difficult. The way she treated me, who would have known? Who would have thought?

Or maybe it was an act, like I had seen before—the theatrics to amplify her point, part of her lying method. Maybe she didn't think I was man enough or emotional enough or conscious enough to need someone other than her. How could someone act so surprised, act like she cared so much, when she was seeing someone herself? That took talent; I had to give her that.

She didn't think I had it in me. That was it. She was trained, an expert on sneaky; she was the lying, cheating, witchy, bitchy one. She was comfortable in what she was doing, because I gave her top cover, mistakenly trusting her, and she used it as an excuse to do what she wanted. How many times had she looked at me like I was an imbecile for trusting her to stay out late for school or work? As she looked at it, I didn't love her enough to be jealous. How squirreled up was that?

Sitting uneasily in the chair as she sobbed and cackled unutterables, she paced the floor, trying to gain composure, but couldn't stop herself from crying. I felt worse and worse the longer I sat there. *I have no evidence of her affair, no physical evidence, nothing really tangible*, I said to myself in my self-questioning trust-everyone-but-myself thoughts.

She went into the hall bathroom for more tissues to wipe her eyes and dripping nose. Minutes seemed days, though time had taken a hard right off the time-space continuum and crashed in another place.

After an eternity in my parallel universe, she brusquely said, "Who is she?"

"Selma, it doesn't matter who she is. It is no one you know, anyway."

"Do you love her?"

"Yes." *A stupid question. Do you think I would go through this mess if I didn't?*

"*What?*" she screamed again. "How could you love her? How long have you been seeing her?"

My first thought was to laugh. *Shit, how could I not love her, with the way you treat me?* But I knew it would add fuel to this four-alarm fire?

I have been here before, where Selma would just sit and sit, waiting for me to say something and dig myself deeper and deeper into a rut than the one she had decided I belonged in. I was used to this from her. Where was her guilt? Where was her shame? Was I not to feel something every time she told me to fuck off—words I would never say to her? Why couldn't she see she had done this to me? But no, she was always the victim, and I, the bad guy.

What can one say once he has pierced the heart of a lover spurned? Granted, I still loved Selma, but I didn't know what to do with her or about her. She was a stranger who happened to be the mother of my beautiful children. Yet there had been times when she too had been beautiful. Where had that woman gone, and what life form had replaced her? That's all I really wanted from her—the woman she used to be, and I didn't even mean physical beauty but the one who could say things that touched my heart.

But what was I thinking?

Our relationship had only been a physical attraction, and to many a man, that was enough, initially. It was for me, until she morphed into this self-absorbed leech creature. To her, the marriage became a what's-in-it-for-me venture, and she got what she wanted, while I worked, supporting her.

"Who is she, Brick? How long have you been seeing her?"

I waited, thinking something should be said, but it could not be said right enough. I should say something but knew I needed to say nothing. As the carnival went, she always won. When one side has a conscience and the other one does not, the outcome is predictable. I felt guilt; she never did. If I didn't answer, I suffered; and if I spoke, I suffered. If I did answer, it would stir up a battery of new questions or comments, like pumping pure oxygen on a spark. We never really discussed anything. She asked questions and would tell me why I was wrong, and then she would reload. She should have been a trial lawyer.

"It started when it became obvious you were having an affair. You have what you supposedly want, so why does it matter?"

"I am not having an affair." She stated it somewhat convincingly. If you do not care about the truth, lying is easy.

"Don't give me your crap. I know you are seeing someone else, and now I have someone who gives a shit about me, okay? Why should you care? You have your mystery man." She was a natural. When I looked at her, I saw fake tears and horns.

I assumed her mystery man was, in fact, a man, but in this day and age, one never knew. Selma was spending a lot of time with Mary Jane Rottencrotch, but Mary Jane was rendezvousing with the Arab car dealer. Maybe they were a threesome, a ménage-a-Muslim.

"I don't know where you are getting this," Selma whined. "If you're talking about when Gaylord came over after work last summer—"

"Let me go through the list. You demanded your own bank account, though we have had a joint bank account with my income for seventeen years of our glorious wedded bliss. My money is our money, but now that you have some income, you think it is your money—special and private. We should treat your money different somehow. It also means you can hide what you spend it on. You have stayed out very late for months, without any explanation. You decided you needed Victoria's Secret underwear that I have never seen save in your dresser. Now, you change in the bathroom and never did that before. I can hear you cleaning up. From what? The kids commented about your 'boyfriend' a few months back. I called you at work to ask you a question several months back. You know what the chief nurse told me? You were not scheduled to work that evening."

I was telling her too much. I wasn't saving anything to follow up with, after all the forthcoming fables would suffice as her answers.

"Speaking of the kids," I continued, "you treat them like hell. You don't act like you want to be around them or me. Life around here is the demon's den. I have been waiting for you to leave. Wondering when I would come home and find out you'd vanished and cleaned us out. Waiting for you to stick it to us. Why haven't you?"

She straightened her shoulders, and lifted herself to her full height, caste her pearls before me. "I don't know what you're talking about. I am not having an affair. I have told you and told you—the checking account was what I needed to do for me. I wanted us to have some extra money. Besides, the accounts are joint now. I have been working really hard. And there's nothing wrong with how I treat the kids! I treat them just fine, thank you."

This was where I needed to leave. I stood up, thinking of the fly touching the web, unable to free itself, as the big, ugly spider crept from dark edges. I didn't believe her. I was tired of her lying to me and treating me like a fool, of enduring her endless moods, of enduring her.

"Just let me stay a couple of nights," I said, "and I will find somewhere else to live."

"No," she spat out, her jaw set. "I want you out of here."

"Where would I go? Give me a day or two to figure this out, all right?"

"No. I want you to go."

With a single truthful proclamation, my world changed forever. I felt the impact crumbling in on me. I felt sick and small. *Shit*. I had wanted her to leave, but it wasn't supposed to be this way. Why, why, why did the man always have to leave? She was the criminal, not me.

What about the kids, the house, my clothes, my stuff, my uniforms, everything? This was my life, and she said I had to leave with nothing. Why couldn't *she* leave like we all knew she wanted? Even the kids said so. She gets to wear her righteousness, and I get the costume of beast. She must have planned this for months—except she couldn't even plan a stupid surprise party worth a whit.

What now?

I grabbed the already packed bag and left. No work would be done today, but I drove toward the office, where I could use the phone. Numb, I was unable to think much of anything, other than my imploding family. As if the past few years had not been bad enough, now they were worse. The only hope I had to cling to in the past five years was being a father. In an instant, it was stripped from me as well.

At the office, a stupefied man pretended to be me. A soulless caricature wandered the halls aimlessly.

In combat, you knew the enemy as best you could and recognized you didn't know everything, so you planned, trained, and made contingencies to expect the unexpected before you struck. This personal adversary couldn't be destroyed. It was as much me as it was her. How could it be defeated or killed? Lost, I was blind, deaf, dumb.

But who was the real enemy—Selma, me, Cameo, luck of the draw?

"Beve, it's me. Nobody died. I need a place to stay tonight," I said. I needed to talk to someone. My brother was the obvious choice, but this was only Monday. We never called each other at work, unless it was bad news to report, someone had died or things of that nature. *Something* was dead, and I needed him.

"Sure, I'll call Jill and let her know," he said. "I'll be home about four. You know the code to the garage right?"

"Yeah, thanks, see you later," I said, and then added, "I met Cameo. And you know how Selma and I have been."

"Enough said. We'll talk when I get home. Have you said anything to Mom yet?"

"Oh, no, that will have to be in person." I needed to sit with my maternal conscience and lay it out. The phone would not be worthy enough for that conversation. "I'll probably go up this weekend. See you later."

It was hard to breathe; my heart was racing. I attempted to call Cameo, but she wasn't there. There was no one at work to turn to, and no one anywhere else. I was alone, cast off, dying with no one caring. I needed to talk but not on the phone.

Low-end sales reps shared a phone in the conference room. Too many people walked by and overheard conversations. I contacted the nobodies I had appointments with and changed them to the next week.

I drove around. Typical February weather complemented my mood—gray, dull, and endless. I had nowhere to go, having just destroyed it. No, she destroyed it and cared only for herself, as always, whatever made her look right. She was the victim and the recipient of all the sympathy, hogging and relishing it, as usual. I'd been vanquished to doom because I did not succumb to her ways. I had fought her before but not on this level, and at this one, no man could win anyway. We're always guilty.

My chest was getting heavy, as if someone were sitting on it. Since I couldn't talk to anyone who mattered, I cruised nowhere in ever larger concentric circles around St. Louis, as if stalking clues. Turning here and there, I tried to be anywhere but where I was. Without knowing I made a turn, I found myself driving across the river to see Cameo. When I realized it, it seemed logical enough, though it wasn't. She wasn't there.

Gliding to Scott AFB below the speed limit, I turned near the front gate and drove on. I prayed out loud. "God, what have I done? How could I do this to my kids?" I swallowed for air, over and over. My eyes clouded the sight of the road.

The sound of the rocks on the shoulder warned me I was headed off the highway too fast. Without a thought, I jerked the car onto the approaching off-ramp at sixty-five miles per hour, the tires griping as I slammed on the brakes.

My heart seized, stuck in the middle of my chest then lurched again. I couldn't breathe. Wincing in shock, I focused on not running off the embankment and keeping the car in the lane. I briefly welcomed the bridge abutment I was closing in on. An old notion flashed.

Should I?

I thought of going ahead and slamming into it. I couldn't work the brake pedal. Was it time to give up?

What have I done? My kids…

What have I done?

My heart broke.

CHAPTER 14

Pearl/Arts District Station

The Texas State Fair was approaching. The fair was infamous for its fried delicacy contests. Each year, vendors attempted to fry the impossible delight. Fried buffalo chicken in a flapjack would be scrumptious. Fried Frito pies, fried mac 'n' cheese, fried salsa, fried bananas—these seemed interesting, but fried butter, fried Coke, or fried bubblegum? Maybe once. Fried beer? How do you do that? If you can, I'll bite.

As I glanced at *Slick* headlines, one of daily column contributors discussed the various roommates she'd had. She listed the quirks that roommates were forced to tolerate in a cohabitation existence. Roommating was an unfortunate temporary financial arrangement. They needn't be friends, she was insisting.

With a career as mottled as mine, friends were hard to come by. Those who used to be friends were no more. Men didn't stay in touch with each other well. No time. A shifting workscape did not help for making or keeping friends. The ones I had in the Corps were promoted, and we could not officially be on a first-name basis. The system said so.

While on duty in Norfolk, I ran into a kid who had bunked next to me in OCS. I had not seen him for eighteen years. He looked twenty years older than the age he was. Wrinkles penciled in his face, and his eyes pooled from the bottom of a well. He was a helicopter squadron commanding officer, who had returned from a Mediterranean deployment.

I had to say, "Sir, how is it going? Good to see you," instead of saying, "Scott, old buddy, you look like shit. Are you all right?"

Seldom would I run across an acquaintance. Most had been forced out of the service in budget cuts of the early nineties. When I did, the scene would repeat itself. Life had been drained from them, and they were marred by their lack of a smile. They were used up, expended. Great characters, full of laughter and vim, had been retooled as statues. Emotions got in the way on the battlefield. The Marines extracted emotions from you over the course of a lifetime.

Valiant tinmen stood vigilant out of reach of their oil cans.

* * * * *

What was the next move when exposed? Nothing—no place to lie my head, no chair to sit and think, no clothes but what was in my hands and on my back, no direction, no money, no children, no laughing, no fun, no sun, no hopes, no dreams, no anything, no nothing. The world was not black because I could not see.

My brother Beve's house was a couple of miles from the house where we grew up but in a nicer neighborhood. Across the highway, behind Bogey Hills Country Club area, his newer subdivision was another cornfield conversion project.

I had bought some coffee on the way there, as I knew I would be sitting alone for several hours, waiting for him to get home from work. His oldest daughter and wife would probably be home before he was. I'd pretend nothing was wrong until I could bare my soul to my brother. He wouldn't judge. He never did. Blood trumped mud.

After entering the garage code, I went into the house that way, taking off my shoes at the door to keep dirt off his wife's pristine floors. Then I went in to sit among the rabbits. Beve's wife, Jill, had a thing. A cast iron rabbit was stationed in the fireplace, a pottery rabbit was against the wall, and other rabbits were on the mantel and in the wallpaper. One would think, with a plethora of rabbit stuff, that they were doing it like rabbits, but they weren't.

Beve was married before, too, in the seventies, to his high school girlfriend. It lasted a year. Then he played the field for ten years. I, on the other hand, didn't know how to talk to women; I married them instead. I needed marriage for entertainment and dead-space clutter.

After my first divorce, I hung around with my brother and his friends, Forester, Eckley, Dalton, and the Sampson boy, whose brothers were older than me and played Canadian football. Forester became a cop and married his high school girlfriend, who was real cute—I would have done her. Never knew what she saw in him. Dalton had a cute blonde girlfriend, too, that he married back then, but like everyone else, it only lasted a year or so. I would have done her, too. They must have been talkers.

Kiley, Beve's daughter, came home. I asked her how school was going and said I was waiting for Beve. She pranced upstairs to watch TV.

The rabbits and I contemplated fate. As I looked around, I saw that Beve had bettered me. He'd bought his first house when he first married. I couldn't remember his first wife's name. She had said once she didn't like or understand the TV show *The Waltons*. No family acted like that, she said. No wonder she didn't fit in with our family.

Jill arrived before Beve. It did not spare me from repeating what transpired that day and filling in the gaps of the past year. Beve walked in and heard the last part first. Beve knew Cameo from high school, too.

"So you haven't told Mom yet," he stated, having asked me on the phone.

I shook my head. "Not looking forward to telling her I fucked up again."

Mom had a sense about these things and was a good listener, even if I was not good advice taker. She told me I did the opposite of what she recommended, but truth be told, more than half the time she never suggested anything. I kidded her that I had to know where she stood, so I could go the other way.

Beve knew bits and parts of the carnival ride Selma had me on for years. This time, we exhumed the charred remains together, putting each ember into its place, bringing him up-to-date on the combustion of the morning and cueing the source of the implosion. Like Mom, he had always asked how things were with Selma, as if I were living with the terminally ill.

I went into more detail about her lying, the change in dressing habits, what Izzy said about Selma's "boyfriend," what Haley's boyfriend disclosed about the previous summer's late-night visitor, the phone call I made to her work to find Selma was not there, and that current state of Cameo's misery.

Beve showed me upstairs, where I could stay. We made a pallet in one of the rooms with no bed. After shuffling stuff out of one room to another, we found an air mattress in the back of a closet. No matter; better than nothing, and glad to have it. I might find myself sleeping on the carpeted floor next to it, if I could sleep at all?

Beve and I went to the Schnuck's Grocery, which swallowed up its corner lot share of cornfield at Zumbehl and I-70. We were buying their week's worth of groceries, but mostly, we went there to buy beer. I didn't feel much like eating. Beve needed me to buy the beer since it was the only way to get it into his house, as Jill was on him about drinking. He used me as the scapegoat, letting his wife accept me as the bad influence. As long the beer made it into the fridge, I could be that guy. I was anyway.

Men don't like to open up or emote; we don't do well with emotions. We don't like them, understand them, or want them. We plant them deep and hide them in order to survive. Early on in their lives, men learn to shut up. They take a lot and learn to get hit and not cry. They play sports more aggressively, naturally, at an earlier age, and it toughens them. Survival of the fittest. In nature, the wounded animal is the most vulnerable. No man wants to be vulnerable. It's why so often they're distant from women, and neither understand. They accomplish more by sloughing off aches and pains and doling out more pain than they receive. Boys play hurt. Men play broken. Men work hurt. Men live broken. It's the way of the world.

Fear is an emotion to hide, suppressed or expressed at will. If man emotes, it is designed to get a response. Expressionless allows men to hide in plain sight. Marines are trained to kill, as an individual or at the unit level, and to accept friendly casualties, if needed, in pursuit of the mission accomplishment. I don't mind killing the enemy and don't fear being killed. My duty, my honor, and my terms.

But even Marines had mothers, and to mine, I could express anything and everything, I was compelled, as if she were my conscience. She had always been there. She was not always right and did not know the way of the world outside the family, in the real world, but she knew the heart. She was a woman once, I would tease her.

Women and mothers think differently. When I commented or complained about girls in my life—Barb, Cathy, Marsha, Selma, or whoever the female antagonist was at the time—I spoke about women in generalities. Mom was taken aback by some of the things I said and reminded me that she was a woman, too.

I used to say, "No you're not. You're my mother. That's different."

She taught me the birds and bees in fifth grade and told me how I should kiss a girl, when I asked. She tried to teach me how to ask a girl on a date, how to talk to them, and how to treat them. I treated women with respect but never learned to actually talk to them. I never wanted them as friends—it never occurred to me that it was possible. I used to be a talker like Mom. But was now, more my father.

Tiny towns slowed the seventy-mile drive north on Highway 79. Every eight or nine miles, the car would slow or stop, then gradually pick up speed. The country highway route had four stop signs and a caution signal, one for each of the towns I slipped through. The car had taken the road so many times before, it drove itself on autopilot. I didn't see much of the countryside along the picturesque route. The dashed lines kept moving back and forth, and I had crossed the line.

As I left the town of Clarksville, I couldn't remember driving.

I looked up at the large smokestack of the Dundee Concrete factory, with its cumulous volumes of smoke and steam pouring out. Aloud, I said, "Haley, that's the cloud-making machine." She was in awe and had believed it to be true, ten years earlier. I choked back the thought of her wondrous smile and of the innocence lost.

The concrete plant was on the ground that was once my great-great-grandfather's farm. Because he treated the Sac Indians as friends in the 1830's, the family was warned of an impending raid and they were able to hide out in the dense woods. Another farm was ransacked, too, but the family was trapped in the open. The adults were slaughtered and a child was burned alive in their Dutch oven. This kin of mine went on to fight the Seminoles in Florida in the 1850's and for his service was given deed to a quarter section of land in Nebraska by Abraham Lincoln. After several years there, they sold the land and returned to Missouri. Over the next rise was the valley where the other branches of my family had lived for 150 years.

Mom had survived her temporary incarceration in the 'burbs and moved back to her real home in the country. From her suburban vantage point, she was not close enough to her farmer father but was closer than she had been during the first ten years of interstate military service. She dreamed of returning to her promised land. Those dreams were shattered when her father fell ill. Mom spent almost every day of that last year, sitting at her father's bedside as the dear man slowly passed.

The bottle she ferried in her purse each day as she trudged to the hospital grew to a gallon jug, hidden in an overnight bag. Once her father died, she slinked about in her empty-nest confines, drinking more consistently. She switched to beer and then to cheaper beer, due to the cost, and she drifted into becoming an alcoholic. The counselors made her proclaim thus when we put her in dry dock ten years later. But none of us ever looked at her that way. She was never loud, or abusive, or ignorant, or even inappropriate. She was just tired, and would fall asleep at seven or eight in the evening, instead of her usual time of ten thirty, after the local evening news. We knew she was just numbing the pain of her broken heart.

Dad and Mom had retired. They'd been lucky to acquire the farm where her father was born but on the opposite hill, where she was raised. A small stone house, nine hundred square feet, stood overlooking the river. In the late 1800s, the local paper called the quaint home the "stone mansion." Well-wishers would disembark at a landing at the bottom of the hill in the days when paddlewheel boats choked the watery highway. Dad and Mom tripled the size of the scant house. The previous tiny structure of less than a thousand square feet had once been home for a family with thirteen children.

When I got there, we talked small talk as I paced the floor. As anticipated, Mom's radar pinged. "Brick, what's wrong?"

"I ran into Cameo."

Enough said. Mental dots connected where blotches had been. This was an easy paint-by-number kit.

"Not again. How could you?"

"Well, it is not as easy as that." I paused and took a deep breath. "Yes, I told her."

Mom had told me with the first Mrs. Me that I screwed up bad enough but had doubly hosed it by coming clean. Women didn't appreciate indiscretion, but they appreciated it more than honesty. I had made a bad situation worse by admitting to it. Wives were not like mothers, not like Mom. You couldn't talk to them to absolve guilt. Carry it or bury it.

Dad, the insurance man turned gentleman farmer, came in from the fields and sat in his chair. He listened to what he could hear. Combined age and years of enduring the constant hammering of the B-25's Wright engines had taken a toll on his hearing. Mom would have to fill him in on missed details.

I told Mom everything, concluding, "Selma is seeing someone else and has been for I don't know how long. I know it; the kids know it. She won't admit it. I have no proof, but it's too obvious. I've known it and sensed it, ever since last summer, but it could have been going on for years. You know how she is. It has been, a living hell."

Mom understood but didn't approve of my counteractions. Two wrongs didn't make a right. "What about the kids?" she asked. She thought about the little ones first. What had Selma told them?

I didn't know what Selma told them. I'd spoken with Haley on the phone the night before, letting her know I was at Beve's for a few days due to issues with her mom. Haley knew Selma was a bitch to be around. She had been for years to all of us. Haley had called Selma such, and Selma slapped her, but it was Selma who should have been slapped.

Mom warned that I needed to sit the kids down and talk things out. The kids needed to know I cared and loved them and that things would be all right. I also must take what I wanted from the house immediately, before the wives' council met to order the seizure of all property and seek the death penalty.

Muddled were the days that followed. The sales production had to be met, but sales were really not me, as hard as I tried. The best salesmen were talkers. Trapped between the have-to-dos and don't-want-to-dos, I longed for the good old days of my meager existence.

Being out of the house made it easier to see Cameo, but she still had to contend with her mother. Her classes provided the best excuse to stay at the Scott Inn several nights a week. A couple of days later, I was to meet Cameo. I had dinner at Beve's. Cameo was in class, so I needn't hurry to the no-tell motel.

The door of her room was partially open. She was busy unpacking her uniform for the next day, as well as the typical cargo her mother had packed for a month. Since we reacquainted, a pattern had developed. We small-talked for a bit, and then the clothes started flying, and our bodies intertwined in the heat of lust.

In the bag Cameo's mother had packed were those damned Tootsie Roll Pops. In hopes of enlivening an already stale routine and feeling cocky for once, I asked Cameo to fill me in on the rest of the story I hadn't wanted to hear before. At this point, what could it hurt? What could shock me?

Cameo gave a flimsy excuse to avert the subject. But I pled my innocence, ignorance, and a desire for the lurid details, playing with fire. She had learned such an enterprise from an acquaintance named Craig, right?

Reluctantly, she said her previous lover was the source, and yes, his name was Craig. He was a master sergeant who had worked beside her.

"You're kidding, right?"

"No," she said sheepishly. "Why?"

"I don't even know an enlisted person by their first name, and you're saying you slept with one who works for you? That's—"

"Oh, well, he doesn't work for me anymore." Leadership's cardinal sin was not failure but being too familiar with someone whom you were in charge.

The pause extended. I was unable to give birth to verbalized words. Partially embarrassed, partially pissed, and partially aware of her history, I was unprepared for the notorious revelations—I was not the only fly stuck on this honey pot.

"Tell me more," the cad in me said, attempting nonchalance while soliciting salaciousness. I loved her but didn't know how low she had sunk. I should have known where she had been and should *not* have cared. *So why do I?* I asked myself. Because this was my Cameo.

"Never mind," I said, usurping command of the inquisition. Challenged to prove I was better than this Craig enlisted character, who got his rocks off doing an officer, I rose to the gauntlet tossed down.

It wasn't just the sex, I convinced myself. We liked each other—loved each other—and had for a long time, despite the minor details of being worlds apart. We were back together as one, erasing the past twenty-some years of pain and married loneliness.

"When are you going to file for divorce?" she said.

The next morning, as Cameo was putting on her makeup, she stepped in front of the mirror, looking solemn. She was someone else. The mask was on.

"What is it, Cameo? What is bothering you?"

"Nothing," she said, applying her rouge.

"I can tell. Something is bothering you. I don't see the sparkle anymore. Did I say or do something? Was it my response when you told me about the master sergeant?"

She reminded me of my previous night's outburst. In a low, cavalier tone, she said, "He was the most current master sergeant. There were others."

"How many others have there been?" These were the '90s, and I tried to be more open, current, and in vogue, tough for a Neanderthal like me. *Why should women be any different from the men?* I thought, *other than the degrading names we have created for them.* I knew men who tore their wedding rings off once they hit a foreign port, ready for the prowl. Women were officially equal, yes, but not the hunters and players men were thought to be.

Cameo enjoyed being with and around men, and they enjoyed her. She casually reveled how she had been with several coworkers—Lt. Col. Gary-something, the time she slept with her boss, a full-bird colonel, the deputy IG, before he was recently transferred to Central Command at MacDill Air Force Base in Florida. At the Christmas party, they had given her a pair of fur-covered handcuffs, and the assembled IG team winked and chuckled approvingly. It appeared the Air Force was one gigantic orgy.

Trying to appear as if I wasn't shocked, I tried not to judge the revelations of her promiscuity. She knew her lovers' wives—their names and often, the names of their kids. She told me she should have given in to the captain who cornered her at Wright-Patterson Air Base, she said. It would have been easier than repairing the damage of the bad officer evaluation he gave her. She should have done him, as he had demanded. He was the one that taught her the most valuable lesson; to not make waves in the system and she would get ahead. There were others as well, she said, but they were too numerous to mention.

"What goes TDY, stays TDY, as they say," she said, repeating the serviceman's under-the-breath motto for temporary duty deployments.

I put on my mask of ambivalence and said everything would be okay. We would talk about it later. A made-up appointment hastened my departure—it was urgent that I get out of there. I tried to forget the line of uniforms on parade and saluting at her bedside. She was no different from one of the boys, and boys will be boys.

Damn country music. The only time I ever listened to music then was in the car or at a bar. The emotions and twang played at a tone and a tempo people could actually understand the words to. I would switch the radio, not listening to words but to beats—Gaelic music, then Smashing Pumpkins, Nine Inch Nails, Garth Brooks, and Shania Twain... ugh.

The male country singers sang about drinking, conquests, their "big Ds, and double Ds, and they didn't mean Dallas," and croon about getting screwed and losing their kids. "The kids needed her, but he needed them," as the lyrics went, filling me with doom. Another was about a young daughter giving her father butterfly kisses. I couldn't stand music anymore.

Convicted and wrong, I hung my head. *What have I done? Why is this on me, while the woman is presumed and granted, by society, the higher ground?* I was not just thinking why me, but why and how—how had I wronged her to have her bring this on me?

The week after Selma and I parted, I tried to contact her to get into the house and reclaim minimal, indisputable possessions. No response. The kids also needed to hear *my* side of the story. Though Selma and I hadn't got along the past several years, I had considered it part of the unfortunate transition to the civilian world—growing accustomed to a new way of doing things. For seven years, we had been out of sync, ever since I left active duty, and she had lost her rank as de facto captain.

A lieutenant colonel and sergeant major with whom I had worked brought the same suffering on their spouses upon retirement. As soon as they left the Marines, their wives did not appreciate their demotion to civilian. Both divorced in the year following retirement. The divorce courts parceled off what remained of their small retirement to appease the veterans' current temporary partners. Military retirements were easy pickings for the thousands of various and diverse county courts, judges, and vermin called lawyers, who knew nothing about serving their country or their fellow man.

No-fault divorce was another excuse to let women do whatever they wanted and protect their future windfall assets. They could screw around, if they wanted, and get their due from their hard-working mates—and keep the kids, too. It seemed a woman could do whatever she wanted to do to a man, and society and courts assumed her irrationality was caused by nature; thus, they couldn't do anything about it.

Men were good for nothing and portrayed as stupid on commercials and in most, if not all, TV shows. They were the only group left that could be officially poked, prodded, and mocked, without rankling some political action group made up mostly of lawyers sworn to protect their honor. We needed to resurrect Spanky and Alfalfa's "He-Man Woman-Haters Club."

And still, I never thought of *not* trusting Selma or of her doing anything malicious. I was naive to a fault.

I drove to the Commerce Bank next to Lindenwood College, put in my ATM card, and punched the button for quick cash. The machine blinked back zero funds remaining. Nothing. There was nothing in the account? Save the receipt. *Shit, I thought there was money in there. Did I mess up the bills again and run low?* I tried it again. The balance was zero. Shit. I put in the card and tried the savings account. It was empty, too.

While I had been recovering the collapse of the family over the past week, Selma had been ensuring I was broke, too—under advice of her council, assuredly.

Where was the pay phone, dammit? I had to call her immediately and see what she knew. She had something to do with this, I was sure. I hated talking to her, even on the phone, but I at least I wouldn't have to look at her. I could counter her parries better when not facing her, but that did not mean I was ever the winner. She always won; it was all she cared about. It is what kept her alive; she ate me for breakfast, lunch, and dinner—and I was her late-night snack.

I barked at her about what she had done with the funds. Her excuse was there were bills to pay, and I had been draining the checking account. Snapping back, I reminded her I was the one paying the bills, not her, which might be why the checking account shrank. Her new revelation, a diatribe of dribble, was she needed the money for food, the kids, clothes, school, her car. I inquired about her separate account. She stated there was nothing in it. Of course, I said, how would I know different. It was exactly what I expected to hear from a rodent.

I now understood murder. I slammed the receiver, breaking it half, hoping plastic and metal shards would shoot through the phone lines into her goo-filled melon. I would have to borrow from my brother until payday and then open a new checking account. Forget savings, there wouldn't be any for a while.

After several hours, I was forced to call Selma back—I needed my things and wanted to talk to the kids. We arranged I would come over in the afternoon, when the kids would be there.

If I had a tail, it would have been between my legs. Thank God and evolution for no telling appendage, but my eyes gave me away. Wracked with helplessness and fear for the kids as much as guilt, Selma's self-righteousness fed the churn of my anguish. I was their father and loved them so very much and needed them, but I was not there to see and care for them in my way. I could see their concern and confusion.

Their eyes matched the misgivings and loss in mine. I could offer no solace or comfort. With Selma, no solutions fit. They were as lost as I was, a fault proclaimed as mine, for not having the courage of endurance, to no longer share the torture of their mother. I should have engaged the pain and then ignored it, given up and given in, put up with it, and never thought of happiness and left things alone.

As I left, the image of my son at the window on the screen door burned a hole in me. Through my puffy, tear-filled eyes, I saw Noah wave back as I waved good-bye to my bud. There was unfamiliar hesitation in his gesture, as if he was questioning whether I still loved him, and if I did, why was I leaving? The noose constricted, and the look on his young face kicked open the trap door on the gallows where I stood.

Turned upside down; it was a polar shift. He and the girls *were* my life. *My son, my dearest son, what have I done?* I waved until he disappeared from the frame of the door and then drove down to the next street, pulled over, and buried my head in my hands.

His image plagues me still.

CHAPTER 15

West End Station

To conserve energy, I tried to quit thinking. It didn't matter where I was going. Anyplace would do. Reading took me away, but some days I needed two sets of headphones.

Everyone had a cell phone, even eight-year-olds. Summer afternoons were the worst for riding the DART home, because of the kid outings downtown, visiting the Red Brick Museum, the Dallas Zoo, or the Brown School Book Depository, now known as the Sixth Floor Museum.

Kids don't adhere well to rules, especially the teens who are inclined to make a mockery of such. Courtesy and quietness is lacking in groups and curdling the rest of us with their slackness and commotion.

Replete with structure, the Corps has its fourteen leadership traits and eleven leadership principles. We have *core* values, general orders, rules, regulations, tactics, techniques, procedures, tips, and made-up acronyms to recall every title with more than two words in it—so many, in fact, that Defense Secretary Rumsfeld tried to rid them. He didn't, of course. There were so many we had to craft a Department of Defense staff, the Joint Education and Doctrine Division, J-7, to build the heap into a three-inch binder—a joint dictionary—and assign a staff to maintain it, or those of us in the military would be unable to speak.

Despite memorizing volumes of tips, traits, and buzz words, I accumulated lessons learned from various leaders, who led by example.

Major Houle, my OCS commanding officer, told us how to set goals. When he joined the Corps, he had set three: to get promoted to corporal, to carry a .45 as a sidearm, and to earn the prestige and luxury of the corner bunk. Once he attained those initial goals, he set three more.

Before he was diagnosed with testicular cancer, Captain Rhett Ward, my boss and company commander at Parris Island, told me an officer's job was to make decisions—as much as the Corps tried to divine rights and wrongs, more remained an assortment of gray. The officer's job was to command the shades into precise blacks and whites in the elimination of gray.

Several of us visited Rhett at his boyhood home months before he died. He would hardly speak to us—hardly could. He was swollen four times his slim build from the chemo that attempted to arrest his cancer. This magnanimous man was beaten. We learned later his Baptist preacher father told him he must have done something horrible to bring this scourge upon himself. Rhett resigned to his fate and had no reason left to live, having lost the respect of his father.

The Baron showed me the value of reading more and running less. Light Pack demonstrated carrying our own load or paying the price of losing respect. A retired reservist friend, Jim, shared how he laughed at himself and had fun. He was the reason I begrudgingly joined the reserves. Staff Sergeant Peek, then later a lieutenant, showed me how to catch more flies with honey than the vinegar I served.

That recruit I spoke to personally about the illicit homosexual play from his uncle taught me that I needed to listen better and take time to understand the rest of the story. As an intel officer, it was not what we knew that ever concerned me; it was what we did not.

3-D taught me to get off my duff, get outside, and enjoy the day, instead of being a mope. I didn't heed his lesson well.

* * * * *

Through all the pain and self-loathing, it was hard to remember I was only partially to blame. The sanctimonious provocateur was not blameless. Though she appeared remorseless and guiltless, she would never admit to having done anything wrong. She was the pregnant virgin, the empress with no clothes, and the kids were her arsenal.

When I ran for the legislature, the party offered classes on communication to fledging politicos. Out of a day-long series of seminars, the phrase that stuck in my mind was, in politics, "Perception was reality." With this awakening, I could understand the political correctness in politics, the yellow of journalism, TV, the evening news, and the Kool-Aid we were supposed to swill.

In other words, truth meant nothing. What a blessing a guilt-free life must have been for Selma, never feeling remorse—with one exception. I considered a letter as one-way, controlled conversation, so I felt compelled to write to her and explain my feelings on her dishonesty and how she had acted. We had to communicate in some fashion about ever-changing details of the kids' schedules and ours and what to do next. I didn't understand her previous contempt and had tried to make sense of it to stop the pain of our relationship. I loved her in some way, as does the battered dog to his brutal master, but also felt sorry for her and for her inability to resolve her problem of me.

I wasn't sure what was wrong before this latest Cameo thing, other than I was not happy with myself for working jobs that were ill-suited for me. But that was my problem, not hers. I brought home money to dent the bill mountain, which was more important. I admitted my guilt to her and tried to see if there was more common ground than the kids I needed.

Selma responded with a letter of her own. With rare openness, she admitted mistakes, with never-before-shown signals of remorse. Selma opened up and told me that when she had worked the late shift at St. Robert's the day of our break-up. Being terribly despondent, she'd given an elderly patient the wrong meds, and the patient died later that morning. In this single instance of transparency, she proclaimed she'd made a mistake and felt guilt for it.

Or was it to illustrate how much I screwed her up? I never knew.

Before I answered Selma's heartfelt admission, Cameo and I were to see each other again. Her classes and her duties remained her best excuse; I was technically free. With March drill approaching, Cameo and I arranged to spend the night at the new Drury Inn on Olive, nearer the drill center than others. I left my gear in the car, except my shaving gear.

Cameo was studying when I reached the room. We talked for several hours, consorting on when we would divorce our spouses. Cameo had called her old friends across the country to reap their adulations on her plans of leaving Trevor. But what would become of her home in Texas? How much could they sell it for in its deplorable condition? Wandering the dismal house in her mind, along with Trevor's shoestring lawn service and his unkempt face, she grinned, giggled, and told me she liked my face.

She reminded me that Trevor had said his beard made him a better Santa Claus for Christmas, and in the same breath, she said Trevor and she dressed up for Easter, too. She had her own rabbit suit.

"Really?" I said.

Admitting nothing to Cameo, I had growing trepidation about leaving Selma. What if things could change? Was I holding out hope for the impossible? Selma's letter did indicate *some* contrition and *some* acceptance of blame. My heart ached as if a piece was gnawed off, not so much for Selma but for my loss and any pain and suffering it had caused my children. Raw and numb, I knew the only way to get back to the kids was to take it or leave it—accept Selma as she was, no matter how much I couldn't stand her.

The next morning, as I opened the car door, I sensed something was amiss. My leather address book was open on the front seat, not snapped closed as I'd left it, a matter of habit. I leafed through it and then flipped to the back inside cover, where I kept loose papers and notes. The letter from Selma was gone, along with any shred of her penitence.

Sonofabitch. She must have been vetoed by her council.

I'd heard the horror stories of what women will do when they feel wronged, but I never would have considered it might happen to me. They were funny stories only because it was another man's misery—a woman going "Bobbitt" on him, Super Gluing his hand to his junk, or having concrete dumped on his car or his house sawed in two—but those outlandish stories happened to other poor bastards as clueless as I. The story of the spurned wife who filmed herself screwing the neighbor and then mailing it to her Marine husband while he was deployed to Desert Storm was real. Another guy in my reserve unit talked about his former psycho girlfriend who stalked him after they broke up. She was obviously crazy, because he was a state trooper.

If a man was lucky, as few seldom are, she would just up and leave. My good friend Blade was on float in the Mediterranean with his CH-53 squadron. His CO called Blade into his cabin to talk in private, telling Blade he had to go home immediately. Blade's wife had left him and stranded their two sons at the base daycare. The CO's wife had to pick them up so the daycare could close for the day. Blade's wife disappeared into the night without saying a word or taking anything. Blade flew back to the States and rearranged his whole life to care for the boys abandoned by their mother. The wife resurfaced eight years later and then wanted to be part of the boys' lives. As traumatic as the situation was, Blade kept his boys and his belongings. This was one of the rare good stories I knew.

I learned Selma had spent Friday night with her girlfriends, the council. They told her what she put in the letter was damning and convinced her to snatch the letter back. Selma, with her bitch posse riding shotgun, tailed me to the hotel and waited for me to go inside. Once inside, Selma used her key to my car to steal her admission back.

More powerful and alarming than one wife, I was against them all. Beware the council of wives. The damned cooked and concocted schemes in tandem, with the unintended effect of ruining each of their lives equally. Selma deferred to their potions.

Normal should have been good enough. The perfectionist in me was long gone, but I did want above average. No one wants average. Longing to be mired in my former mediocrity, I was living a scoundrel's soul on a floundering barge. Daily routines established a sense of normalcy. Inventing a new set was required to create a new grind.

The St. Louis Alert alarm systems' sales job was not meeting my financial or professional needs, but pleasurably off-setting was the boss's perpetual open-bar tab at Novak's, our usual watering hole in Soulard, several blocks from the Anheuser-Busch world headquarters. AB was our St. Louis office's largest client. Drinking beer and socializing were the best parts of this job in sales and the only grasp of normalcy with which I was comfortable. The real Tony and I had little in common. He was ten years younger and respected the Marine Corps, and I appreciated the kinship. There was also a bevy of lookers working at Novak's, as well as a great lunch menu.

One lunchtime, Tony and I were seated next to a covey of four young women. We joked how each rated on a scale of one to ten, based on legs first and then working up to portrait and hair. As Tony and I sputtered on about their ratings and bantered about world politics and current events de jour, our curiosity spiked when we overheard one of the girl's request. Soliciting support from the others seated, she wanted a consensus on whether a blow job was cheating. Tony and I looked at each other inquisitively and tried not to be obvious as we strained to hear the various declarations and suitably veiled excuses. The dark-haired cheat, whom we had rated an eight, needed post-affair corroboration, as said seedy deed had already happened. The gaggle lunched away, justifying the guilty one's action. Tony and I shook our heads, marveling at the vixens' spirited acceptance to their friend's indiscretion.

From the beer in my veins, I would switch to coffee to get going in the morning. Now racing between seeing the kids, seeing Cameo, arguing with Selma over the phone, drill weekends, and socializing with the sales gang, I had to find time to work.

A couple of days after drill weekend, Cameo called my pager. When I called her back, she was in a panic.

"He *knows!*"

"Who knows what? Slow down."

Trevor, she told me, had ripped into her about me, and their wounds were torn anew. He threatened her that she had to stop the affair immediately.

"How the hell did he find out? You didn't file for divorce, did you?"

"No, I haven't done it yet."

"How could he know?"

"He said he got a call from someone? It had to be Selma."

"It can't be. She doesn't know who you are! I never told her a thing. She tried plenty of times, but I never told her your name." I hadn't seen this coming. Hell, blinded, I couldn't see anything. "Damn. I can't believe it. She must have taken the letters you wrote me from my car when she stole her letter back. She does this kind of shit. This is who she is. She digs and digs until she hits pay dirt. Cameo, I am so sorry."

"I told him I wanted a divorce and that I was talking to an attorney. He threatened me with the letter."

"What letter?"

"You must remember. I told you I fell asleep with a love letter in my hand from a friend named Tim. Tim wanted to take me away from Trevor. Trevor found the letter, and he has been holding it like a knife to my throat ever since.

"Cameo, I told you; that is old news. The Air Force won't concern itself with something from the early eighties. It's too old to dredge up any pertinent facts. It is a hollow threat and the only leverage he has. He knows it will eat at you, and he does his best to manipulate and contain you, but he has nothing."

"I'm scared. He wants me to come home and talk before I hire an attorney. He pretends we can work it out. He warned me not to see you again. He says he knows people. He is going to have me watched."

"Well, too bad for him. He's probably bluffing anyway. Show him you aren't scared. Meet me at the Cracker Barrel tonight at seven. Everything will be fine. I promise you; he can't reach this far."

"He will stir up more," she said.

"What can he do? If he has someone around, we will know right away, but again, so what? I love you, dear. Don't let this get you. We can do this."

We met as scheduled. She parked in a different place than usual and walked in before I did. She told me about the phone conversation all over again. Trevor was using her girls as leverage, saying she would never see them again if she went through with a divorce. We rehashed old issues. We needed to concoct a plan to put the two spouses together, since misery loved company. Trevor and Selma would be perfect for each other.

The highways on a week night were an interesting place. Most people were tucked in front of their TVs, carrying on their married lives in boring bliss. I often wondered about the odd vehicles with crazy-ass drivers who appeared late in the evenings. With less traffic, it took me no time to get home.

At Beve's, I slipped in as best I could, given the grinding gears of the garage door opening and closing. I took off my shoes and went upstairs to my plastic bed. My pager went off. It was Cameo.

Stepping lightly downstairs, I called her.

"Trevor did have us followed! He described you and the clothes you were wearing. He is threatening to call the general. Don't panic if Selma relays something from Trevor. He is trying everything to convince me to drop this divorce talk and come back, and then he tells me he knows it is over. He says *he'll* decide if the girls get to live with me. I know it's been a trying week since you and I have questioned the rightness of our situation. But we both know we are right for each other. You ended my fears by deciding not to go back this morning when you said you'd wait for me and that I had your heart."

What a mess created by people like Trevor and Selma, the bearers of apathy doused with intolerable hostility. Why did they act like they cared now, when before it was not worth a plug? Before this explosion, there was no spark. Letting all the shit pile up must have caused a fermentation of gases that now splattered the place.

Cameo's attorney served Trevor too early and without warning Cameo. She was to see Trevor first but not until April. Within days, the daily telephone lectures, with hot charges and denials, elevated Trevor in the eyes of her combustible eighty-year-old mother. He had called her to fill her in on the dirt.

In the nick of time, Cameo neutralized her mom missile and scrubbed the launch that would have had her mother calling me. Separate skirmishes escalated into all-out war. Selma put her self-serving spin on late-night communiqués with Trevor, while coordinating the supporting elements of the wives' council and her boyfriend. Our old bedroom was converted into a command operations center. Trevor, whom we highly suspected of bedding Cameo's waitress friend at the Officers' Club at Hurlbert Air Base, enlisted the waitress's help to turn Cameo's daughters against her. And my calls to Selma to keep her pie hole closed were coming in garbled and unclear. But Selma, the talker, the slash-and-hack Sherman, didn't know when to shut up. She had to win at all costs. Collateral damage was an unfortunate side effect of combat.

After weeks of enduring incessant barrages from her mother, Cameo retreated to an apartment on the Illinois side, closer to work—a coworker had a lightly furnished basement apartment. Cameo only needed a few uniform changes and a place to hunker down. The rest of her life was packed tightly in the car's trunk. Her Operational Readiness Inspection suitcase was ready for upcoming inspections anywhere in the US.

The fog of surreality cloaked our temporarily tranquil landscape. Things were different now, completely. Tortured by having to speak to the opposing battle captain to schedule visiting her prisoners, my kids, I weathered torrents of arguments about our pitiful situation, but I sensed no desire for a truce or to redraw the lines. We grappled like old times, but Selma never admitted errors or weakness and never her affair. She held fast to her exalted claim of innocence, and Cameo and I were the grandest of offenders.

For the past seven years, she had ignored our invisible children; she was tired of running to soccer, baseball, and school events; tired of homework and housework; and scorned the daily drumbeat of the family routine. Now, her most cherished possessions, her long-lost loved ones, were cover and shield against me. They were all I wanted now, not her—even Cameo was fading. Selma knew to get me was to keep the kids her prisoners.

Cameo was again the only one I could speak to about everything. She had a quiet and accepting tendency. We could discuss the future, where Selma could see no further than the closeout of the week, if lucky. Cameo and I seldom argued, but when we did, it was in a tolerable, understandable tone, more in common than misery.

From one of her Operational Readiness Inspections, Cameo wrote,

Dearest Brick,

I love you, sweetheart. I really miss being with you when I'm on the road. Your phone calls definitely brighten my day and make me appreciate your love every day. Your love is so warm and caring, and I can hardly wait to be with you all the time.

Guess I'd better finish this since I'll hand deliver it tomorrow evening. Sorry about the teary eyes last night. Don't really know what got into me, although I imagine it was a combination of things, including being close to that time of the month and the thoughts of not seeing Beth going to prom. Thank you for caring so much about my thoughts and feelings. I still am amazed that I deserve your love and why/how you can love me. I'm not trying to open the guilt box, but...

Selma would have never told me about her time of the month. It was dead obvious to all around her, and hers lasted the whole month. I was surprised she hadn't bled to death.

Simply imagining Cameo's slight smile and glimmering eyes made me more alive. Her soft, serene voice closed each night and welcomed each morning. I took silent comfort in following her across the country by phone, calling to wake her or to talk in the middle of the day and in the evening, to put her to bed; in hearing her speak from the heart. It was comfort I had never known. I needed her to be independent but welcomed her dependence. I admired her aggressiveness and enjoyed her passiveness. Unknown to our consciousness, our hearts beat their beats, emanating radii of impulses that sought comfort. The heart alone defined its harmonic balance. In speaking with or writing to Cameo, I could not adequately express this feeling.

Cameo's mother wore her out. Trevor also called, doubling her displeasure. Ironically, Trevor and her mother merged as one. For years, her mother's rage was reserved for Trevor and his failure to get a job, but her mother held plenty of contempt for Cameo, too. Her mother never forgave the two sinners for living together in college. She also felt Cameo did not belong in the Air Force, to her mother, it was man's world, making Cameo a poor mother for being with her girls so seldom.

Trevor held the high ground, and on this occasion was with her mother, who held holy ground zero. It was Cameo charging up the ignoble hill. Trevor's greatest weapon in his arsenal was Cameo's mother, and he mowed down her advancing charge. In the crosshairs of her mother's ire, Cameo defied what was right, good, and decent and went against the old ways, the tenets of the church, and her mother's religious beliefs. Trevor exacted a deafening staccato of shame, weakening her, and keeping her trapped in the depths of the valley of despair, where he had kept her for years. Fronted and flanked by walls of guilt, he would bring her daughters and her beloved Air Force to bear to complete the destruction.

Tidal waves of emotion overtook sensibilities and our new reality, confusing our love for something bad and wrong. Her spouse knew, my spouse knew, and our mothers knew we wanted to be together. What was old was dead, and the new was fresh and alive, yet the dead haunted and confronted us, not dead enough to be dust but only dead in that it could bring down the others against us. If not us, who would quench their thirst for vengeance?

We deluded ourselves into believing we could hold on to each other and the kids. Unfortunately, my kids had their mother, and I was tired of playing the fool. Courts are automatically sympathetic to women;

the liberation movement never made it officially to the divorce courts. Equalization in the courts was unnecessary. What was mine was hers, and what was hers was hers—except in Cameo's case. She wasn't a woman but an Air Force officer, a woman in a man's world, and as such, less a woman in their eyes. She altered the rules. Boys will be boys, but women can't be like the boys. Never could be, never would be, never should be.

Cameo and I had not enjoyed her new living arrangement in the basement apartment but a few weeks before I got a page from her and learned that Trevor had railed to the Commanding General of the Air Mobility Command that Cameo was not caring for her family in Texas. The general called her in and to explain herself. After seventeen years of service, she was subjected to questioning that bordered on ridicule and had to explain her familial responsibilities to her chain of command. Private affairs in every other level of government, or in private and public business, were kept private, but the military leadership stuck their noses in, sniffing for signs of distastefulness or disloyalty. Humiliated, Cameo dispelled the accusations and disarmed the situation. The general, out of courtesy, ignored Trevor's call— temporarily.

Several weeks passed. Trevor saw no action and heard no alarms of distress from Cameo. Trevor called the general again, demanding attention. Trevor, the civilian loudspeaker, berated the general and demanded action. The political leader acquiesced to the threats of a congressional inquiry. Twisting the knife, Trevor hinted Cameo was seeing someone but failed to mention he and Cameo were legally separated and she had filed for divorce. This notification would have warned the general to stay clear. Since separations and divorces happened daily, the general surely knew, none were clean or pretty.

The general, an otherwise smart man, was unable to put two and two together. Couples in splits have issues; the losers were always the ones in uniform. Their civilian spouses orchestrated the system that paid them. The civilians nibbled and munched on the military carcass, using the military legal system to pursue and prosecute anything suspicious, to prey on their military spouses with investigations, juries, and prosecuting attorneys. The non-military spouse didn't have to lift a finger or spend a dime, it was taxpayer time, just dream up an allegation and let the wheels of military righteousness grind the once-honorable one to shreds. The armed services made it too easy for the pissed-off spouses, deferring to them when they knew they should ignore them. Loyalty works but one way in the military—up.

Now, out of concern for himself, the general had to run for cover and shield himself by putting the uniformed spouse, actual offender or not, on a skewer. In all good bureaucracies, ass-covering is art. In getting promoted, perceptions are altered and realities are jaded. Generals make general by not making waves—clasp hands over ass and send in the hounds. All branches of service are full of senior officers with spaghetti backbones but plenty of asses, having covered and polished them their whole careers. The best and brightest officers are lucky enough to make it to twenty years and then escape and retire. The potted plants, the stale doggy bags—these make generals.

Cameo's general was no different. He did not want to appear to lack empathy for a spouse by protecting his own. He alerted his local Office of Special Investigation (OSI) to create a fire where bilge smoke blew from this pesky spouse who threatened to get a congressman involved to look into the general's business. The OSI initially was established to keep fledgling nuclear secrets safe but morphed into a catch-all to investigate anybody for anything.

Interrogating Cameo as a suspected terrorist, they called her in and quizzed her coworkers. The OSI looked for abnormalities in the manner in which she conducted her assignment. They interviewed the married Lieutenant Colonel George-something—the one she once had slept with—whose newest girlfriend was at another air base. He stated he knew nothing out of the ordinary. They confiscated material that Cameo was working on and decoded her uncooked files. They reviewed the financial data to see if she was stealing and went to her new apartment, just rented from a coworker, and talked to his wife.

OSI agents asked about the female lieutenant colonel tenant in the basement to see whether anything strange was occurring. They asked whether she was seeing someone. The wife said nothing as the agents pretended to take notes, waiting for her husband to return.

An hour later, Master Sergeant Craig stepped into his living room and saw the men waiting. He excused his wife to tend to her daughter from a previous marriage and remove her from the situation. Once alone, the husband immediately threw up his hands, proud of his conquest, and burst out that he had been the one to bag Cameo.

Being enlisted, he sheepishly begged for immediate immunity, so his current wife would not find out and become his third ex-wife. Granting such, as Craig was of lesser rank than Cameo, he spewed on what he knew about "someone." If he could have, he would have named all Cameo's lovers, going back to high school, in the hope of a promotion to super master sergeant.

The Navy Criminal Investigation Service (NCIS), service sister to the OSI, called me. They had received a phone call from OSI and wanted to know the secrets I knew. The more mature NCIS was not interested in flings but national security. Frankly, they had better things to do with their time than chase stories from spurned lovers and affairs of the heart. The agents asked if I knew Cameo and if I could assist them with OSI, who were pressuring them to get what they could. I had no idea to what they were referring, I said, and concluded the call.

Cameo was apprehensive. OSI warned her not to talk to anyone. Cameo learned Craig had spilled his guts, having waved the white flag at the first hint of injury to himself. His betrayal was damaging enough—nothing more was needed.

"Deny it all, word against word. Proof of the claims are required," I said. "Tell them Craig must have been vengeful for not getting the evaluation marks he wanted. Never agree to any claims, I told them nothing. It was all speculation. You needn't worry."

Cameo needed legal counsel for covering her back, now that Trevor had the whole air farts preying on her. Trevor had run like a whiny school girl to the teacher—in this case, the general—who relieved Cameo of her official duties.

Cameo wasn't listening. The infamy was working. She felt she had it coming.

"No, dammit, you don't!" I hollered over the phone. "Trevor deserves it, and the only way to give it back to him is by denial. Deny, deny, deny. You have done nothing horribly wrong. You haven't stolen money or taken Air Force or national secrets to sell to the highest bidder. Share with them that the complaint only came after Trevor was served for legal separation. It's vindictiveness. It is a typical, ugly divorce case. It doesn't mean anything about your character or work habits. Tell them about his extortion to trap you in marriage all these years. How about that? You can't get weak on this now. You have to stay strong. Fight them on their own terms. Use the legal system. Do they have anything in writing that might be damaging? Get that lawyer to speak his legal garbage only they understand, okay? Do you hear me?"

"I guess you're right," she timidly said, but she wasn't grasping the seriousness of it all. She agreed just to shut me up.

Her silence bothered me. She was giving up. Condemnation was eating her alive, and she didn't have much left to feed it.

Unknown to us, both NCIS and OSI called Selma, unfettered by conscience, to ask what she knew. Selma, the open-mouth espouser of all, had no problem clattering and disclosing Cameo's and my doings, whereabouts, and whatever else she could pontificate on to cause discord. Selma, the talker, found in OSI another willing accomplice for her command center speed dial and found the right butt and button to push. She chatted away, as OSI became her newest "BFF," as my teenage daughters might say.

Days passed. Selma paged, and I reluctantly called back. Acting innocent and absentminded, the nobly placid Selma stated she'd had a long talk with OSI, and I needed to talk with them.

"Shut up!" I screamed. "I will be right over."

The puppeteers now had their marionette, but I wasn't getting tangled in the strings. Racing over to Selma's house—my house—I fumed at Selma's engaging outside sources into our lives. It was like her to do whatever it took to twist the rusty knife in non-lethal regions to keep the tortured alive. I was furious.

Nothing else mattered but her—no reason was necessary, no excuses given. That was who she was. Attempting to figure out what she had told NCIS and OSI and what she had not, I could not get her to see that if she had cared anything about us, she would not be doing this.

"Are you fucking insane?" I snapped, even though I understood her warped justification to jeopardize Cameo. But she *had* come after me and my career, what little was left.

After several hours of beating my head against the bulkhead, I had to leave, starved for oxygen. No intelligent life existed there. As I opened the front door to leave, I demanded she not speak to OSI again, not ever, not if she had a shred of decency, and we were ever to try to work things out—I lied about that. I was done. No way in hell could I ever stay with her. Her true colors were black and putrid.

But if that wasn't enough, days later, OSI called her, and she spoke to a "nice" guy named Dave. He made up some story about having no interest in me but wanted to know what she knew about Cameo and anybody else. They prodded and probed, having no real idea whether Selma knew anything, telling truth or dare. OSI assumed it was conjecture and hearsay when Selma declared she could prove it and invited OSI over.

During one of many difficult phone calls made to check up on the kids and see what grinder Selma was stuffing me in next, she slyly and matter-of-factly told me that OSI knew about Cameo, because she had given them the *letter*—the one Selma had stolen from my car. Rage exploded from deep within me. I could have killed her instantly, had I been standing in front of her.

Once again, I drove to the house and confronted her.

"What the hell were you fucking thinking?" We went back and forth again for hours, taking us into the darkness of our marriage; then, thankfully, the kids came home. We put our parent faces on to ask how school was that day. After enough of the niceties, we scooted them off to the living room TV downstairs, out of sight and distant their hearing.

Game on.

"Are you just fucking stupid, or do you just subscribe to *Jackass* magazine?" I didn't want to say it but said nonetheless, knowing it was not stupidity but pure evil I was dealing with. Selma only understood hatred; she didn't understand love. In all the years we had been married, she had expressed more hate than love.

Warbling poison-tipped words were getting us nowhere. I had to craft some way to get out of there. Finding the kids downstairs where they had been planted for several hours, I hugged and kissed them, told them I loved them, and then went upstairs to leave. I blurted a retort to Selma, and as I stomped off the front porch, I noticed a broken brick under one of the bushes.

Realizing at that moment words like "I love you" meant nothing to Selma; no words of any kind would show her the wrath consuming me. I stood for a second and consciously debated whether or not it would work and decided it was better.

The last few hours had been wasted. She needed something she could understand in her strange non-verbal Venutian language. I picked up the brick, walked to the back of her car, and threw it at the rear window.

It ricocheted off and landed harmlessly in the yard.

You gotta be fuckin' kiddin' me?

Pissed at being rejected by a brick, I picked it up again and got more directly in line with the window then shattered the window over the backseat.

Now maybe Selma would get the picture I was pissed, and could understand something in her fucked-upped-ness. I was not a talker anyway.

I heard nothing from Selma about the window. No condemnations, no lamentations or fiery commentaries. It flippin' worked.

In her twisted, mush-melon way of processing, she thought I had expressed a type of affection and she had won me over. She must have thought that if I could be driven to that, she actually meant something to me. To her, the busted car windshield meant love.

I went with it and used it, though I didn't understand it. It bought time and space for Cameo. She was on the ropes, and I was at wit's end, trying to mollify Selma on one hand and keep Cameo's spirits uplifted on the other. I pretended to care for Selma and spoke to her more about reconciling, in hope she would do no more damage to Cameo by talking to the OSI or NCIS.

Cameo was fighting her mother, Trevor, two attorneys—one in Texas and one at Scott—the OSI, and the most damning of all, herself. Forced by the situation to remove herself from the apartment, she faced the daily trumpeting of doom by moving back in with her mother.

Torturing myself to the nth degree, I played both ends against the middle. I would see Cameo when I could and continued negotiations with Selma. Cameo was intoxicating. Often, we could meet only on a Saturday at a distant park or commercial parking lot, but when we were alone, I had to have her, as she had to have me. It was all we had left, but it was more than we had separate and married. We wandered to different car paths around St. Charles to find a private place, such as behind a billboard along Highway 370, just off Second Street.

Cameo defiantly kept watch out the window. Nobody would deny her what she wanted and needed—except they had. Now they knew—everyone knew, and they had turned the daring and dicey into her embarrassing vice.

In the living room of my former house, where our lives played in surreal-a-sound, I came unhinged.

"I don't know where all this shit is going," I railed at Selma, "but if you think there is a fucking hoot in hell chance that we are even going to start thinking of working on us without your coming clean and finally admitting the truth—that you cheated—you are out of your fucking mind. Is there somebody you haven't told that you are not the poor little victim but that this precipitated because of you? You have involved those air farts, OSI, NCIS, the Marine Corps, my work, your sister, my family, your family—hell, have you thought about calling the fucking evening news? Maybe Tom Brokaw or Katie Couric want to hear your pathetic lie."

"Brick, I have told you and told you over again that there was no one. Study is all I ever did and that incident of Gaylord's coming over after he got off work at three in the morning—he had some questions about our class. That was all it was."

"You used to be good at lying. You are the best liar I know. The State Department needs to call your ass up and put you to work in negotiations with the Bosnians and Serbs. You can heal the world with your lying talent. But just because you lie about something long enough or loud enough and never veer off your dribble, does not mean shit. You are guilty as hell, and I deserve the truth for once in my fucking life."

Another hour passed.

Finally, she said, "It was one time and only a blow job. It doesn't really count."

"Oh, fuck no. Don't give me that stupid shit, and it wasn't just a blow job. I am not your idiot. Is that really the closest you can get to the truth?"

"But—"

"Shut up. Now this is what you are going to do. I am not paying the mortgage anymore or any other fucking bills until *you* tell *everyone* in your family the fucking truth." I still didn't expect her to do it. She lied all the time. She had no idea what the truth was anymore.

The game went on for another hour, her bitching fastballs and sliders, my batting fouls.

CHAPTER 16

Park Lane Station

A blonde strand drafted its curl, like a maestro's baton, as it floated and glided across my nose. *A spider web,* I thought and jerked. Blondie's hair spilled over from the seat in front of me. Lifting my head to check her out, will her reflection match her hair?

My thoughts roiled and pinged a divergent, recessive nerve. No transition in the way men think.

"It is what it is"—that seemed to be the current version of "Shit happens," another daft expression. In the movie *Forrest Gump,* Forrest was given credit for it. Seems I led his bump-along life.

"If it wasn't so sad, I'd cry." Was that the saying? "So sad, too bad," was it? I was not sure what those oft-repeated little phrases meant, other than to generally cast aside responsibility with one swoop.

"In a hundred years, who will give a shit?"—a quote I heard thirty years earlier. It was another version of "Don't worry, be happy," in a way.

A hundred years ago, we didn't have a personal income tax; women could not vote; horses and wagons were the mainstay means of transportation; factories poured mercury into rivers; masses died of influenza; and minor infections could be deadly. We should give a shit; living was much better. Nowadays, no one had patience. It was an immediate-gratification generation; only here and now mattered. They would not give a shit, but some of us did.

A hundred years ago, my great-grandfather died. He had helped his father clear two hundred acres of forest with axes and two-man saws. It took them eighteen years to build a two-story frame house to replace the one-room log cabin that the family of six lived in. The country was agrarian, independent, hard-working, and proud. I gave a shit about what he did. Who would care a century hence for me?

Wally Fong, a buddy of mine, always said, "It's all good." What the hell did that mean? It wasn't. But he had a brighter outlook on everything. It was his mantra, and he believed it enough to make it happen, whereas I repeated mine laughingly. In my hierarchy of needs, if I had factored in friends, I'd hang myself. I didn't do friends, but Wally stuck to you like Elmer's and wouldn't let you get away. I never had a puppy, but that is what Wally reminded me of. He never met a person he didn't want to like.

When I was stationed in Miami, I ran my three or four miles alone until Wally came along. He asked if I wanted company, and I said no. He suited up and met me at the pull-up bars. When I took off on my run, I was a bit faster, but he kept tagging along. If I ran too fast to get away, he might not have found his way back. My solitary regimen was past. Wally was a talker and provided the step-by-step color. He was and is one of a kind.

Wally was one of my best friends in my single-digit collection but not because of anything I did. He reminds me of 3-D, the year after Little League. 3-D tried to get me to come out and play when I didn't want to.

I needed friends more than they needed me. I am glad the few I had stuck around.

* * * * *

Cameo and I were forced to separate. We didn't want to but had to for the sake of appearances. Selma was out to get Cameo. I was trying to fix what I could, but too many conditions were out of my control.

Cameo tried to understand and suggested we break off our relationship completely.

Dear Brick,

Please forgive me for all the pain I've caused you. I wish I could have been stronger for me and for you and us. However, I guess I've been in a downward spiral all my life and just wasn't able to get out of it earlier. I do wish I could have loved you better so we could have had that future together. You told me Selma had the same look I did when you first met her. I'm sure if you both seek counseling and learn to comfort each other, your marriage will be able to start anew. I was going to include your letters but decided it would be best to toss them so you can start the healing process and getting on with your life.

Please don't start another guilt box because of me. I was never happy with the choice I made or those I allowed to be made for me, but I just didn't know how to say no.

Please, please take care of yourself since I can't be there. Thank you for all the joy and love you gave me these last few months. I'm sorry for all the lives I've brought to shame. Please tell your family I apologize for the grief I have caused in their lives.

I really loved you but just couldn't love myself.

Cameo

Loving her more than she loved herself, I couldn't let her go. It seemed I was the only one left in her world who cared. She had nowhere else to turn, and had reached out to me the previous November, when I was most vulnerable. She had no one.

Selma called and informed me of news she needed to relay and said I should come by. I thought, *This is it, the day of reckoning. She will admit she lied and manipulated all these years.*

"Oh, great, what the hell is it this time?" I sniped "California is missing, and they think I took it."

"No, but I can't tell you over the phone. Just come over."

212

When I got there, I learned that 3-D was dead. He had found a couple of acres in southern Missouri, around Pevely. While camping and clearing brush with his dog, a sharp pain in his shoulder didn't seem right. Calling in the dog, he made it to his truck and drove several miles into the nearest town to find a hospital. He left the dog in the car, but typical 3-D, first he had to take care of his companion. He cracked the window and searched for water to leave with the dog. In the hospital, he asked them to check out this pain he had never had before. The hospital, alerted by his condition, could not take care of him locally. 3-D waited for a Life Flight for transport to a larger St. Louis hospital, designed to handle more complex traumas. He died on the way. He was only forty.

Cameo knew 3-D and should have attended the viewing with me, but she would have had to tap dance for her mother. Selma knew 3-D, too. Although I didn't want to take her, I wanted less to go alone. She was the one to tell me about 3-D's death, being home when 3-D's wife called. It was only right that she go, but we wouldn't bring up the separation.

3-D was a good guy, and I should have shared with him what I was going through. He would have had choice words regarding my current situation. He might have set me right, having clarity for such things. I hadn't seen him often enough in those trying, preceding years. As we aged, too many things filtered our friendship—day-to-day entanglers, wives, and kids. We forgot good old friends, as I had forgotten mine. I wasn't the best friend, but he was the better of me, always there when he needed to be—and now he was gone forever.

It had been a year or two or three since I had seen 3-D on New Year's Eve. We'd visit at each other's house once in a while for holidays, trying to remain connected, yet workdays kept pulling us in different directions. I was better for having known him. Had I added anything to his life?

3-D would argue I was better than him, but we were both right and both wrong. We were both better because of the other. In addition to not collecting or keeping friends, I didn't see my brother enough. Maybe that was my major malfunction—trying to live life on my own. A part of me was gone, another notch on the pistol grip. Eclipsing years meant accepting loss, like it or not, despite whatever triumphs might come. No one wins all the time. Hell, if we recognized what small victories enlivened us, we should consider ourselves lucky. In the end, we are losers—time's up, game's over; you either lived it up or you hadn't.

Selma and I embraced 3-D's wife, Sue, hoping to comfort her. Sue was taking it better than I, which was unsettling. I wondered if 3-D and Sue had been like Selma and me, and 3-D's death was the result. Perhaps Sue was the conquistador and 3-D, the Mayan.

She took his death too easily in stride; she was too composed, a stiff upper lip, and had not shed a tear in the name of my late friend. It would have been a shame, if that were so, but maybe Sue was stronger than I was.

He left four children mourning his death, a death that was not his fault. This brought things into focus for me. I had not intended it so but felt I left my three children behind. I could not help thinking what my children thought of me. Did they mourn my loss? Who was the better off, 3-D or me? The one in control of his life or the one without a life? And which was which? The living have questions; the deceased do not. I hoped my children knew my leaving was not up to me, that I was forced out by their mother.

As I tried to atone for my transgressions, I started, easily and innocently enough, on the road to reconciliation with Selma. Wicked and her evil step-sisters decided couple's counseling was in order. I marginally decided I would try it. Selma found a male counselor, knowing a female would not work at all. I agreed to entertain the idea in a session or two.

The session went about as expected. The counselor asked us each about what we thought, as if each did not know enough.

Cameo sat in purgatory all summer. Her attorney hammered out details of her defense and had good arguments to make in her calculated defense. In discussions with the Staff Judge Advocate's office, representing the Air Force and the general, the prosecuting attorney of Cameo's affairs indicated acceptance of less harsh punishment and a fine of several thousand dollars for a guilt admission from Cameo. Cameo was content with her defense and concentrated on battling Trevor.

The only support I could give Cameo was mostly over the phone and in writing. Letters went each way. Selma tried her hand at writing, trying to be more like Cameo, expressing longing and emotion in her compositions but none seemed to fit her.

They weren't Selma; they were a façade, part her treacherous plan. If it were really her, I could not give her credit, because I could not recognize which rendering of her was the fake and which was not. She waited too late to show her true self, whoever that was. The brooding, churlish one's lasting impression tainted all the other versions.

Selma and I entered a tempering stage, discussing in letters, back and forth, ad nauseam, the ills of the marriage between us and burning issues. The book *Men are from Mars, Women are from Venus* recently had been published. Selma and her council read it and sent a copy to me, with their editorial comments on pages' margins, as my flaws were noted.

I was aboard the USS *Ogden* on its twilight tour before being mothballed, but it was still the command ship of our amphibious exercise. The hours I stood watch afforded little time for sleep, much less reading the book and their prescriptions. When I did have time to sleep, it was too hot and sticky to force my eyes closed, so I picked up the book and whipped through its pages as quickly as I could. I could have read the book, front to back, had the ship not lost all power. Trapped in the sweltering darkness, I was unable to see or do anything other than lie on my rack and try to doze. We both were dead in the water, bobbing helplessly where the currents took us, instead of underway with our own power.

Once electricity was restored, the mounted lamp over my head illuminated each page. I highlighted with a yellow marker the apt details and attributes of a man and a woman. I penciled my own comments in the remaining margin of the pages that mattered. More important, I wanted Selma to see her own biographical sketch overlaid on the pages, to see that she was oblivious, built different, and incorrect.

On the inside cover, I signed and dated when I'd read it and included a collective summation: "See? Aren't you glad I am not like that?"

The counselor preached his psychotherapeutic incantations, stirring a cauldron of bobbing questions to brew up a batch of loving couple rehash. My skin crinkled and cringed in the heat of repeating myself for the millionth time about Selma and her affair, my life and my blunder, only this time with an extra set of eyes ogling me. Selma had moved past denying her affair and never stated my charges were true, she was probably afraid I wore a permanent wire on me and I would capture her telling the truth. No, that would be her a few months back, who planted the tape recorder in the basement and recorded not only my conversations but also those of Haley and Izzy.

Her indifference was more incendiary than the carnal infraction. Selma's role in the room seemed akin to counselor's assistant, as she tossed inquisitive slashes into conversations as she wanted.

The session leader coerced Selma into apologizing for what she had done, but that was just it. She didn't act or seem sorry; she was only mouthing the words as her part in this play. She wasn't really sorry— that was evident—and with her words, I was to move her direction toward center and then cross over to her side, without a budge from her.

I expressed to the counselor that hope was lost unless Selma laid it on the table to the kids. She was the arsonist for this flare-up, and I was not settling for less. Unconvincingly, the counselor relayed that the children did not need the additional burden and hurt of their mother's marital violations. They had been sufficiently disturbed by what they had already gathered and collected from Selma's interpretations. Writing this guy off as a whack-job female enabler, I figured Selma was probably sleeping with him too. Once the session was over, we signed up for the next proctored gutting.

But that was not going to happen.

The resplendent topography and beauty of the San Diego Bay area was not lost on me. I decided to have Selma and the kids come out—for the kids' sake. *The last vacation as a family*, I thought, as I tried to forgive myself and forget the claxon extolling—man overboard. Unable to afford vacations before, and having neither the time nor the money, I leveraged another decade in bank servitude from the newest credit card that had been mailed to me.

Except for its high-rise buildings downtown, San Diego is one of the most captivating places, for a city. The slight deviation between high and low average temperatures makes it a garden spot every month of the year. Too bad so many people discovered it and called it their home, sending prices orbital for a parcel of paradise. The Spanish architecture, even in the petite ranch style homes, was evident westward around the bay to Point Loma.

Selma and I pushed our associative displeasures aside. We visited Pacific Beach, Ocean Beach, Disneyland, La Jolla, and Black Beach. We took drives along the coast, visited the Gaslamp Quarter, the waterfront downtown, and we stopped in Kansas City Barbeque, made famous for its depiction in *Top Gun*. We would have checked out Sea World, but vacillating Selma could not decide. Since she couldn't, we didn't, leaving time for other sightseeing.

We arrived back home a family again. Not knowing what to say or how to say it, I stood, warm and friendly, in my former living room. I did not want another painful dismissal from my newly reacquainted kids, I essentially moved back in.

Selma didn't say anything, but things were never the same or better. To Selma, I was more open and blunt with the problems I had with her. She didn't appreciate my abrasiveness, where before I would have said nothing. She told me to never see Cameo again. With Gaylord, Selma pretended to break up, but he had reconciled with his estranged wife, leaving Selma in a lurch.

To Cameo, I said that I had to do this to keep my eye on Selma and keep her in check. The job was a job. At home, I watched a lot of TV with the kids and let Selma run the house, since she was used to being her own boss. She took offense at my doing less than the little she thought I did before, so we lived there together but separately. We shared the bed, each clinging to opposite corners.

On a self-appointed errand one Saturday, I met Cameo in the parking lot of Blanchette Park and unveiled the new hairball of a living arrangement. We had to split. As I drove away, I could see in the rearview mirror, she was sobbing. I went back and told her none of it was true. I couldn't leave her. With limited availability to be together, I would do what I could.

Time crawled, reversed, and then turned murky and muddled. Cameo and I would see-saw, saying we should have done this, thought about that, could have waited, and kept our attraction in check for a couple of years, so she could retire. Our romance was under control of the air farts.

A former associate of mine had a friend who was former CIA. He and I talked at length on many occasions, discussing mostly philosophical juxtapositions on science yet discovered, politics, and crossovers into possible business ventures. We shared notions of the best current opportunities, based upon the situations here and there.

While I was at Quantico at a school, I met him in DC to see what business opportunities he might have that I could be part of. He discussed wanting to establish an offshore bank in Antigua, where banking regulations were fluid enough to allow unique financial exchange transactions. Sierra Leone was falling apart. There would be opportunities ripe for the picking as opportunists similar to us moved in to fight it out.

What he was saying was all too foreign, but I needed to enliven the dead in me. When I returned to St. Charles, we continued discussions, and I applied for a passport. Details were fuzzy, but I went along with the notion I was leaving. Too numb to do anything, I was trapped in walking circles outside Cameo's bubble and living in the clutches of the black widow Selma, waiting to be eaten.

I wanted to leave, needed to leave, but could not bear leaving my three small hopes of salvation.

Cameo's prosecuting attorney was discovered in his own adulterous dilemma. The legal arrangement he had been prepared to offer, with which Cameo was comfortable, vanished with his reassignment. A pretentious new attorney arrived to prove he was more worthy and capable than his philandering predecessor. He threw the arranged deal out the window, along with Cameo's chances for negotiating a reduced fine with no jail time.

In my new secret-agent mode, thinly guarding a need for a sales appointment here and there, I met Cameo in the parking lot of the Scott AFB commissary one afternoon. I believed she had given up on me, had written me off, or was just not reaching out. I'd had to do my best to convince her to show up.

Cameo handed me a letter and said I was lucky to see her. She refused to relay additional information. Word games were not my forte. I shared with her my hesitancy for the planned mission to Sierra Leone. Cameo had plans of her own to leave but didn't want to talk.

An old black-ops ally was willing to help her. Trevor was not the only one with dark friends in strange places. Someone named John from Chicago was to appear and make it all happen. She wasn't supposed to tell anyone, but when I talked her into meeting me, I had forced this delay. She had planned to be gone.

Selma and I circled on auto-pilot over no-man's-land. What existed limped and lingered along with the summer setting. Lively jade foliage turned to flushed crimsons, cold golds, and furious oranges, and to crinkling rusts, and then let go under the oppression of another winter.

Letters between Cameo and me dried up. I met Cameo at a dent-repair center down Highway 94. Cameo needed to replace her windshield. A hailstorm had fractured the windshield away from the epicenter of a near-perfect small hole.

The court-martial process slithered as Cameo withered. Under her mother's hints, slights, and overtures, she was unable to recuse herself and winced instead. The merciless barrage from every quadrant intensified when Trevor enlisted Cameo's daughters to strike the final blows. Their barbs cut deepest. They could not properly attend school, as pet programs were no longer affordable this semester. Cameo updated me on her unchanged status. She played with the elusory comparisons of us as Romeo and Juliet.

Hearing her erratic constructs, I would parry in the same breath that nothing would hurt my children more than the loss of me. Everything I stood for would not blow up by my own hand, and life was not fair; it was rough. I tried to lead by example and kept putting up with it nonetheless and never quit.

"The slicing feels more gouging when spoken by your daughters. You knew he would resort to this. He is no different from Selma Iscariot. It is all about them. We had to take our hearts in hand and beat them back with it. How did this hole get here, Cameo?" I pleaded with Cameo to not take it so hard.

She held her head.

"Cameo," I said. "You need to see a doctor. You need to get some professional help, some therapy. Or talk to your preacher. You are not the first to go through the mental torment you are dealing with. Christ preached salvation, saving us from ourselves, not perfection. It doesn't exist. He knew guilt weighed and preyed upon us, doing as much damage as the deeds themselves. Your daughters still love you, despite what they sound like now. They're teenagers, stuck in their own twisted version of the world. They will come back around, if you let them. Cameo, save yourself for your daughters."

Looking up at the hole in her window, she said, "I found my father's pistol in the closet. It seemed the right answer. It went off when I pulled it out of my purse."

"Don't give up or give in. Fight to the end, whatever it is, but never let the enemy see the look of fear in your eyes, or he has you. Never let him see you sweat. Doing the right thing is always the hardest; it's too easy to succumb to the flow of the under current," I said. "Talk to your attorney; you are depressed. He can recommend someone. Talk to your doctor, okay? Please, will you do that for me?"

"I will," Cameo said. "Why couldn't you be more like Trevor and pretend not to give a shit what anyone thinks? It would have less impact. You might even convince yourself it was okay to be you. You are a great person. You are not evil, dear. It is okay to be you. Another way to look at this is that you have won—to break the bondage at the hands of Trevor. You weren't holding out for sainthood, were you? Where was the fun in that?"

"No."

"No perfect man ever existed, save one. You are a Christian; you believe in Christ. He forgives you. Forgive yourself, and relinquish your guilt."

Cameo visited her doctor. As was general practice, a complete physical was conducted. He referred her to a mental health doctor. The results of the physical found she had a lump in a breast. More tests would have to be scheduled, though. Along with counseling, she began taking antidepressants.

"Cameo, I am so sorry. The last thing you need is more bad news. Let's pray it is only a cyst, I hear many times that is the case. Let's not jump to conclusions that it's worse than it might be."

"I know. We'll take it slow. One thing at a time. I have to get this trial over with first and then I can get this bump checked out."

"That's the way to go—first things first. How are things going for you?"

"Well, I don't have a job anymore, so I spend the days studying for class. My friends in the IG won't talk with me, but I talk with some of my long-distance friends back in Texas and California."

"That's good."

"But every day, like a drumbeat, Mom is on me, telling me I am going to hell. I have sinned against God. It's wearing me down. I can't stand it."

"Hold on there, Cameo. Try to stay out of your mother's way and keep reading or studying. This will be over soon.'

Christmas turned out fine, because Selma had to work. The kids and I went to the country as we always did, and Selma was pissed, though we had no control over her schedule. In retribution, she went out on New Year's Eve with a friend or friends. I stayed home and enjoyed the evening with the kids. I had the better end of the deal. We ordered pizza, watched Dick Clark drop the ball in Times Square, and ran outside at midnight to bang spoons on the bottom of pots and pans.

Had I been smart, I would have moved from the house and taken the kids with me, or at the very least, changed the locks on the doors. But those types of actions are *reserved* for damsels in distress, women. The men in our society can't push the women out, though it is patently accepted for women to do so. It is what they do. The laws can't fix it—no one can—and so we all give them exception and line up in support of kicking the men in the jimmies.

That is what Selma did. While lying in bed, a discussion boiled into a feud. She kicked me in the back and then between the legs in a random fit of rage, until I was off the bed and holding myself on the floor. Time was up. She wanted me out. She didn't want me in that bed, and I didn't want her there either. She is the one who should have left, since she was the most discontented with the surroundings.

Moving out this time as hard as the first, but we split up furniture. I was able to get my hands on a few more things. The greatest comfort and surprise was that Haley declared she was moving out with me. She wouldn't stay in the house undefended.

Selma had wanted me to decide what the rules were and weren't for the kids, adding her minimal input. After the decision was made and announced, she would pounce on me for being too strict or too lenient. Later, in execution of said plans or arrangements, Selma would blow her stack at the kids for violating *her* hidden expectations for rules they knew nothing about and have it out with them.

While I was packing, I heard Haley crying on the couch. I went into the living room, sat down, and put my arms around her. Selma was sitting across the room, telling her she couldn't go with me. "Haley, what's wrong?" I asked.

222

"Nothing, I don't want to talk about it."

"Obviously something is bothering you. I know it is about your mom's and my situation."

"I hate her."

"Hon, I'm so sorry." Tears blurred my vision, and I swallowed heavily. I hugged her so tightly I thought I might break her arms, curled up inside mine. "You don't really hate her. Your mother and I just don't get along anymore, and we are trying our best to resolve that. Neither of us has done the best job of keeping you all insulated. I know it affects you, your sister, and your brother, but we really both care about all of you. We both love you."

Looking in Selma's direction, I was glad I couldn't see her perched in the red stuffed chair in the corner. It was dark outside, and no light was on in the room. "Your mom loves you. We both do. Don't you, Selma?"

"Of course, I love you, Haley," Selma said.

"Haley, I don't want to leave, and maybe you should stay. What would your mother do without you? Your sister needs you, and your brother needs you. Your mom depends on you."

"Nothing I do is right. She wants me to run Izzy around and Noah. I am supposed to do the dishes, fold the clothes, and she yells at me when my friends call on the phone or come over. I always seem to be in her way. I can't go anywhere while she is gone because I'm babysitting the other two. Plus, Izzy is perfect and never does anything wrong. She is always on my ass."

"She just depends on you to help her. We both do."

"She doesn't depend on me. I am her bitch."

"Hon, that's not fair, is it? You have chores that are yours, and Izzy and Noah have theirs. I stay on top of you as much as she does, to make sure you do them. I am hard on you too."

"But you're the good Nazi."

Haley and I found a two-bedroom apartment within two miles, to keep Haley close to school. I gave Haley money to pick up groceries and odds and ends from the store, so we had toiletries and basics for breakfast and the like. Without beds, we put mattresses on the floor.

A week or so passed. Noah was visiting, and I posed the question to him of where he wanted to live. He said he wanted to live with me. Calling Selma, I told her to bring Noah's things. She rocketed over the dozen blocks separating the apartment and house, and a frantic blast came at the door, as I set the phone down. I tried to talk to Selma through it, but she refused to leave me and the neighbors alone, continuing her wailing. I had to let her in to reduce the disturbance in the apartment complex.

"Noah, your dad says you want to live with him. Is that right?" she asked.

Noah was cornered. "Yeah," he said.

"You don't want to leave your sister Izzy, do you? How do you think she is going to feel? She will be all alone. And what about me ? I am your mother. Don't you love me?"

"Yeah."

"Don't you think you need to be with me?" She didn't plead; dishonor and disloyalty charges were unleashed upon him. "How can you do that to me?" she asked. She would not let up until she had her way. I had been there too many times.

Noah was confused in the wake of her admonishing. Broken, he didn't stand a chance, and he held his head. I couldn't bear to see her torment him anymore, even if it meant he wouldn't with me.

"Noah, it's okay. You can come to visit any time. I love you and will try to see you as much as I can. Stay with your mom for now." I felt like I had reached up and cut the rope he was hanging from, and he could finally breathe. The feeling hadn't been there before, but now, I could hate.

Freedom from Selma did not make seeing Cameo any easier. She was trapped in her own hell. Fear kept her from seeing me where others might notice. Her mother's ire had her trapped, She suffered the judgment from ages past, as lorded by the queen high-and-mighty mother.

She was able to get away once, and we tried to love, but she wasn't there. The cancerous regret had consumed her, and not much was left of us either. She offhandedly commented perhaps we could all live together—the two couples and our five children.

I told her the idea was barmy. No one could put up with Selma as long as I had. Besides, once the children grew up, there was no reason to suffer. I was out, and there was no turning back. Selma was Selma, immutably.

She had a self-righteous affair with herself, and no one else could love her that much.

CHAPTER 17

St. Paul Station

Black… alone… am I awake, or is this my unconscious self? No sensation. Can't see or hear anything. No lights, nothing faint, no hints. Listen closely.

To what? There is nothing… nothing there. The damn ringing in my ear is even gone. It's been there ten years. How could it be? Is this death—this nothing. Not really black but blank.

What happened? I was on the DART, dozing on and off. When was that? Was that the last I remember? I thought… I thought, *How can I think, when other feelings are gone?*

Am I dead? That's stupid; my mind never quit. Here and now. So, what the hell is going on?

Hajiville—we passed it several stops back. The mosque along the line. That kid got on. Not really a kid; everyone younger than me is a kid.

Wake up, dammit. Try screaming. My mouth doesn't work. *Bite.* I can't—no tongue or teeth. *What do I have? Can I wiggle a toe? What's a toe?* You need a leg to have a foot and a foot to have a toe. You need to know you have them to have them. *Am I locked in unconsciousness? What is this?*

He was maybe twenty-five.

Ow, shit, what the hell was that? Was it my whatever consciousness or this thing, swirling?

His face was thin, but his body didn't match, did it? Not really, but I didn't seem curious then, did you? How come?

Am I talking to myself, or thinking to myself? Which is it? Is there a difference? I guess—context, tense—does it matter? No more judges. It's only us, you and me. We can say whatever we want. No one can see or hear; neither of us can see or hear. You don't have to watch what you say. You can scream fucking, fuck, fuck until the cows come to roost. You like saying stupid shit like that, don't you?

Are you losing it, or am I? You are all over the place at the same instant.

We are the same.

No, you are the evil one.

Ha, you would like to think that. We are one and the same, both good and evil, past, present, future, blended, like a fine wine, aged.

Huh? What are you talking about? A fine wine? Are we red or white?

Both, everything, and nothing. Is this how a guy's brain works?

Well, I know I am a guy, I don't know about you. I am straight.

Oh, shut up, we are both straight. We are the same, stupid.

Shut up, yourself, self.

I wonder how a woman's brain works.

A total vacuum, a marvel to modern medicine.

Don't give me that. You say modern as if in the future, it will be discovered how it works. They never will find out how their brains function. What does go on in there, even God doesn't want to know. Probably nothing in and nothing out. Kinda like this with us now, but without pants.

We don't have legs. How can we have pants? Does it really matter? Yes, everything matters.

No, nothing matters. Was there a guy sitting up forward? He sat on the left. You remember anything?

I think so. Are you still trying to figure it out? We are here, nowhere and everywhere; time stopped.

But where is that? Where? Time can't stop. We can't stop; we are but we are not? How?

Wait—wasn't there a millisecond you recall.

No, nothing but the past.

Forget about the past. Except when was the last time we saw light—anything, sound, the tinnitus?

Oh, big word for you. Just say "the ringing." Wait. Remember? It pierced, shot up a pitch, extreme.

An explosion?

Shit, there it was again. Did you feel that? Ha-ha, I forgot; we can't. What was that?

My mind kept writing the story. I didn't want to be in this one or the other.

I woke to find Blue Hair sitting on the aisle seat, her umbrella spiking my ribs.

* * * * *

Cameo's funeral was this morning.

The court-martial proceedings had been held and a verdict levied. Cameo called the previous Thursday late, to tell me the results, but we had already known she was guilty. She admitted so, against my advisement, because she was afraid of jail time more than anything else. She put up no real defense and admitted the affair with the enlisted man, Craig. She needed to know from the pious officiators if her request for leniency would be heard or if her Air Force would hang her out to dry. Cameo was found guilty of fraternization, the infraction she admitted. The adultery and trumped-up sodomy charges were dropped. She was sentenced to be dismissed from her beloved service and lose all benefits—though the Vice Chairman of the Joint Chiefs of Staff General Ralston, admitted he was in an affair at the same time. He just would not receive the nomination for Chairman of the Joint Chiefs of Staff. He had his twenty years plus and the elevated stature of generalship. So he could retire; she did not. So he was more or less guiltless; she was not.

He was part of the military wing of the good ol' boy network. Cameo wasn't a boy.

She got the best she could have hoped for—she did not get the jail time she was afraid of. We hadn't expected the Air Force to be benevolent and allow her to remain another eighteen months to reach her twenty and retirement. It was up or out in today's service, and she was out with nothing.

We talked again and again over the next several days. Cameo said I should reconcile with Selma. The only way I could heal was to be with my children. She was probably right, but that left me with Selma.

Cameo asked me to forgive her for the pain and anguish she caused me. I told her there was nothing to forgive her for. We were in it together. I said she needed to forgive herself, to start looking at what she would do in the future.

The funeral was scheduled for ten in the morning, and the clock said nine. Mom pleaded with me not to go and make a scene. I sent three dozen long-stemmed red roses to the funeral home, with the simple words, "I love you," on the unsigned card. Pacing in the apartment, I wondered aloud if they had been delivered or if the oaf Trevor had disposed of them.

Cameo's coworkers attended, some who had slept with her and had been relieved she knew how to keep her mouth shut. The IG paraded through, breathing his sigh of relief. Dozens, if not hundreds, were part of her story.

Unable to go to work, I plopped down in a chair, sat for a few seconds, and then darted around again. I watched the clock tick. I told myself to ignore my mother and make a scene. I was the only one who cared for her anyway. But no, I was as gutless as the other bastards around the country. I hid in the shadows, denying anything to do with the silent whirlwind, Cameo. "Think of her daughters," Mom said. This was the last they knew of their mother. They needed this time undisturbed.

I drove to the funeral home and then drove slowly past to catch a glimpse of Cameo's daughters and their father, the hoodless executioner. Parked on the street, I watched people arrive, seeing no one I recognized. I had seen pictures of her daughters, but Trevor would stand out more than they. He would be the ugly one, sporting the bearded smile.

Opening the door, I closed it. I twitched; I couldn't bring myself to approach. I might go off. Trevor had won; his revenge was paid for by the government. He used the military as a threat for fifteen years to keep her trapped in an unwanted marriage, and then he ruined her, when it looked like he was losing his sugar mama.

As a result, he was paid an unexpected bonus—the $200,000 in life insurance Cameo had signed up for. Cameo needn't know math well to realize that without the Air Force or retirement, finances would be tough for her family. If she were dead, she could leave her children something.

Cameo must have immediately hung up the phone the past Sunday, when we last spoke, and while her parents were still away at church, she'd slipped downstairs to the basement of her parents' home, taking her father's shotgun with her. She deftly laid out plastic, as if she were stretching out a blanket for a picnic. She didn't want to leave a bigger mess than she had already made for her mother. She paused on the landing, halfway down the steps, and propped herself against the wall in order to find a way to manipulate the trigger with her toes. She took the full blast in the face.

On the following Tuesday, while cleaning up and taking care of Cameo's affairs, her mother called to let me know Cameo was gone. She had wanted to give me a piece of her mind at different times for the past twenty-three years. At first, I thought that was why she called.

She said Cameo was gone, as if she was out of town for the week. Then she went on to say how she had discovered Cameo's body upon returning from church, and then she gave the details of what had happened to Cameo and her despondency. The woman was more concerned about the horrible mess it made on the basement wall and the stairs. She left me with the ill feeling that she was more comfortable at having been proven right in her lecturing and arguing with Cameo on the rights and wrongs of her sins than in grieving for the loss of her only child.

"She wasn't there anymore," Cameo's mother said. "Last weekend we were cooking Sunday dinner, and she picked up the frying skillet with both of her bare hands. She nearly fried them off. They were so burned and blistered, we had to bandage them. Made a mess of that meal, too, and the kitchen floor. We had to go out for dinner; it was getting so late after fixing her up."

"I appreciate your calling."

"You have keys to her car, right?"

"Yes, ma'am."

"I thought you did. She left some letters and things with your name on them. I'll put them on the front seat. You had better hurry, though, to pick them up. Trevor and the girls will be here from Texas tomorrow."

Racing out of the house that night, I let myself into Cameo's car, parked where it always was on the side street. The car's peach scent was Cameo's signature, and I paused, drawing in my breath as slowly and fully as I could, swallowing hard. The letters were in the middle of the seat, with a new one atop the bundle of the string-wrapped old ones. She also left the butterfly earrings I'd had made for her.

"Cameo, what have you done?" I said softly. "We could have worked this out. Couldn't you see this was all temporary horrible? We could have made it, if you hadn't given up."

I had to go. Driving away, I went past the Quik-Trip where I bought her roses and turned around. Buying every rose in stock, I went to the next one to find more. Back to Cameo's, I parked in the middle of the street by her car and honked. Taking my time, defiant against the stares from the kitchen window, I placed seventeen roses under the windshield wipers in honor of the Lost Flower of Youth picture. It was the title of her favorite picture, her most cherished glimpse of herself, featured in the newspaper the week she graduated high school. She left it with the additional letter on top of the bundle.

231

Cameo—my most endearing love, one I couldn't quite grasp and hold, and the only friend I sought to love.

As the funeral mourners emerged, I waited and saw Trevor and the daughters with the small crowd of people, waiting for the procession to line up. Trevor was raw and unhandsome, as Cameo described. He quickly lighted one of the cigarettes she hated. One of the girls looked just like her mother.

The procession departed up Jefferson and then to the main city thoroughfare, First Capitol, in honor of St. Charles' place in Missouri history. It proceeded to the intersection with Highway 70, past the sign noting the place and year Eisenhower's interstate highway system began—1956, the year Cameo was born. Turning west, it traveled two exits down and pulled into a newly expanded cemetery that had once been a small farm, owned by folks my parents knew back in our camping days. As the column of cars slowly entered the hallowed grounds, I diverted from following and went the long way around, waiting for them to settle at Cameo's final resting site. I slowly entered the entrance road but turned an alternate way at the roundabout, to go where I could observe from a distance. Raining, tents sheltered three separate funerals. I couldn't make out which was which.

Waiting for parties to disperse from the three sites, I drove and parked near each, looking for some marker for Cameo. Knowing she wasn't at any of them, I prayed God was a kind and just God and took pity on her soul. But still, I wanted to know where they laid her remains.

Continuing my circuitous route between each plot, I quit driving around and began walking the soppy ground, but found no indicator of her anywhere. Panicky now, I retraced my steps to gauge the perspective I'd had from afar. I set new reference points and started all over. Several hours later, finding no trace or anything signifying Cameo had lived, died, or existed, I took my battered heart back toward the apartment to hold my own funeral.

A year would pass before they marked her grave.

On the way home, the fuel indicator lamp came on. I pulled into the Mobil station at the top of the hill near the intersection of Droste and Duchesne, a block from where I grew up. I climbed out, taking little notice of the dingy old Dodge parked across from me, but I saw a young boy Noah's age sitting in the passenger seat.

With the rain subsiding, the sun came out, stewing the noxious air from the spilled-over trash in the can near the pump. It wafted in the rising heat. I favored the fumes from the gas filling the tank. I bent over and breathed an especially deep lungful. As I rose, I shuddered.

The Little League coach from my childhood was standing on the other side, as nasty-looking as I had ever recalled.

"Get out!" I hollered to the kid in the car. "Get out and go inside—now."

The kid looked about, searching sheepishly and then noticed I was yelling at him.

"Get out! Go inside, and call your mother. Now."

The coach looked at me—poison-green pus pinholes for eyes and a scab for a mouth. He opened his chancre but nothing came out as I lunged and shoved the gas nozzle deep down his throat, breaking his teeth. My free hand gripped his throat—pig fat.

"I don't want you to utter a single fucking syllable, you wretched piece o' shit. You are not going to do it anymore. You are not going to wreck another life."

He shook his head.

"I'll bet you've raped so many boys, you cannot remember one from the other. You cannot remember any of the boys you polluted, but it stops now—today. Enough is enough of you and your kind."

I kneed him in the groin, dropping him, and pulled the trigger on the nozzle. The gas sprayed over him. I aimed for his mouth. Startled, he squirmed to get under the car until I kicked him in the head. A boot to the gut, and then I stood with one on his arm and the other on his throat.

"I was one of your victims forty fucking years ago. You have probably molested that many since, because I was too weak and powerless to do anything about it. Haven't you? How do you like it now, asshole."

He tried to speak under my weight.

"Don't say a word. I don't want to hear excuses. It is the decade of excuses. I'll take none from a scumbag like you." I stomped in hopes of hearing a crunch.

A crowd had started to form. Harry, the old man at the sales counter inside, stared at me in a state of horror. He knew me. We had talked. He had survived five years after his terminal heart attack diagnosis.

Wretched compassion started to stifle my disgust. *No, dammit, the time for compassion is gone.*

I kicked him again. Hands were grabbing and clawing at me, trying to pull me off him. I raged on and broke loose of their grips.

"Leave me alone. He deserves this. He ruined my life when I was eleven. He has harmed others, many others, boys in this town—who knows how many. Death is too good for this vile puke of a being. You can't even call him a man. He will not—*he will not*—hurt another kid as long as I live. He has done enough damage to this town."

The crowd looked at me and backed off. They did not know what I was capable of. I didn't either.

"Stand up, asshole. Tell everyone here what you are. Tell them. Say it loud, so they can all hear you!" I shouted at the top of my lungs. "Let everyone assembled for this spontaneous occasion know what type of shit you are!"

"Na, 'ou kick me ag'," Coach mouthed.

"I will kill you right now if you don't get your ass up and tell these people what you do in your freaking free time, you sick bastard." I reached down and yanked, ripping his shirt to stand him. "That's it—stand," I said, as I round-housed the nozzle across his face. "Stand, dammit, and tell them."

"I like ba's," Coach uttered, stumbling. He was trying to get out of range of the hose.

"Come back here. You're my bitch now, pig." I flung the hose over his head and around his neck, flipping him closer. "Like *ba's*? Hell, no. You don't like sheep. That would be okay. Nobody would care. No, that is not what you do is it?"

"I like boys," he muttered.

"Well, son of a bitch. No, you don't like boys. What do you do with them?"

"I play with them," he said.

"Play? What the hell is that? You mean like this?" I dropped the nozzle and slammed my fist into his nose. The crunch was audible to the onlookers.

"I fuck little boys," he said, "and I make them suck me. Stop, please stop. I can't see."

"Grandpa?" said a voice. I turned around to see the boy I warned to get out of his car.

The coach turned, wiping the blood from his eyes. He struggled to see who matched the voice.

"Grandpa?" the grandson said, flicking a Zippo.

I put down the nozzle as shock washed over me and rage waned. "No, son, you can't do that." My eyes welled up, unable to comprehend what the boy was telling me. He was Noah's age. "Lord knows, he deserves it, but other people might get hurt here, too, if you do that. You don't want to hurt others, like he has, do you?"

"I hate him. He hurt me. He is a bad man. He is not a real grandpa. I hate him. I—"

"I understand, son. But I don't want you to live with the guilt. Whether you feel justified or not, it will haunt you for the rest of your life. What he did still terrorizes me. You don't need it—the guilt." Guilt kills everyone it touches.

The coach dropped his lifeless eyes to the fuel at his feet.

"Let me do it."

CHAPTER 18

Cityplace/Uptown Station

Fathers rendered useless.

The *Slick* offered little today but a short article on deadbeat dads. We knew men as deadbeat but exalted single moms. What the state seemed to care about was latching onto the money, forcing economic equality to the lesser women, the anti-males. The last generation grew up viewing men as bumblers, failures. Women were proselytized, the saviors of humanity. They could bring home the bacon and fry it up in the pan, and they could do everything on their own. Several discussions I had seen on the Communist News Network argued whether fathers were needed anymore; mechanicals yielded any urgent sexual needs. The enlightened talking heads ballyhooed that women earned their own way now. With full independence from men, *they* did not need them to confuse the relationships with their children. The only requirement to create families could be acquired from well-stocked sperm banks.

The article went on to cite a different source that repeated studies that showed lesbian couples made the best parents and, of course, better than gay male couples. Both were better than traditional hetero couples.

The next generation will act like women. Hope they have eliminated snakes and roaches. Probably start offering classes in college on how to hang curtain rods, too. Yeah, I watched it on *Sex in the City*—once.

The pattern rarely altered in the scramble to whack-a-mole land of office cubicles. I glanced from time to time to check for the deltas in the landscape, inside and out, nothing new. The DART entered the tunnel for the Cityplace station. No one would get on the DART here, but two would debark, like clockwork. One is Ditz, with her entourage of luggage, and the other is a middle-aged geek, with reading glasses clinging to the tip of his nose, wearing a thick, navy blue button-down sweater with a curled collar; the sweater the same despite the weather. He is missing the pipe to complete his professorial ensemble.

Why would I know or care about such things? I cannot recall where Burns or Blue Hair unloaded for their workdays. And Fro Bro was a random.

Slowing to a halt, Ditz and Professor stepped out and strolled to the escalator. The dark-haired Haji, who flew onto to the DART at Spring Valley, stood up, a red wire dangling from underneath his thick jacket. He glanced back and caught me looking. He promptly reseated himself.

No sooner had he sat down than he bolted and jumped onto the platform, scurrying quickly.

I didn't think.

I ran.

Haji reached behind to pull the red lanyard.

I slowed, ready to pounce.

His iPod headset had fallen out of his ear and trailed behind, under his jacket. He looked at me and smiled. He slipped the red earpiece into his ear and waved good-bye.

* * * * *

I drove away from the Mobil station, expecting to hear police sirens. I didn't speed away but drove the speed limit. I only lived a mile away. I learned from Harry a week later that he had asked the onlookers if they had seen anything, and before they answered, he reminded them they hadn't. He pointed out that the grandson was spared further abuse. The boy's mother was called and filled in on the gruesome details.

Harry had asked the coach if he wanted the police called. He reminded him the officers would have to interview each of the witnesses in detail. The crowd of strangers, each one, had heard his admission of rape. It was sure to make the evening news.

The coach opted out.

One of the witnesses spoke up and agreed with Harry in convincing the witnesses to say nothing. A Lindenwood student admitted he, too, had been a victim, ten years prior. Then he came forward and kicked the coach in the groin, like he was kicking a field goal.

"Those balls of yours better never work again. I hope I kicked them into a million fucking little pieces of shit." Turning to the crowd, he announced, "If anybody calls the police or talks to them, tell 'em I did it. My name is Kilgore Trout."

The coach struggled to stand but chose then to crawl to the edge of the street. He painstakingly rolled on his back to light a cigarette and then rolled onto his knees and stood with great difficulty as the flames erupted. And he stepped in front of a oncoming bus.

* * * * *

I married the next woman I met after Cameo.

With Cameo gone, I was left holding the Selma bag. She would not vanish or implode under her own ignition. Hanging on for several more years, Selma never made overtures to me, nor I to her, other than *my* sick willingness to attempt reconciling. She never acted as if she cared. Better, I supposed, I did not want to cross over to her lunar reality. I could not bear the thought of divorce but had to do it, to move on, whatever it took. After failed attempts at being a civilian and after a decade of applying to return to active duty, this time I was accepted.

Approved with an age waiver and written acknowledgement that I knew I was too senior to expect further promotion. I received word I was accepted the month before the divorce went to court. A divorce proceeding had been scheduled the previous year, but I could not bring myself to do it, though there was never that positive traction from Selma. I clutched at faulted hopes, burying the evils done to me.

Haley was in college. Izzy was soon to go. The one left behind was the man in training, my only son. Izzy felt left out when Haley moved out, and I fought to get Noah whenever I could. Izzy asked why I hadn't fought for her. She was a young lady, turning eighteen, I told her, and could make up her own mind. She could live with me or not, and I would appreciate that. But I told her I knew she wanted to remain with her mother and I didn't want to set myself up for the rejection. I left the question unasked. Uncomfortable choices had been made. I hadn't liked any of them.

I told Selma I wanted to take Noah with me. I would leave for duty after the divorce was final. She cried and said, "Why couldn't it have happened sooner, while we were still together?" She was concerned more for the return of her military stature. Her telling, tearful response sealed the deal. I harbored no further doubts about the scheduled split.

The courts care about their jurisdiction, with no understanding, care, or tolerance for federal issues or those of us in the military. If you want a divorce and have children, too bad. They don't want you to take them out of *their* state. They are intolerant of the familial needs of the military father, nine out of ten times—other than, of course, for ensuring they apportioned the money to their community standards. Take money out of the equation, and the divorce rate would drop precipitously. The courts forbade my son from departing with me, though that is what he wanted. My family was stripped from me if I wished to continue serving my country. It felt as ceremonious as Chuck Conners having his sword broken over the thigh of his superior officer in the '60s TV show *Branded;* he was branded for cowardice, stripped of his dignity.

I could not do what I needed to sell my case to the judge. The requirement was for my son to appear before the judge. Selma and her attorney would grill the young lad mercilessly as to why he would want to live with his father, in perceived rejection to his mother. I couldn't subject him to this legal abuse, suspected ridicule, and coerced maligning. He was subjected to enough of that by his mother. I settled for long-range joint custody arrangements, more akin to never seeing him. Thank you, inflexible and thankless court system. Go fight your own war next time.

On the last day I lived in the family home, I tried to forgive myself and forget. It is not a trait I am good at. I had not divorced my family, but it felt like it nonetheless. Movers had taken what little I retained in a shoebox of a truck. Unable to scream, I was alive at my own funeral. The miserable Missouri January air spit slush in my face as I carefully packed legally sanctioned leftover belongings in the vehicle bound for Twenty-Nine Palms, California, two thousand miles away.

I did not want to go, but had to. Those three children were my life, but I was no good to them if I didn't have a job that helped me stand up straight. I was broken, but words kept running through my head: *a man has to do what a man has to do.* I had laid out the situation to Noah, and that was what he told me, my own words coming back to haunt me. He was as right then as I had been when I taught the phrase to him, as much as it hurt. Izzy wrote in a project for school the following year that it was the worst day of her life.

Having said good-bye to the kids the night before, my heart was in pieces. Snow melted on my wind-burned face and covered the tears as I pulled away from the house for the last time. The stark image etched in my mind was of my brother, who had helped me pack, as I saw him in the rearview mirror, waving good-bye and choking back similar weeps of snowy tears.

* * * * *

I could not make it alone. Two weeks before I left and with little thought, I was married. I had not planned to remarry, as all divorced men say. But she wouldn't leave me alone. Virginia hounded me from state to state as I went on any active duty assignments I could pick up to make ends meet. I called her Jenny instead of Virgie—that was before I knew a jenny was a female ass.

I was fired by yet another company that did not want to comply with federal law about employing and retaining reservists who had to perform drills or active-duty training. The federal law exists, but hundreds of employers break the law every day, regardless. The law does not force compliance; only lawsuits do. It does no good unless the offended takes the matter to court and suffer through that process, legally and expensively.

Several Marine reservist friends who were state employees sued the state of Indiana in the early nineties to get their old jobs back after Desert Storm. Noncompliance and lack of understanding of federal laws seems to be the careless general rule of thumb at the local level.

Jenny said she adored me. I could not understand what she meant. Adore? No one had attached a word like that to the likes of me. What was she talking about? I was nothing but a miserable louse, an empty house, with no job to speak of or be proud about. I was nothing for anyone to love. How could she even tolerate being around me? But she said she did, and I could not ignore a beautiful lady with a large enough heart to include me and my skeletons.

Caving in to her whim to hang around, I accepted fate more for myself than for her. I don't do "alone" well. I was embarrassed to live; I needed color to fill in the white space. Not doing friends very well, she was a natural at delivering fresh air in all the dank bars we haunted. Jenny had a buoyancy—all smiles, grins, and talk—and everyone was her friend. She said she was perfect for me. She was yin to my yang, she would say.

In sowing middle-aged oats, as I catted around in the days after Cameo, I didn't hold anything back and was blunt, macho, and irreverent—no airs, just being myself. Anyone who wanted to be with me had to know and deal with what I really was: the real me—warts, farts, Copenhagen, beer, Cheez-Its, opinionated, cussin', fussin', bitchin', Democrat and Communist and socialist intolerant, and now jackass lawyers- and judge- hatin'—all the rot.

What I wanted was a roll in the hay. With her, I found myself needing more than a one-night stand. Maybe a two-, three-, or forty-night stand would do, and then I would break free of her clutches and go to the next barfly.

I expected her to change. Female chameleons hid their true identities during the mating stages, emerging ruthless and demanding once harnessing their horse to the marriage cart. Painted ladies, young and old, proudly strutted their goods to be sold, but once you bought what they had to offer, the product's warranty expired, and you were left holding the bag. It didn't go unnoticed that young women kept their hair long and alluring until they married, then chopped it off for convenience or children or work demands, as claimed, as if the need to be attractive had dissipated.

Jenny said she could meet my demands. She was what I saw, not a changeling, and she could follow my simple rules and become the next Mrs. Me. She would do the girl stuff, and I, the man stuff. Simply put, she had to 1) keep putting out, which was the most important and inflexible rule; 2) stay cute, doing whatever that took; and 3) keep working, at least long enough to help reduce the debt burden I had accumulated.

Come to find out, she also could cook, an additional benefit, though not required, and that was all I needed. Nothing else; the rest was mine to shoulder.

Jenny was a talker. She talked all the time to anyone about anything—and often too long to me about nothing. We argued every day about this and that, but it was all good, as Wally Fong would say. It got everything out there so it didn't build up, forming a layer too hard to break through. She had been married before, making me number five. She grew up off Union Boulevard near downtown St. Louis, when the whites lived there. She pointed out her grade school as we drove out of the area (not quite fast enough), a two-story brick building, oddly not in decay, along the I-70 corridor.

As an elder teen, Jenny hit all the jazz and dance scenes and once rebuffed amorous advances from Ike Turner, during an early show of Tina Turner at Club Imperial. She was as gorgeous then as now but sported waist-length hair in her youth and was offered a job as a

Playboy bunny. Her first husband beat that notion out of her head. The wannabe Marine, spent most of a failed boot-camp attempt in the brig, never making the grade but falsely claiming a heritage of being a Marine and Vietnam vet. Jenny finally left, after seven years of his brutal matrimony; the last straw was putting her in the hospital with broken ribs.

Jenny raised two boys alone, and her ex later left the country to work the oil fields in Venezuela, still owing her a hundred thousand dollars in substantiated unpaid child support. She tended bar in a joint owned by a Mafia bent-nose type—her boss and protector, as one would suspect. Her second husband was a rebounder; the third turned out to be a coke-head and her fourth had too many kids by various other wives for her to deal with. I worried a little, wondering what unforgiveable sins I had would repeat the cycle of her seven-year betrothals. From her second ex came a daughter, who loved me like her real father. I am afraid I loved her, too. I liked being a father, teacher, and mentor. But distance and mixed marriages are never as fun as you read about. (Oh, yeah, you *don't* read about that.)

I liked being a father, but forces stripped my role. I feared my children might have transferred affection to whomever assumed my place with their mother. One would think I could have been a father and serve my country too but not in accordance with the ruling court judge. Fathers didn't rate in his eyes.

Jenny and I tolerated each other's foibles. No one was perfect—not her, certainly not me, and not even my mother. Jenny claimed she loved me more, because she had loved me longer. I told her that men love differently.

Jenny loves my being the man, and I love her being the woman. She is a wuss and plays that part against me to have her way a lot, but she places a hand on my shoulder when I am deep in thought or despondent in missing my children, and I feel her love—a love I respond to in kind. She knows I am damaged goods and need time to mend.

I could not have survived without her, on what would otherwise have been a short, solo ride.

A couple of years later, I reread Cameo's suicide note, trying again for a sense of closure, whatever it was (really, there is no such thing). I read it and then read it again, and a quirk caught a tearful eye—something hidden to me before. I must have missed it the last time I had read her writing, because this time I discovered a hint in one of those bulbous dots she put above her i's.

Clutching the note in hand, I ran into the living room to get a better look at the letter in the light.

"Don't look at anything except what I am showing you," I said to the newest Mrs. Me. "What does that look like to you?"

Jenny looked at it for five seconds. "Looks like a wink to me. It looks like one of those smiley faces, but this one is winking. Why?"

"That's her letter, her suicide note."

"Whose? Oh, Cameo's?"

Slowly, a grin spread across my face and then I emitted a hearty chuckle, as I recalled the night in the parking lot when Cameo told me she was not supposed to be there. A plan had been hatched to which I was never privy, but someone else was. Given the situation as it played out, suicide was understandable to friends and family—and the Air Force. *What an excellent cover*, I thought. *No one would dare check her dental records, making a horrible situation for her elderly mother worse.* "Yeah, do you remember my telling you how she had talked about 'disappearing' six months before her court appearance."

"No."

"Well, she did. I never thought about again, because of the horror of her death, but this note is the one she left for me. I remember she said she had been instructed not to tell anyone, but then when I convinced her to stay, she told me what she had been up to and told me to never mention it again. She wouldn't go into details, other than a SpecOps guy she knew named John was coming out of Chicago."

"How can that be possible?"

"I don't know. They have their ways. You watch some things on TV or at the movies and think it is only Hollywood and not real. Which ones are and which ones aren't—you would have to be on the inside.

There is too much hidden power and money in this grand democracy. Those with power like to keep their options open. Ever wonder about the blurred lines between black ops and organized crime, especially out of a place like Chicago?" Then another thought occurred to me. "And remember, Cameo was immediately cremated."

Special ops meant special favors, Cameo had once said.

Jenny asked if I was happy.

I thought about it and said, "Yes, happy, but not content."

A content man cannot write.

CHAPTER 19

Union Station

I don't ride the DART because I want to; I ride it because I have to. I saw her once, for a split second. Her eyes connected with mine. That was two years ago.

My head was down, reading. The book was *Somme*, the bloody battle of trench warfare in World War I. The battle lasted four and half months, from 1 July to 18 November, 1916. Killed or wounded was one million men. Slaughter wasn't a big enough word to describe it. I was engrossed in the details and not paying attention to my surroundings at the time.

Union Station is the nexus of the multiple lines of the DART coming in and departing Dallas. From there, you take a DART anyplace within sixty miles, as well as DFW Airport and Ft. Worth. The Trinity Railway Express, or TRE, runs several trains an hour east and west to the airport and past, during peak hours. The Amtrak Texas Eagle, with direct service to Chicago and Los Angeles, boards its passengers here. I didn't know where she was going to or coming from.

I looked up briefly and saw her thirty yards away, waiting for the TRE. Then I looked down without registering what I had seen, as my mind percolated and processed. Two seconds past, I looked up again. She was gone.

I raced to the front of the train, but the doors were closing. Couldn't get there fast enough. I ducked to look at the train platform and saw the back of her, disappearing around the train.

The DART train traveled north in slow motion for the two minutes it took to get to West End Station. Launching out the door as soon as it opened, I looked for a train going back to Union Station. I did not see one close enough and started running back to where I had spied her. I ran along the railroad behind the Brown School Book Depository, through their parking lot, and quickly tucked my bags in a hole on the Grassy Knoll as I took off in a sprint. The TRE had left the station and all I could see was the tail end slipping into the west.

I ran to the platform to check out the remaining travelers. A small crowd trickled in to await the next train arrival, but I couldn't find her anywhere. I saw a gray head and started to run toward it. As I closed in, I could see it wasn't her but a gray-haired dude. I took off in a trot, south to the underground tunnel, under the tracks that ran toward the Reunion Tower and the Hyatt Regency. If she was checked in, I wouldn't know what name to ask for.

I bolted into the lobby and then back to the doorman to describe her. He told me he had not seen her. I hustled around the lobby and looked in back corners, in front of the elevators, and went back to the front desk. I described her to the female attendant, and she told me she had not seen a person matching that description in the last few minutes or in the past day. I wished I could remember what color her coat was, but for some reason that detail was lost to me.

I raced back to where my gear was stashed and trampled a path in the liriope that I stepped through each day to get to work. I went in to the ticket counter at Union Station and bought a ticket for the next TRE train to the airport… and I waited; it would be forty minutes. Might as well have been forty years.

I didn't know what I was doing. How the hell was I going to find her at the airport—which terminal, which airline, which gate— if she was even headed that way? I took the ride over there anyway, contemplating the amazement alone, the chances of having caught a glimpse of this ghost from the past. When I arrived at DFW, I took a seat and looked around at the impossibility of finding her. The sky was the most beautiful blue—the color of her eyes—the airport so vast, the chances of finding her so few.

Her hair had been different; her manner of dress was too. She looked more fashionable than she had been before and exuded more confidence. She looked happy—radiant, almost. Her shape was altered—a tattoo wrapped from inside the neck of her sweater and halfway around her throat. Her bosom appeared flatter, and silvery-gray short hair adorned her thinner face, and her eyes were no longer blue. Her gaze hooked on to my random glance. She was talking to me, telling me something, captivating me. She said she was doing fine.

But how did I know? How was I so sure? Her tattoo was familiar; it was my design. It was the butterfly with one blue orb on each wing, like the earrings I had made for her—*her eyes.*

CHAPTER 20

2003
Kuwait Border

Sitting behind the Line of Departure, I was giddy and had to pinch myself. We were operating out of a C-square that comprised part of the mobile command operations center (COC) for Regimental Combat Team, RCT-7, call sign "Ripper." We were the Seventh Marines, First Marine Division, out of the desert oasis of Twenty-Nine Palms, California. The COC was set up to get on the move in less than ten minutes. Two command-variant light-armored vehicles (LAV-C2s) were backed up against each other with the ramps down and a tent placed over the middle, to give the officers and staff space to operate.

The Commanding Officer, Colonel Handle, operated out of his Humvee, parked just outside. He had a chair to occupy, as needed, in the middle of the tent hood on the ground, just below the leveled overlapping ramps. The colonel was one of those genuine good guys, who would make general without stepping on others.

This was it; I was part of something historic, I could begin to live with myself. Coalition forces had been building up since January. We had been planning and rehearsing our attack for over four years—contingencies—this but a variation in one of the many war games we played. This time was for real.

The Marine Corps tried to transfer me, but I told them no way. I was staying put. An associate had made the statement that President

Bush would never go into Iraq. I tripped over several chairs in the conference room to place my wager. I knew, hands-down, little George was going to take care of what big George had left unfinished. He was going to put Saddam out of power, like we should have done in '91. The silver-spoon offspring had to prove his mettle, and we were the metallic chess pieces to make it all happen.

The Iraqis and Saddam were in violation of UN resolutions and if not the UN and not the United States, then who else was going to make them toe the line? Who else was going in to look for suspected nuclear weapons-making material? All knew the UN was weak and powerless to do anything worthwhile, other than a pretense for global unity and a soapbox for whiners to trash the United States. What we needed to do was the same to Iran, but this would be strategically easier and more tolerable for now. This should let some steam out of the Middle East tempest. Iran was and is the greater threat to counter, the one on which to keep our celestial steely eyes and hidden microphones. We will face them soon enough.

After years of sitting on the sidelines, I was part of something real, instead of being ran, marched, trained, rehearsed, and paraded to death. It took thirty years. I was the oldest one standing there, including the Old Man, in a world that favored the youth for its vigor and its seniors for their experience and knowledge. I had none of those traits, but I was glad to be a there.

The shackles of pain from the breakup had loosened, and the oldest skeleton closeted. Disquieted for most of my life, I could move on. I was exactly where I wanted to be at this time and place. My life was not wasted after all—not that it should have been, but being a father was more than simply DNA transference, there had to be more substance, something I could lean on, having experienced or achieved. There had to be more. A father had to earn the respect of his children and teach them discipline and responsibility. He had to show them resilience as he battled his own imperfections, mistakes, and demons. They had to know a man, a father, was not perfect, but he would not quit trying to be more. But...

A man has to be somebody. He has to work day to day to prove he was worthy of stealing air. "I am happy, I am rich, I am successful," I say to myself. *Getting there.*

My son, Noah, joined the Marines and would go to boot camp in three months. He wanted to be like me. Could a father ask for more?

Mark Twain was quoted as saying, "The two most important days in your life are the day you are born and the day you find out why." This was my day. Success defined is singular to each soul. No one can determine what it is for you; no one can for me.

JUST—me.

Skittish, waiting for H-hour at midnight and the invasion launch, we relaxed in our Humvees, packed, staged ready to go. I had to ask one of the Marines what the empty ammo box draped over the upright exhaust pipe was for and he told me it was a toilet seat. I looked around at the other Hummers and they had them on their pipes as well. "That way you don't have to squat," said my primary driver, seated in the back left seat, manning a radio. Lance Corporal Troy Moul, nickname "Pig Pen," didn't mind getting his hands dirty, or his uniform, and he seemed to relish staying that way, but he was a loyal, hard worker.

To my left, in the driver seat for now, was the a-driver, Corporal Eric Melnyk. He was half-sleeping with a headset on. I could hear the music bubble out from under one of the ear pads. It was "Nights in White Satin" by the Moody Blues. Perfect timing—Vietnam era music for our Iraqi adventure. It suited, the music was me, the only I music I *felt.* I never knew most of the words to any of those songs, the emotion of this one became part of my DNA. With Vietnam going on then, the talk of MIAs and KIAs, ours and theirs, rights and wrongs, and fear, and of riots against the war on campuses and in the streets, I felt the meaning of the song was more.

To me, it was "*Knights* in White Satin," and it was about me, it was us, it was the gallant warrior dead returning from war draped in satin funeral shrouds of innocent white, not innocent to the what, but to the why. "...what the truth is, I can't say anymore..." And the love he spoke of, was the love of his country, of those who remained behind and would not do what he had to do, what *we* sacrificed ourselves to do. The few for the free.

As Saddam launched rockets over our heads to where he thought we were but weren't anymore, I turned to the colonel standing next to his vehicle and laughed.

I feared not death but a life insignificant.

Printed in the United States
By Bookmasters